Prais

HIGHL

"The is enchsharp into th

—

Legend of the Highland Dragon

"An outstanding read! A fast-paced, smartly written plot—fraught with danger and brimming with surprises—makes it impossible to put down."

—*RT Book Reviews* Top Pick, 4.5 Stars for
Legend of the Highland Dragon

"Mesmerizing, ingenious, slyly humorous, and wonderfully romantic, this unusual charmer is a winner for fans of paranormals. A Highland dragon? How can it miss?"

—*Library Journal* Starred Review for
Legend of the Highland Dragon

"With a well-developed plot and rich language, Cooper's tale is rooted in romantic suspense and aligned with fantasy, making for an excellent crossover."

—*Booklist* for *The Highland Dragon's Lady*

"The fantasy, interesting characters, mystery, danger, sensuality, romance, and love will keep readers intrigued right up to the very satisfying ending."

—*Romance Junkies* for *The Highland Dragon's Lady*

"Another incredible, unique romance from the ingenious Cooper. Smartly written, fast-paced, and brimming over with magic and surprises, this is exactly what readers crave and what Cooper continues to deliver."

—RT Book Reviews Top Pick, 4.5 Stars
for *Night of the Highland Dragon*

"An imaginative historical fantasy... I can only hope that there will be more stories about these fascinating shape-shifters."

—Night Owl Reviews for
Night of the Highland Dragon

ALSO BY ISABEL COOPER

Dark Powers
No Proper Lady
Lessons After Dark

Highland Dragons
Legend of the Highland Dragon
The Highland Dragon's Lady
Night of the Highland Dragon

Dawn of the Highland Dragon
Highland Dragon Warrior
Highland Dragon Rebel
Highland Dragon Master

HIGHLAND DRAGON MASTER

ISABEL COOPER

sourcebooks
casablanca

Published by Sourcebooks Casablanca, an imprint of Sourcebooks, Inc.
P.O. Box 4410, Naperville, Illinois 60567-4410
(630) 961-3900
Fax: (630) 961-2168
sourcebooks.com

Printed and bound in the United States of America.
OPM 10 9 8 7 6 5 4 3 2 1

PROLOGUE

THE TENT SMELLED OF TALLOW AND SMOKE AND BLOOD. MORTAL men said they got used to the reek after war had gone on long enough. Erik doubted he ever would.

At least the blood was mostly old by now. Dragons weren't carrion-eaters: the inhuman part of him stayed quiet. It was the human side that wanted to howl with fury, a longing that had become familiar in the days since Balliol's treachery and only intensified now, with the moans of dying men only a few paces outside.

In the face of Erik's rage, Artair MacAlasdair's calm stillness would have been offensive had Erik expected any other reaction. He'd rarely seen his uncle roused to any emotion, and never to passion. In Erik's youth, it had been a joke between him and Artair's younger children that the MacAlasdair patriarch wouldn't have done more than lift his eyebrows if someone had cut off his head.

Now Artair sat in Erik's tent, drinking bad wine and picking weevils out of bread with the same air he'd used when presiding over holiday feasts in his own castle. He'd seen as much fighting and death that day as Erik, but his white hair and beard were neat, his blue eyes as impassive as the glaciers they echoed in color. Under their scrutiny, Erik could give voice to but a bare fraction of what he felt.

"I'd thought," he said, his own wine cup neglected, "that we'd *done* with this. Years ago. Will they not stop until the Day of Judgment itself?"

"Likely not," said Artair. "I don't know that stopping's in their nature."

The devil of it was that Erik didn't know if the older man meant Englishmen or mortals. Like Artair's daughter Moiread—now married to a Welshman and unable to take an active part in the war, lest other lands be drawn into the conflict—Erik would have ardently voiced the former view. Artair himself had argued for the latter on more than one occasion.

We've never tried to take London, Douglas, the MacAlasdair heir, had said once.

Artair had tilted his head, dragon-like, and peered at his son. *Because we wouldn't, or because we can't?*

There'd been no good answer then, there wasn't one now, and it mattered little. Four years of fighting already, nearly twenty before the treaty the English had broken, and many days it seemed as though the wars would go on until there was no man left able to lift a sword—or until the vindictive bastard who'd taken the crown at Westminster felt his father's honor satisfied, whenever that would be.

"Your eyes changed," Artair observed with neither fear nor admonition. "Maintaining your form becomes harder?"

Not wanting to voice the words, Erik nodded, once. For the most part, the MacAlasdairs kept firm control over their shapes once they'd passed through the trials of youth. Dire sickness or wounds could make the matter more difficult, though, as could great strain on the mind or heart. Spending the days killing didn't help either.

Artair finished his wine. "I'm sending you away from the front. Douglas and I can take command for a time—and after this, there's likely to be a lull, for the winter if no longer."

"My lord—"

"Soon you'll begin to see them all as prey." The single

sentence, delivered with only fact and no feeling, cut Erik's voice off entirely. Artair crossed the room and put a hand on his nephew's shoulder. "Be at ease. It comes to us all in time, and you've not failed me. Indeed, I need you for another duty just now."

Erik bent his head in acquiescence. "I'm at your service, my lord."

"I've had a message from Cathal's wife," said Artair. "You wished a way to make the invasions end? She may have found one."

ONE

Bordeaux was far emptier than it had ever been in Erik's long life. In the past two centuries, he'd been accustomed to seeing the cities of men grow greater and more crowded, pushing out their borders every time he visited and building new houses almost atop the old.

Now many of the houses sat empty, their windows black as the empty eyes of a skull. The noises of the street were almost a whisper compared to what they had been. Sellers of fruit and fish, meat and leather still plied their trades in the markets, but there were far fewer, and their voices sounded muted, afraid. The rumbling of carts easily drowned them out, and while most of those carts held goods for the market, still there were many with a cargo of the dead, open eyes oft staring up to an unseeing heaven.

Man was a fragile creature. Never had Erik seen that more clearly than in the last ten years.

He walked without fear down the pitted cobblestone streets. The dragon-blooded took no harm from mortal plagues, save perhaps to their mind and soul. That horseman might ride after him and the other MacAlasdairs in vain—or perhaps simply leave the duty to his brothers. Certainly they were War's creatures often enough.

War was the root of Erik's mission, after all.

Although far fewer ships sat in the harbor, there were yet enough that their masts made a bare-branched forest against the blue summer sky. Men crossed the docks with their burdens: barrels of goods, pails of tar, even the occasional horse or cow. Other men stood or sat in mere idleness, fishing off the docks or talking over mugs of ale.

Some such idlers stopped Erik, as men in their position always had done with a well-dressed man who carried a nobleman's arms. They asked him to join them in drinking—and doubtless stand them a round later—which he declined; asked if he'd found himself lodging and care for his horse, which he had; and asked if he'd need of fresh fish, which he didn't. He did accept one offer from a young towheaded man for directions.

"I look to hire a ship," Erik said. "And men. I wish to make a voyage westward."

"Hmm," said the young man, and put his head to one side like a spaniel seeking a bone. He had great brown eyes that only heightened the impression. Those eyes scanned the ships in the harbor with alertness, though, and he gave answer promptly enough. "The *Hawk* might do it, m'lord. She's small, but she's been known to take human bundles from time to time, and she's not beholden so far as I know."

It sounded promising. "And where might I find her captain?"

"Aboard, most likely. They made port but two days ago. She'll be looking at every board, if the past's any measure."

"She?" Erik asked. It was no shock—among his line, the women fought nearly as much as the men, and such had been more common even among mortals in his parents' day—but it was a surprise to hear as much from modern lips.

The young man rolled his eyes. "Not that there hasn't been a bit to say about it. But her husband's dead, and they'd no children, so…" He shrugged. "The world's not over-blessed with men these days, no?"

He crossed himself as he said it, and Erik joined him. "The *Hawk*," he said.

"Down at the end," said the young man, and waited expectantly until Erik handed him two pennies.

The docks creaked beneath Erik as he walked toward his destination. That sound, and water lapping against wood, brought back memories from his youth: fishing out in boats on the loch with his cousins, with more joking than actual fishing being done in the end. Cathal and he had been of about an age, or close enough to make little difference among the MacAlasdair youths. Together they'd hidden from tutors, run races, and later planned to court kitchen maids.

Cathal had been the one to explain Erik's current mission—or, rather, his wife had. A charming woman, unnervingly intelligent and more unnervingly familiar with the magic that Erik had only half learned in his youth, Sophia had been the one to unearth the relevant legends. Sophia and Cathal's two daughters had served the evening meal while Sophia told stories, their eyes as grave and brown as their mother's, but with a dragonish gleam in their depths.

Such an evening left a man brooding, apt to consider his own past and perchance the future to come.

Such a man, Erik told himself, would do well to concentrate on the task at hand, ere he fell into the harbor and earned himself an unpleasant evening. He turned his attention to the ship he was approaching.

The *Hawk* was a flat-bottomed cog, its oak boards weathered smooth by the ocean but to all appearances solid and sturdy. As it lay in harbor, the single sail was furled against the mast. Above it, a blue flag displayed a single yellow silhouette that might have been a hawk, an eagle, or indeed a giant bat. For certain it had a head and wings, but that was all Erik could make out from a distance. The ship looked to be a good length, eighty feet or so, and sat well in the water.

Two figures stood on the deck. At such a distance, a mortal man might not have known that one of them was female. The dragon-blooded had better eyes, but save for her sex, her height—greater than that of most women—and the gleaming copper-red of her hair, Erik could make out no more of her.

Approaching, he hailed the ship. The captain set her hands on her hips, considering, and then nodded. "Wait there," she called, gesturing to the docks, "and I'll come ashore."

Erik heard a familiar note in her voice, but he couldn't place it. Not until she reached the docks and he looked into a tanned face with wide, almost-black eyes, in which gleamed small specks of golden fire, did he know her. Then, laughing in amazement, he saw the joke of the flag.

If the man before her hadn't gaped and then broken out laughing, Toinette would have thought herself wrong about his identity. The world had big men in plenty, and blond men—whole countries full of big, blond men. There might even have been a few big, blond men with the same shimmering blue-green eyes as this one.

But his expression convinced her.

"Erik MacAlasdair? What are the odds?"

Not so great as all that, come to think of it. The world could be small, and it was growing smaller of late. In truth, there'd been times when Toinette had wondered if her blood would be all that was left.

Best not to brood on death. Better to step forward and let Erik embrace her. His lips brushed lightly over hers: a quick kiss of greeting, as between any friend and another, quite unlike the rather messier and more daring one that she remembered receiving behind the forester's cottage at

Loch Arach so many years ago. His arms were stronger, though, and Toinette stepped back feeling a tingling echo of the same thrill she'd had at sixteen.

"A pleasant surprise," he said, and the accent of Scotland in his voice called back memories of hunting and hawking, of stone halls and the triumph of controlling her heritage for the first time. "Captain Toinette?"

"Captain Deschamps, rightly."

"I heard," he said, and bowed his head. "I'm sorry for your loss."

"Thank you. It was ten years ago now, so—" She spread her hands, smoothing the air as time did pain.

Erik looked slightly surprised. "Ah. Not the plague, then?"

"Only mortality—though you might say the plague counts. He was middle-aged when I met him. A very kind man, and not a very curious one."

"God rest his soul."

"Yes," said Toinette. "Quite likely. And how many times have you wed since we last met?"

"Two." He made sure that none of the crowd were likely to be listening, and then added, "Both longer past than your man."

"Quite a crowd in heaven, I'm sure. Children?"

"No."

"I'm sorry." He didn't ask in return. Toinette would not bear to a mortal; the blood didn't cross that way. Men could crossbreed, with difficulty and rituals. The older ones, like Toinette's father, didn't even need those. Whether mortal or magical, though, bearing the child of a man with dragon's blood had certain risks unless you yourself had it to begin with. To Toinette's mind, it was a bad deal either way.

To her relief, she saw no great pain in Erik's face, nor

heard any in his voice when he spoke again. "It happens. You look to have done well."

"I have." She smoothed her hands down the crimson wool of her skirts. "Amber and wax from Muscovy this trip. Lighter than furs, and less likely to leave the crew scratching."

"Only half frozen, I'd think." Erik laughed.

"As long as it's the right half, gold does a lot to thaw a man again." The setting sun glinted red-gold off the water, catching Toinette's eye. "Here, you didn't come all this way just to compare our lives or ask for a rematch at archery, did you?"

"No, no more than I did to let you redeem yourself with a falcon. I need to hire myself a ship."

"Welcome words. There's a tavern down that way"— Toinette jerked a thumb to indicate where—"that's half-decent if you watch the landlord while he's pouring the wine. I've a mind to talk over meat and drink."

The tavern was small and reasonably clean. The table wasn't sticky, and the rushes had been changed within the last fortnight. Toinette had been right about the wine too, and the pottage, though mostly cabbage, tasted as if the bits of meat might truly have been rabbit.

Such qualities drew a number of guests, mostly the quieter sort of men from the docks by the look of them. None sat very close to Toinette or Erik, and all seemed absorbed in their own affairs. Still, Erik switched into Gaelic as he put down his spoon and asked, "You've perhaps heard of the Templars?"

Toinette thought for the time it took her to sip wine and put the cup back down. "Crusader knights, weren't they?

And maybe devil worshippers?" A hundred-odd years since their parting had left her accent rusty, but Erik could understand her well enough.

"Aye, so the king said at the time, I hear." He hadn't bothered about it much on that occasion. Moiread MacAlasdair had said she didn't care if they'd each kissed Satan's cold arse in person; the men didn't matter, only their artifacts. "They had a great deal of treasure."

"Had?"

"Philip claimed most of it." Indeed, those who felt safe speaking of such matters suggested that greed had been the fuel for those pyres. Erik wouldn't have been surprised. "But there are those who say he didn't find all—that a small company of the knights smuggled some out and brought it to an island west of England. Of those tales, a few say that it wasn't only gold. They speak of magic enough to reshape the world, or a part of it."

Toinette's crimson lips pursed. "Ah," she said, amused. "And I daresay you've no wish to hire an English captain. The war progresses?"

"It does. That's the reason I'm going," Erik said. "It's a small chance, but I'll take it for my people's sake."

"How very loyal of you."

As it had always done, her gaze grew remote when speaking of such matters, and the humor in her voice was lofty: *These affairs have so little to interest me*. When Erik was fifteen, he'd blushed and stammered and grown angry. When he was eighteen, he'd blushed and stammered for different reasons, and the anger had taken a distant place.

Toinette had been his first kiss. He'd never asked, but he was dead certain he hadn't been hers.

Older, he drank wine and composed an answer. "There's not so much fighting these days. We're preparing for David to return. I've been told I can be most helpful in this manner." When Toinette's dark eyes didn't waver, he added, "And I'd like a reason to be away just now."

War grew weary for most men. For the dragon-blooded, it could be dangerous. Too much death without a respite could lead to bloodlust, or to enough distance from mortals that their lives became playthings. Artair MacAlasdair was very careful about such tendencies in his kin, even in the cadet branches.

"I'd imagine many people would," said Toinette. "For all there are fewer men about, we'll likely find a crew easily enough. But first," she added, raising a slim sun-browned hand, "let us talk payment."

TWO

"And half the treasure," said Toinette, pulling off her second boot and propping her feet up on the end of the bed.

"If treasure there be." Marcus, already as horizontal as it was possible for a man to be, gave her a skeptical look from the depths of his pillow. "He's chasing legends. Will you start too?"

"I *am* a legend."

"Captaining one merchant ship doesn't make you an Amazon."

"A girl can dream." Toinette didn't correct him. While Marcus knew a great deal about her, his knowledge did not extend to her other form, and she was content to leave it that way. "Besides, that's why I'm having him pay in advance, and pay well too. I've not gone soft in the head just because we made land."

"Oh, I was just crediting it to old age."

"Bear in mind," Toinette said, giving him a baleful look, "that you sleep sounder than I do, young man."

Marcus laughed. "You'd not kill me. What other man would you trust to share a bed and not to turn you out for better company half the nights?"

Desire, whether for men or women, had never burdened Marcus overmuch. If he'd been a more faithful man, or a less adventurous one, he would have made an excellent priest—which would have been a great loss to Toinette, as he was a damned good first mate. "And I suppose most of them would snore worse than you do, at that. Smell worse, almost definitely."

"I can live, then?"

"Oh, for now. It's late, and I'd as soon not go to the trouble of cleaning your blood off the mattress. And innkeepers make an unholy fuss about corpses in their rooms."

Toinette stretched herself out, luxuriating in the length of the bed and the softness of the straw mattress. She'd chosen shipboard life freely and had yet to regret it, but all the same, it was lovely to have her back truly straight for a night or two. She wiggled her toes.

"Speaking of better company," said Marcus, "will *you* be needing the room to yourself while we're here?"

"Doubtful."

On the occasion that Toinette took a lover, she generally either went back to the man's accommodations, hired a room herself, or—at times—found a stable loft or similar convenience for an hour's privacy. When none of those options presented themselves, Marcus took himself out to find his own amusements for a while. It was never very long. The last man Toinette had let stay afterward had been Jehan. After he'd died, it had seemed a slight to his memory for others to remain.

Marcus was different. Wherever Jehan was, Toinette was sure he understood.

"Ill-favored city, is it?" Marcus asked.

"When I was young, it might have seemed otherwise. Now?" She shrugged. "The more men I've had in my bed, the more they all seem the same—and the less worth the trouble of getting them there."

That might have been true after ten years; it was certainly true after more than a century. The exception who came to mind... Well, he was paying her, and they'd be on a ship full of her men for months. Best not to even think about that one, much as she might like to.

From the street outside came off-key singing: men drunk enough to take their chances in the darkness.

"They left out a line there, I think," Marcus observed.

"D'you want to go out and correct them?"

"I might, if they don't stop soon."

"It always is a shock," Toinette agreed, retrieving her share of the blankets, "how noisy cities are after the sea. Though the beds make up for it. And the food. I can't say I'm looking forward to biscuit and fish again."

"You're the one who took the man up on his offer. And how does he intend to *find* this island, come to that?"

"He managed to get his hands on a map. He says it's a long story. I'll have it out of him by the third day at sea, I'll wager—but meanwhile, I've seen the map, and it does look real. Besides, MacAlasdair's not the sort to chase nursery tales without any solid sign. Never was."

Punctuating her sentence, she blew out the candle and settled down into the bed. Marcus, a foot away, was a comfortably warm presence. Even summer nights in Bordeaux almost never got very hot.

His voice came out of the darkness, half drowned in a yawn. "How do you know this fellow, then?"

"Oh," said Toinette, her own voice slurred as her eyelids grew heavy. "Long time ago. You might say we grew up together."

In a way, she thought as she slid down under the waves of sleep, it was true. Only growing up meant more to the dragon-blooded than it did to mortals—and she, looking back, could never have said when it had happened to her. Adulthood had come in fits and starts, blood and pain and madness.

Toinette supposed that much was common enough even for mortals.

Loch Arach had long been familiar to Erik. As great a distance as it was from the island that he called home, it was still close enough for frequent travel in dragon form. Lamorak MacAlasdair held the island with his brother's backing, and both knew it. A year or two sometimes passed between visits, but never more.

When Erik was fifteen, he'd gone to Artair MacAlasdair's castle. To mortals, that had been the fostering common with most young men. For Erik, as for the others in his line, it had been more: his transformations had begun. Unlike the island, Loch Arach had room to keep changing and hunting a secret. Moreover, Castle MacAlasdair had rooms with magic woven into the walls that could hold a dragon if one's nature broke free of control.

However many branches the family had, the youth came to Loch Arach. Erik came to suspect that Artair was fond of the arrangement. He was as canny as he was old, and no stranger to the advantages of strengthening blood ties with a bit of mingling.

Young Erik had welcomed the journey. He'd had a glorious few months at first: training both of his forms, playing games with his cousins, hunting in the forest, and swimming in the lake.

Shortly after harvest, a small band of traders had come through. With them had come a girl.

Erik still remembered his first look at her. She'd been thirteen and spider spindly, her hair a roughly cut shock of carrot-orange and her face all outthrust chin. Her clothing had been patched and too large; her hand had lingered near the dagger at her waist too long for any sort of courtesy. Standing in the tower room at Castle MacAlasdair, she'd watched the assembled MacAlasdairs with barely disguised skepticism.

The girl was named Antoinette. She had no last name; Fitzdraca would do if one was needed. She was dragon-blooded. She would stay with them until she learned to control her abilities. They would treat her as one of the family. Artair had explained those facts briefly, and to say that his tone had brooked no disagreement would have been untrue only in implying that any tone of his had ever allowed for argument about anything. Antoinette was staying. It was a fact, from that moment as unchangeable as the hills around them.

Later Erik had discovered that Toinette had marched up to Artair, told him of her situation, and offered to demonstrate her powers. He and Cathal had speculated about whether she'd *started* by sticking her hand in the hearth fire just to get Artair's attention. It had seemed like the sort of thing she'd do.

Poor relations, especially illegitimate ones, were supposed to conduct themselves with a certain humble gratitude, and while Toinette had never seemed ungrateful, she'd been far from humble. From the first, she'd kept up with the MacAlasdairs, refusing to be left behind or to keep her questions to herself. Erik, fifteen and very conscious of his dignity as a young man, had thought more than once about throwing her into the loch. His own status as a guest had tied his hands, though, and he'd never managed to persuade Cathal to do it, not even when Toinette had won all of their pocket money at dice.

He outdid her in hunting, in both forms, and he was far better with dogs and falcons. Those were his consolations.

Over three years, he'd found out very little about her past. Her father had been a scholar calling himself Antonio. He'd not bothered marrying her mother, which explained some of Artair's interest in her. Since the MacAlasdairs had settled Scotland, if not before, no man of their line had accidentally sired a child on a mortal woman. Toinette's father, by inference, must have been only a generation or two removed from the Old Ones, the true and immortal dragons. Toinette didn't talk about her mother.

She'd grown up in London, not quite a child of the streets but not far from it either. At twelve, on the cusp of womanhood, she'd started changing in more ways than one. She'd managed to make it out to the countryside before her first full transformation, she said, and since Erik had never heard stories of a dragon rampaging in London, he was inclined to believe her.

He'd never heard exactly what rumors she'd followed to find the MacAlasdairs. Toinette didn't talk much about that either.

Not that she'd been silent, by any means. As a girl, Toinette had been full of questions and opinions, songs and stories and challenges. At fourteen, she'd broken her arm trying to outdo the others in flight, and even the quick healing of their blood hadn't spared her a week of miserable boredom. At fifteen, she'd taken to writing bad poetry. Erik and Cathal had found some and read it aloud, and Erik had gotten a water pitcher to the head for his pains.

By the time he'd been eighteen and Toinette sixteen, she'd been tall and willowy, finally graceful in skirts. Her hair had grown. Braided about her head, it had looked to Erik like a flaming halo, though she'd never achieved any kind of sainthood.

He'd more than reconciled himself to her company.

Their fights had continued, but with an undertone that had left him with a spinning head and embarrassing dreams.

Then Artair had sent her away. He'd been kind about it, letting her choose her path. She'd ended up leaving with the traders who'd brought her, with enough money to give her a good start regardless of her sex.

"I could go to a convent, too," she'd said as they'd sat behind the forester's cottage on her last day at Loch Arach, enjoying an adolescent refuge for the final time. "But I couldn't see myself among nuns."

Neither could Erik, but he didn't consider it the better part of chivalry to say so. "I can't see why you have to go in the first place," he said. "To go back on hospitality after so many years—"

Toinette had rolled her eyes. "Don't be a fool if you can help it. You and Cathal are old enough to wed now. Any lord who's thinking you over for his daughter will go sour on the whole idea if Artair has a ward around old enough to warm your beds. He cares more about land and arms than blood, so I'm a hindrance right now. Sensible man."

"Heartless, you mean," Erik said, trying to pretend his face was red from outrage.

"Hearts don't do anyone much good. He's been nicer than I'd a right to expect. Besides"—she shrugged—"it's about time I saw more of the world. But before I go—" .

She'd leaned forward, awkwardly since they were both sitting, grasped his shoulders, and pressed her open mouth to his.

Girls hadn't been *rare* in Loch Arach, but Erik had never gotten the nerve to approach one. They were servants, or villagers, and he was a guest at the castle. He'd no wish to risk Artair's wrath. He'd looked, and dreamed, and thought things might be different when he went home.

At the touch of Toinette's lips, his body had lit up with internal flame. He'd kissed her back clumsily but intensely, their tongues sliding against each other, and wound his fingers into the red silk of her hair. He was leaning toward her, trying to figure out how to get closer without falling over on her, when a voice called her name from a short distance away: Agnes, Cathal's older sister.

Instantly they broke apart, and Toinette sprang to her feet. "I'll be there directly!"

Erik—not inclined to stand up just then and unsure he'd be able to any time before sunset—had stared up at her. "What... Why did you do that?"

"I wanted to know," she'd said, "if it'd be better now I'm older. And it was. Thank you."

Then, skirts whirling as she turned, she'd left him to his confusion and lust.

THREE

CREW VANISHED AT EVERY PORT. SOME FOUND NEW SHIPS, SOME tired of life at sea and headed off to seek a farm, and a few met a more final end, whether by tavern fights or spoiled food. Toinette was only thankful to be seeing fewer deaths from the plague.

Erik's mission meant losing more than usual. Men who'd been quite content to sail from France to Muscovy, or London to Spain, heard *mysterious island west of England* and shook their heads. Sailing was dangerous enough on the routes men knew practically by heart. They sailed on respectable merchant ships, not as pirates or explorers. The whole venture sounded foolhardy.

Knowing that very well, Toinette didn't bother trying to convince them. It wouldn't have done any good, and she had a conscience, shriveled and shrunken though it might be. Risking her life and those of willing men was as far as she would go.

Thus she drew more heavily than usual from the taverns. The *Hawk* would sail decently with ten men. Counting herself and Marcus, that left eight. Erik would likely be useful if they met with pirates, but she didn't want to count on him for running up the sail or manning the wheel.

"And you don't *have* to come," she told Marcus as she made her plans, the notion having occurred to her while she slept. "I'll not hold it against you."

He made a *pfah* sound through his beard. "And will I live forever if I stay?"

"I don't know," said Toinette. "Make friends with an alchemist, and you might manage it yet."

"I'll take my chances. If this island *does* exist, I want to see it. If it doesn't… Well, you're a woman of some sense. I'll wager you'll turn back before we run through our supplies."

"That I will," said Toinette. They both knew that the matter wasn't so simple. Storms and calms interfered with a captain's best will, often to the cost of lives.

But Marcus knew that, and he was a grown man. Toinette made certain that the rest of the men she hired knew it too. Five were from her old crew, loyal enough to stay with her no matter how dubious the voyage, or young and adventurous enough to welcome the risk for its own sake.

Of the other three, Raoul was a branded poacher, Sence a dark and morose man who spoke little, and Emrich a scarecrow who looked around constantly and sat with his back to the wall at all times. Toinette was doubtful of their company, but they all spoke knowledgeably about their time on ships. If nothing else, they were reasonably young, strong of back, and whole of body.

Taking no chances, she had a shipbuilder come aboard and tour the *Hawk*, keeping an eye out for any gaps in the boards or unsoundness in the wood.

She didn't think of speaking again to Erik. The preparation was hers to handle. She'd taken passengers before. When she was ready, she would send a message to his inn. Until then, she had no time for nostalgia.

"'Ware the barrel, there!" Toinette shouted as Erik approached the *Hawk*.

He sidestepped quickly out of the way as two men

carried an immense tun up to the ship's gangplank. Their fellows were rolling or lifting barrels of a similar size, as well as vast boxes and sacks. The docks near the ship were as busy as an anthill on a sunny day.

Toinette took her sharp eyes off the activity to walk down and meet him. "Rather chafes to know the two of us could have all of this done in an afternoon," she said.

"We could put our shoulders to the wheel even in this form. It'd make your reputation," Erik joked, looking at her. She wore a light-blue gown of thin wool with green and white embroidery, and her hair was pulled simply back into a white net. There was nothing ornate about her, but she looked every inch the well-to-do merchant's widow, and while she was tall and tanned, nobody seeing her would have credited her strength.

Toinette laughed. Her eyes thinned a trifle, though, and there was sharpness in her voice when she first spoke. "I don't doubt it. That's the problem." The mood lifted, or seemed to, and she gave him a freer smile. "Come for inspection?"

"Gawking, you might say. I don't know what *should* be going aboard."

"Biscuits, wine, cheese, salted pork, turnips, and peas, enough for three months." Toinette gave him a flat look. "If we've not found the place when we're six weeks out, we're turning back, and I'll hear no argument on it. Understood?"

"Completely."

"Good." She turned back to look at the ship. "Also fishing nets and lines, soap and brushes for the ship, sailcloth and wood for repairs, which God willing we won't need to make at sea. Medicines."

Erik glanced at the ship. "Do you have a physician?"

"Not as such. I know a few things, and Marcus and I are both decent with a needle, should it come to that." She gestured to a tall, bearded man in black who stood super-vising the loading. "Marcus. He's my second-in-command. You'll treat what he says like it comes from me—and you'll treat what *I* say as law, at least until we hit land."

"Of course," said Erik, affronted. "Do you think I wouldn't?"

"I don't think you'd be a fool about it," Toinette said, and her expression added *unlike most men*, "but if aught goes amiss, there'll likely be no time for debate. I know the *Hawk* better than you do, and unless you'll truly surprise me with your recent history, I know the sea better than you do."

Erik nodded assent. "I helped my cousins on my moth-er's side build a *drekkar*—one of their ships—once, but it was only fit for a few boys to row about in and pretend. Other than that, I've only been a passenger, and that rarely."

"We'll not hold it against you," she said with another grin. "You're a well-paying passenger, and it's an interest-ing journey you've got for us."

"Is that why you agreed?"

In his own voice, he heard the echo of his eighteen-year-old self asking *why*. If Toinette thought of the kiss, she didn't show it, but her smile was that of the brash, sharp girl she'd been. "I agreed because you offered me money," she replied, "but I'll say it's a more exciting job than I've had in a few dozen years. And you're a better employer."

"True," said a lanky and dark-haired young man coming off the gangplank.

"You've never met the man before in your life, Gervase," Toinette said, shaking her head at him.

"No, but he's not having us ship goats anywhere, nor swine, and that's a high virtue already." Gervase's words sounded of Paris. He'd a gold earring in one ear and a non-chalant look. "Sir, I'm most sincerely at your service."

"Even if I'm taking you into uncharted waters?"

"Ah, but I know in my heart that the captain will bring us back safe. And if my heart's wrong, my nose rejoices still that I'll have only a dozen men in high summer to endure."

"We're all likely to be bad enough, by the end," Toinette warned him and Erik both. "Water's for drinking, not bathing, unless you fancy a dip in the ocean, and quarters are close."

Erik shrugged. "I've been on battlefields. It can't be worse." He remembered the stench of blood and offal at midday and grimaced. "We'll have the sea around us. That can only help, aye?"

"That's the spirit," Gervase chimed in. "And men, unlike beasts, clean up after themselves."

"They do on the *Hawk*. That reminds me: if Marcus hasn't yet given the new hands the word about drunkenness, see that he does. And—" Toinette turned back to Erik as Gervase bowed and ran off. "How's your stomach for the ocean?"

"Decent, or I'd not be doing this." That wasn't entirely true. Loyalty and the force of Artair's command could probably have gotten Erik onto a ship even if he knew he'd keep nothing down for a month. As fortune had it, he was a fair sailor, but Artair hadn't bothered asking.

Toinette's thin lips quirked up at the right corner. A suspicious man might have thought she knew damned well what Erik wasn't saying. "Good. Buy ginger, in case. The sea's rougher where we'll be going. And I'll tell you the same as Marcus will tell the men: if you disgrace yourself, whether from motion or drink, you'll be cleaning it up. I don't have the hands to spare."

"Quite a tone to take with a customer," he said.

"You hired a ship, my lord, and sailors." The title wasn't

quite sarcastic. "If you want a nursemaid, you'll have to find one separate."

Erik made a slight bow. "In truth, Captain, I can't imagine you nursing anyone."

"Nor can I. Oh, and if you fight with the men or otherwise get in the way of our tasks, I'll have you in chains until the journey's end."

"And what…" Erik took a step toward her, so that Toinette had to tilt her head back a little to meet his eyes. Although it hadn't been his intent, the gesture made him notice the slender length of her neck and the shadowed hollows behind her ears. He smiled. "What would you do with me then?"

"You couldn't break free of irons in human form." Mindful of the crowd, Toinette spoke softly. The words hit Erik's ears in small puffs of air. "And even a dragon couldn't fly all the way to your destination. I'd assume you'd be reasonable."

"I could be *very* reasonable," he said, his voice low and his body tightening both at her presence and at the images in his mind. "I'd hate to disappoint you, Captain."

She flashed him another grin, even as she stepped back. "Then I trust you'll behave. I've a ship to run, after all, and a duty to my men."

FOUR

They cast off on a clear dawn, with the sun rising gold in the east and the sea stretching out clear and shining before the *Hawk*'s prow. As many times as Toinette had made the slow journey out of Bordeaux harbor, as many more times as she'd left other ports, she never ceased to feel a thrill in those first moments. She could pretend to forget the danger and boredom that were both nearly certain to lie ahead. For a little while, the world was new and she could go anywhere.

"A fair wind," she said to Marcus, watching the sail snap briskly above them, "and a good tide."

"Yes, for so long as it lasts."

"Your constant cheer is one of the things I cherish most about you."

"I'm surprised. You have such a wide assortment to choose from."

"I try to vary my preferences from time to time. Keeps things fresh." She leaned on the railing and sighed with contentment. "How are the new hands?"

"Shaping up. The rest of the men have a wager on about what Emrich's fleeing. I only pray he settles once we get further from land," Marcus said, shaking his head with the air of an exasperated tutor.

"What are the current favorites?"

"Theft's well ahead, though none's so sure as to specify what. Next is that he's a serf who's run from his lord. Murder's half and half. Longest odds against an angry father or a jealous husband, given his looks."

Toinette laughed, finding double pleasure from the way the open air caught the sound and sent it back to her ears. "Oh, have they not heard? You never can tell with women. And he might've been quite comely back when he ate more."

"How generous of you," said Marcus. "How fares our passenger?"

"Asleep, or so he declared his intentions when he came aboard. As I've not seen a hair of him since we cast off, I can only guess he slumbers like a babe." She shook her head.

"The privilege of rank, or at least of wealth."

"Aye," said Toinette, leaning against the rail. The deck rose and fell steadily beneath her feet, a gentle rocking motion that could easily have eased her into sleep herself, no matter how hard the berth. "He's welcome to such luxuries."

"For now," Marcus said, giving her a knowing look.

"Everything is for now, isn't it?"

Marcus snorted. "I've no objection to you turning philosopher on us, Captain, as long as you don't abandon the ship for a convent before we get paid, but in this case I think we can both see the future without the help of any stars."

"You could go to bed yourself," Toinette suggested, falling into a pattern the two of them had danced many times. "I can keep order, whether you believe it or no."

"I'll have to eventually." Marcus turned to look behind them, where buildings were becoming indistinct and hills were rapidly receding. "But I've a mind to enjoy what might be my last sight of land."

"Before what, this time?"

"'Eaten by serpents' is the favorite," said Marcus, speaking not only for himself, as Toinette knew, but for prevailing opinion among the men.

"Well," said Erik from behind them, "I'd be inclined to pity the serpents in that case."

The years had taught Erik to get up at dawn when the need arose, but they'd never taught him to like it. He'd come onto the *Hawk*, found his quarters, and stretched out. The pallet and blankets in the corner of the hold were no bed, not even such a one as he'd had at bad inns, but he'd had worse in war and managed.

For that matter, he remembered his last voyage, seventy-five years before. That ship had been older, without the shelter of a sealed deck and a separate hold. The men, Erik included, had slept in what little shelter the sides of the ship could provide, with hard planks beneath them and leather bags lined with fur for warmth. From what he'd seen as he picked his way back to his not-too-private quarters, the crew had the same bags and little cushioning beneath, but not being at the mercy of the rain and the waves was a pleasant change.

Waking, he'd come up to the deck to discover that he'd not slept very long. The sun was still low in the sky, but they were well on their way, perhaps three hours into the journey. He'd spotted Toinette leaning on the forward rail and gone to join the conversation.

The looks of shock he got from both her and Marcus were not surprising, though not particularly flattering either. He'd met Marcus briefly the night before, and the man had struck him as experienced enough to be jaded about the habits of the wealthy. Toinette's cynicism he knew very well.

"I don't *think* that was an insult," she said, turning to face him. "Or I choose not to take it as one."

Marcus chuckled. "I like the idea of not being a pleasant meal. Suggests we'd fight too hard, even from the inside."

"You take my meaning well then, sir," said Erik, with a small bow.

That had indeed been part of what he'd meant. The other part was a joke between him and Toinette, one which would have betrayed their other shapes to explain. From her slight, skeptical smile, he thought she'd heard it.

"The captain was just saying I'm a man inclined to look on the bright side," said Marcus solemnly. "Even going to the ends of the earth."

"Not quite so far as that, I believe—and hope."

"If I see an edge, we're turning around," said Toinette, shaking her head. She was facing into the wind now, but it didn't budge a strand of her bright hair, tightly coiled as it was into its net. It did ruffle the crimson folds of her gown, showing her slim curves more clearly.

Erik allowed himself a moment of indulgence before returning his gaze to her face and laughing. "Nonsense. You've read Aquinas. I know, as I was there when you had to recite."

"How did she manage that?" Marcus asked with enough interest to make Toinette glare in his direction.

"Badly. I'm surprised she's gotten the use of her hand back."

"Remind me to have you both thrown overboard when I can spare the men." Toinette made a pretense of turning back to the rail, only to reverse course and add, "And my Latin wasn't half so bad as your figuring."

"A very cogent argument."

"Hmph." She looked at Marcus, who was standing in silent but obvious amusement. "Don't you have supplies to check, or men to flog?"

"Or sharks to be eaten by? I take your point, though I don't know how you'll send *him* away."

"I can't," said Toinette, mock-groaning. "He's paying."

"How long has he been with you?" Erik asked as Marcus strode away over the deck.

Toinette hesitated a moment, searching his voice for prying or possessiveness, the sort of quality that would demand a sharp answer. She heard none, only a friendly question. It was a pleasant surprise from a man. "With me alone, these ten years. He sailed with my husband for five years before he died."

"And he thinks you're…"

"An adventurous young woman who married an older man. Hardly a creature of myth. He also doesn't ask inconvenient questions."

"A good quality in a companion."

"That it is." Toinette clasped her hands at the small of her back, lacing her fingers together, and stretched. The surrendering crack of her spine felt good. So did Erik's eyes on her outthrust breasts.

She'd never been able to be very dishonest with herself. As a boy, Erik had been handsome in a gawky kind of way. He'd grown into himself in the last century, into a long nose and a square jaw, arms that rippled with muscle and thighs that filled his hose nicely. Jaded as Toinette was, she couldn't stand near him and not feel desire ripple through her.

After Jehan's death, she'd never taken lovers on board the *Hawk*, be they crew or customer. Men were too unpredictable, too apt to resent each other's access to any woman's bed or to think that their presence there gave them authority. Erik was *possibly* less dangerous in the second case, but the crew were no less prone to the first.

"What sort of birds are those?" Erik asked, sensing and then breaking the silence before it could become too awkward.

Toinette looked up and out. She spotted white wings, black heads, and a profile she knew well. "Terns. They'll follow us for a little while, but they don't go very far from land. Once we get further out into the ocean, we might see porpoises."

"Do you catch them?"

"No. The men think it's bad luck. For all I know, they might be right. No sense tempting fate on a voyage like this, is there?"

"Not in the least." Erik grinned. "I've a fair idea of how daft the whole venture makes me sound."

Toinette glanced back from the water to meet his eyes. "Do you think it's daft?"

"I don't know," he said. "Artair doesn't, and it's seldom that he's far wrong."

"I'll take that as a compliment too."

"You're very quick to seize those."

Toinette shrugged. "I've an eye for a good thing, and I'll take what I can get." She turned back to the waves, watching them rise and fall. White foam broke around the *Hawk*'s prow, and the boat rocked steadily onward. She could feel the wind as if she were the sail herself.

"Almost as good as flying, in its way," said Erik.

"Oh," Toinette laughed, "better to my mind. Much of the time, anyway."

"Truly?" Perhaps remembering how quickly she'd taken to the air at Loch Arach, Erik sounded completely surprised.

"Mm-hmm." Toinette turned around again, facing into

the wind and taking a deep, salt-scented breath. "Flying, you're above everything. You see it from a distance. It's you and the stars and the clouds. The birds if you're staying low enough. Don't mistake me, there's a glorious sort of freedom in all of that."

"But…"

"But on the sea, you're a part of things. You smell the air, you see the way the water changes from place to place, the difference in what you catch for dinner or the whales in the distance. You get to know the ship too." She smiled. "I wager I could tell the *Hawk* beneath my feet even if I were blind. It's a place to come back to, a thing you make and maintain—and I'd say *that's* the mark of souled creatures, though I'm no priest. Craft."

"Earth and water, not air," Erik said thoughtfully.

"And not fire, God willing. Rather the opposite of your line."

"Yours too—or rather your blood," he amended the statement quickly.

"Ah, well, perhaps it's the mortal in me. Drawn to what will outlast short-lived men and so forth." Toinette waved a hand in the air.

"That could be on both counts," said Erik, looking out to the water. The wind played with his golden hair. He had less to disturb than Toinette did, yet it still ruffled in the breeze, and strands clung to his neck. "The Norsemen carve dragons' heads on their boats, you know."

"They might just want to frighten their enemies."

"We are often things to be feared," Erik agreed, and his smile was devilish.

Toinette returned it. "Some of us more than others," she said, "and perhaps for different reasons. Depending on who it is we're frightening, of course."

For just a moment, before she went to check on Marcus, she let Erik see the veiled challenge in her eyes.

It would be a long voyage. With no privacy, there was also no danger that either of them would get carried away. And few people were more qualified than Toinette to play with fire.

FIVE

"THE ROPES NEED TARRING," TOINETTE WAS SAYING TO MARCUS, "especially toward the bow. The spray's been eating into them in no small way."

Erik stopped to listen as he came up on deck with a loaf of bread in one hand and a wineskin in the other. He couldn't have said why he listened—since none of the duties were his, there was no need—save for the pleasure of hearing Toinette speak with utter assurance. He'd always found a certain beauty in watching tasks performed by those who were skilled at them, even when they didn't possess Toinette's other charms.

She was standing at the wheel once more, talking to Marcus, with a few of the men nearby. "There's a bit of the deck there"—she gestured—"needs sanding and oiling. Keep a close eye for woodworm. Otherwise"—a shrug—"the wind's fair, and we'll make a good distance before sunset, God willing."

Marcus took a few of the men off, nodding to Erik in passing. Gervase and a towheaded man with a sharp chin went to fetch a bucket of sand, and only then did Toinette glance in Erik's direction. "If you're looking for duties," she said with a playful smile, "I can likely think of a few. You might even enjoy them."

Her voice didn't make it entirely clear what those duties would be, but had hint enough to warm Erik's blood. If there'd been privacy, he would have investigated further; he'd have wagered a great deal that Toinette knew as much.

Teasing wench. When they returned to Bordeaux, Erik vowed silently, he'd see how far she would follow through on her suggestions.

For the moment, he contented himself with saying, "I'm sure I'd rejoice in any command you gave me," and letting their eyes meet for a few fraught heartbeats before adding, "by way of making up for the hardship I'm causing you and your men."

"There's hardship and hardship, isn't there?" Gervase said from the patch of deck nearby.

As Erik had seen on land, Toinette let her men speak freely, but he flattered himself he saw a flash of irritation cross her face at the interruption. She stifled it well, though, and only asked, "How do you mean?"

"Well, this voyage we're on, it's the Atlantic, and it's further north than I'd like, and we don't know the route exactly, no?"

"Aye," said Erik.

The tow-haired man grunted a "Hunh," which Erik took for displeased agreement.

"Dangerous," said Gervase, giving his companion no attention. "But so too are the winds off Tyre, and storms anywhere, and men always. Three times I've fought pirates. I lost a good friend and three toes. Then on land there's war, plague, bad meat, brigands, women—so I say to myself, Gervase, you have the span of years the good Lord gave you, and you know not what that will be, no more than does any man. Best to spend them more eventfully than in taking salt fish from Calais to Dover and back."

Erik nodded. "'The coward believes he will ever live if he keep him safe from strife, but old age leaves him not long in peace, though spears may spare his life.'"

"Yes, just so! Your words?"

"No, I'm no poet. A saying of my grandmother's people. Translated, more or less."

The other sailor glanced up at Erik from under lowered brows. "A Norseman as well as a Scot, then?" he asked in an English accent. "My lord?"

It wasn't quite sarcastic, but skirted around the edge. Toinette's lips went thin. "The *Hawk* bears a French charter, John," she said. "You'd do well to keep that in mind, if we're suddenly minding kings and nations."

"Captain," said John, and bent his head back to his work.

"Don't mind him," said Gervase. His hands made quick circles as he talked; he worked without looking, a man for whom it was second nature. "You should be bled a week into every voyage, John. It'd improve your temper considerably."

"For two pence, I'll improve *yours*," said John, but the threat sounded almost genial, and he looked at Gervase without any of the resentment he'd shown Erik.

"No improving perfection. You're only jealous that *I* know I'll not drown."

"Not drown?" Erik asked, both curious and eager to turn the conversation from his allegiance.

"The earring," said Toinette, and gestured. "Tales say it's the best protection a man can have, unless he can lay his hands on a caul."

"And I keep saying you should have a pair, Captain," said Gervase.

"One day I might. Meantime, I can take care of myself," she said, and gave Erik another grin before turning back to the ocean and adding, under her voice, "in all the ways I want to."

Conditions aboard ship being what they were, it was a few days before Erik found Toinette alone. She did her best to give him the opportunity, but always there was work to be done, or men around asking questions, and no easy way to put them off. Knowing the question Erik would ask, she also didn't feel much urgency.

It was to his credit that he braved the weather to find his chance. To Toinette, the squall didn't amount to more than a few bumps and a shower. Landsmen often felt differently. Then again, she admitted to herself as she saw him walk toward the forecastle, ignoring the rain on his face, Scotland and particularly its islands would make a stoic of anyone where weather was concerned.

"Here," he said, holding out a skin of wine. "It must be cold work out here, even for one of us."

"Cramps the hands, after a while," she admitted. The wine wasn't good, but it was warming. "I'd let you take a turn, but I'd rather live."

Erik laughed, not offended. "I'll start wi' the ropes, should I take a fancy to seafaring, and learn from there."

"That's how all my men did it, as far as I know," she said. The other meanings of *my men* came to mind then. Toinette looked up into the strong, wet face near her, and felt her heart beat faster than wrestling with the wheel would explain.

"A worthy lot to join, I've no doubt," said Erik. As Toinette waited for more, eyebrows arched, the flirting light died from his face, and he said, a man recalling duty, "I'd a mind to talk with you on that subject."

Toinette considered misunderstanding him and continuing the banter, then rejected the idea. This was business. It was best to get it out of the way; they both had responsibilities. "John?"

"Aye. He…knows what we're about?"

"As much as any of the men do. I told them the basics. Not about us, or too much about magic, though I did say that legends had it that…"—she waved her free hand—"and so forth. But he knows who you are, and that your mission is like to benefit Scotland. He signed on regardless. I'll not say he likes you, but that's not required."

The rain kept splashing down above them, steady and even. The deck would likely need inspection afterward, Toinette thought. Damp bred rot. She glanced from the sea in front of her back to Erik, who was hesitating.

"You don't think him likely to…" he finally said, looking embarrassed by the suggestion.

"To let the English know what you're trying? No, he's no way of contacting them, and nobody who'd listen, from what he's said of his home. To stab us in the back at the last minute? It wouldn't work on either of us, and the rest of the crew would tear him apart for trying."

"Ah. Yes." Relief joined but didn't chase off the embarrassment. "I'm sorry for raising the question, only I felt it necessary."

The wind shifted northward. Toinette turned back to the wheel with another shrug. "I would've, in your shoes. But John's like the rest of us, no matter how he grumbles. Wars are for kings and knights, and the poor bastards on their land."

"And your men are loyal to you."

Both the emphasis Erik used and the half-grudging admiration she heard made Toinette a trifle warmer from pride. Out loud she laughed. "And pay. It comes to the same, in the end."

"Does it?" Erik asked.

When she glanced over her shoulder, Toinette saw him studying her with an expression that was serious as well as heated. She cleared her throat. "I'd not care to test it too far—by knocking them about on this water, say. Best you get back below, and I to my duties."

Flirting was one thing. It was best, even for her, not to get in over her head.

The storm, such as it was, cleared up, and they had another few days of fine weather. Erik grew used to the sea air, the rocking boat, and the voices of the men blending with the lapping waves or the rippling sail.

Slowly he began to know a few of them: Gervase, of course, and Raoul, new and lovesick for a girl who'd "likely married already" in the words of cynical Sence. Most talked to him more reticently than they did to Toinette or Marcus, without long familiarity to smooth down the difference in their ranks, and John avoided him when possible, preferring suspicious looks from across the deck.

Yet there were days when general merriment overwhelmed them all, such as the time when the men brought in a vast blue fish, more than twice Erik's height. As it lay flopping on the deck, Yakob and Samuel stretching out their arms, the general laughter and cheers expanded to include Erik.

"This place you're taking us," Samuel said, with a flash of teeth, "is it full of such creatures?"

"We can but find out," Erik replied. "For all I know, it could be Prester John's kingdom and all its wonders, though I'd not hold my breath in hoping."

"Wise of you," said Marcus, striding up with a more serious countenance. "Good work, but we'd best have it butchered and salted quickly, and return to duties. Captain doesn't like the look of those clouds to the east."

SIX

BARELY AN HOUR LATER, TOINETTE LIKED THE CLOUDS EVEN LESS.

Not content with being large, dark, and fast accumulating—any of which would have been ill chance enough in the middle of a strange ocean—they'd developed a sickly greenish undercast. Never in Toinette's experience had that color failed to mean an unpleasant time ahead.

"Looks like we're in for a blow, men," she said when Marcus had assembled the hands in front of her. "For the moment, we'll run before the wind and try to get ahead of the worst. Raoul, Samuel, Marcus, trim the sail. The rest of you, to the hold. Lash down everything heavy, and have buckets ready to bail if the water gets high. Should this thing catch up with us, we may drop anchor and furl sail. There won't be much warning, so listen for my shout."

She glanced toward the new men in the crowd. Emrich was looking pale, Sence watching the faces to either side of him, and Raoul surprisingly composed. None of the three looked close to breaking, thank God. All she needed was to have a man go off his head in the middle of a storm.

"Be wary, all of you. This is new ground for all of us… well, not ground," she joked, by way of easing the tension, "but new. No knowing what storms in this part of the sea might be like. No foolish chances, aye?"

"Aye, Captain," came the chorus.

"To your duties, then, and may God see us through this safely. Marcus, I'll take the wheel. Come to me with any questions."

"And what should I do?" Erik asked, falling in at her side as Toinette hurried toward the prow of the ship.

"Help below, if you've a mind. Try not to go overboard. Unless you can magic away this weather, you're a strong back at the moment."

"I fear that it'll be the second. Weather..." he spread his hands. "John's already been silvering the water, same as the fishermen used to do back home. I wouldn't be capable of much more."

Toinette nodded, unsurprised. No wizard she'd ever met, Artair or his daughter Agnes included, could command the weather well enough to stop a storm in its tracks—particularly not at sea, where ocean water played merry hell with magic in any case. Throwing silver coins into the waves and being careful not to whistle was the best any man or woman could do, even if they were sorcerers.

"Get on below, then," she said. "Keep your head down and your wits about you. Even we can drown if the sea's bad enough, and if a falling crate takes your head off, I doubt it'll grow back."

"So noted." Erik flashed her a smile. His skin had tanned over the last month, and his teeth were very white against it, another legacy of their shared blood. "A man might be forgiven for thinking you cared, with talk like that."

"It looks bad to let the passenger die. Especially if he's paid already."

Below the deck, the men had uncoiled great spools of rope and were tying them around the barrels and boxes of provisions, making them fast to the wall by means of iron hooks. Gervase and Franz were telling Emrich about storms in the past. The others were silent, save for Yakob, who was steadily praying as he worked. Erik caught the names of saints Elmo, Peter, and Brendan: nicely scattered among nations, though he'd no notion of whether that would make the prayers more effective or not.

Descending, Erik joined the group of them. He got a few startled looks at first, but the men accepted him quickly and without question, save for saying "m'lord" when they told him what to lift and where to put it.

It was hard work, but physically well within his means: the dragon-blooded were slightly stronger than most men even in human form. Lifting and carrying were almost an enjoyable change from the last month of enforced idleness.

The worst of it was the hot airlessness of the hold. Neither heat nor cold could truly harm Erik, but they could be damned uncomfortable, and this was. The whole place also reeked of unwashed sweat, which he was mostly used to, and of terror, which he hadn't smelled in a good few months. Franz and Gervase might talk a good game, Sence and John might maintain a stoic silence, but all of them were afraid.

When the ship veered hard to port, Erik stumbled and fell against the wall. A brittle scratch of laughter went up. "Should've stayed out of the wine, m'lord," Gervase said, extending a hand. Even his joking voice was shaky, and the hand Erik clasped was cold.

"Och, I'm weak and a sinner," Erik jested in reply. "Especially about the legs, it seems."

"No better way to learn than a storm," said Franz. "Here. Hold while I tie up. My lord," he added.

Obediently, Erik took his place in front of a great barrel of salt beef. As the ship turned again, he braced his arms against the weight and considered the prospect of being killed by a cow—several cows, in truth, but that would do very little for his pride. It might, however, be a fitting vengeance for the beasts.

"Do you think we'll outrun it?" he asked Franz.

The sailor, tall and dark with a luxuriant mustache, shrugged. "Could be. Captain knows her trade, but none know these waters. Or these winds. There." He yanked a knot tight and then stood back, prompting Erik to warily do the same.

Ropes held. Barrels stayed in place. From above, a clap of thunder rolled slowly across the sky.

Profanity in three different languages filled the hold. Yakob's prayers got more intense, but he also grabbed a stack of large buckets from the corner. "Half of you go, half stay," he said to the others, motioning toward the ladder. "I'll pass them up."

Erik followed the other men, climbed swiftly, and emerged into a world of greenish-purple light.

Saint Elmo's fire. Toinette had seen it a time or two before. Some held it to be a good omen; she knew only that it went with storms and sea.

Usually it came toward the end of the storm, though, not at the beginning. Then too, it had typically been blue or green, without the violet hue that made it look sickly and diseased, and it had confined itself to the mast rather than spreading all across the deck. The difference might have been down to the sea, yet a feeling in the pit of her stomach said, *This is uncanny*.

Gripping the ship's wheel, she uttered the Latin words— *visio dei*—she'd learned at Loch Arach in her youth, calling on the aid of spirits that would let her see the hidden world of supernatural forces—and nothing happened.

What in God's holy name?

She didn't let herself clutch the wheel as tightly as she wanted, lest it break. She told herself that an absence of magical sight was the last thing she needed to worry about. It had been a while since she'd bothered, and there was the chance she'd done it wrong, or perhaps the spirits who made such things possible wouldn't come near a lightning storm. Toinette had never tried invoking them in such circumstances before.

She had more urgent considerations. Lightning was flickering through the clouds above, and growls of thunder followed it, growing steadily louder. Toinette eyed the motion of the sky, looked at the rising waves, and made a decision.

"No outrunning this one, damn the luck," she called to Marcus. "Strike the sail and drop the anchor. We'll try to ride it out."

She didn't wait to see the order carried out. Toinette knew her men, and knew that Marcus would ride herd on Raoul if need be. She turned back to the wheel. A hard, spitting rain began to fall, blowing horizontally into her face. The *Hawk* rocked from side to side.

The first stab of lightning hit the sea about a hundred feet off. It lit up the sky, which had otherwise turned dark as midnight. Everything looked vivid in that second of illumination. The restless sea stretched far out ahead of the *Hawk*, with nobody and nothing for hundreds of miles, as far as Toinette could tell.

They were alone in the storm.

It hit them hard and suddenly, one long scream of Nature roused to fury. Toinette was no stranger to storms, even to perilous ones, but this outdid everything she'd seen, everything she'd even heard of, save for the tales of men who'd been to the Indies. Lightning struck again and again, turning the sea around them into blue-green flame for a few seconds at a time. The thunder rolled in constant baritone to the higher voices of the wind and the sea, but all were rendingly loud.

Soaked, breathless, Toinette clung to the wheel. Even with the anchor, the *Hawk* could capsize without a steady hand, and Toinette knew very well that she might do so even with one. Ships were wood and men were mortal, and she was close enough to a man to fail. She'd done that before, but never with others' lives at stake.

The ship rolled from side to side, and waves beat at the hull with fierce, wet noises. A few washed over the sides. More followed, swamping the deck, and behind Toinette the men ran back and forth with buckets, throwing the water back overboard. It was a perilous business. Cries and oaths rang out as someone slipped; from the tone, she didn't think he'd gone over the rail. Toinette had learned to identify such things.

She couldn't have named the moment when she knew they were losing. Time lost meaning in any storm, and this one made her half forget it ever had existed, that there'd ever been a normal world outside the pandemonium of wind and water.

Her arms ached. She thought, *We're not likely to come through this one.* That was everything she could muster of words, since all else was simple instinct to clutch and stand and turn. She probably should have prayed, but she couldn't remember anything past Ave Maria or Pater Noster.

Then the mast went up in a blaze of lightning. Even with her back turned, Toinette saw the strike: it filled the world. A shriek followed, human but inhuman, as men sounded in the final extremes of agony. She couldn't turn to see who it was, nor shut her eyes in sympathy, for the ship, unbalanced, rolled in that moment and only the full extent of her strength kept it from overturning completely.

A hand grasped her shoulder. She snarled.

"Change." Erik stood behind her. Of course it was Erik. Anyone else would have known not to approach her. She was doing the only thing she could do, for whatever difference that made. "We need to change."

Words flooded back, borne on anger like a tide. "I'm not a rat, damn you, whatever else I am. I'll not leave my crew!"

"No!" he shouted back, straining to be heard over the storm. "One on each side—keep the ship upright!"

Toinette's first instinct was to say that he knew nothing of ships or the sea—but she did. And his notion might work.

Moreover, nothing else likely would.

"Get Marcus," she said.

In an eyeblink, her second-in-command was there, blood sheeting down his head but upright and otherwise unharmed. "Take the wheel. Try to keep the men calm. We won't hurt you. I'm sorry."

"What?"

There was no time for explanation, but old habits were strong in Marcus. He grabbed the wheel as Toinette left it, and didn't let go of it to catch her as she ran to the rail. He shouted as she leapt.

She didn't hear the sound he made when she transformed.

SEVEN

POUNDING WAVES GRASPED ERIK AND PULLED HIM DOWN. THE water was dark, cold, briny where it seeped into his closed mouth, and heavy. He'd never thought of water as heavy before. It weighed on him like lead.

Water slowed the shift too. His muscles twisted, expanding around bones that grew and changed. Claws slid from his hands and feet. His neck rippled outward, vertebrae multiplying; spines sprouted from the back of it. Erik felt it all, as he hadn't done since years before he'd come to manhood. His lungs burned through it, lack of air blurring his vision, until his wings sprouted and let him thrash his way back to the surface.

There he gasped the storm-ravaged air. Above him, on the tilting deck of the *Hawk*, the sailors were crying out in panic. Erik hoped that Marcus could calm them. For a mercy, none of them had tried to attack him yet.

He swam awkwardly sideways toward the ship, learning to move with the waves as best he could. Filling his lungs in case he sank further than he intended, he let his body fall downward, then rise, taking the weight of the *Hawk* along his right side.

In dragon form, Erik was far stronger than he was as a man. He'd lifted cows into the air with no more effort than a man might use to heft a brace of rabbits after a day's hunt. The *Hawk* was still a vast weight. He made no attempt to lift it out of the water, only to keep it upright in the waves, yet for a few moments the mass of it was almost overpowering, certainly more than he could hold for any time.

Then the weight balanced onto the other side. The ship righted itself. At the edge of his vision, just ahead of the prow, Erik saw the great dark shape of Toinette's head, long horns curving back like stylized lightning bolts themselves. Her eyes met his, fully golden in the darkness. They couldn't speak in this form, but Toinette gave a faint nod, Erik nodded back, and both knew the words that would go with the gesture: *I can do this for a while.*

With Toinette to aid him, he could. His muscles had carried his whole weight up into the air more times than he could count. Now the water would support him, turbulent as it was, and the *Hawk* through him. They had only to balance themselves, balance the ship, and wait.

The storm kept up its assault for a long time. Waves slapped Erik in the face, even though he held his head up high. Lightning pierced the water around them and sent sharp tingling sensations crawling across his skin. The itching was the worst of that, making it devilishly hard to keep still.

Occasionally he turned his head toward the *Hawk* and saw the sailors at the rails. Most were still running back and forth with bailing buckets. Good thing: the less water the ship took on board, the less difficulty he and Toinette would have carrying it.

Most of them stopped a moment when they poured the buckets overboard, staring down at Erik with eyes so wide that he could practically see the whites at his distance. In a brief break in the storm's noises, he heard Marcus call one of the men to stop gawping and be about his duties, or by God he would get a reason to move faster.

All around them, the green fire lit the ship's deck. The air smelled of salt, lightning, and a trace of blood.

Erik began to think that the storm would never end. Common sense said that it had to, that all storms did. Anywhere else, that would have been more of a comfort. As best Erik knew, the only men to sail to that part of the world had been the Templars, years ago, and no man knew what had become of them. Such an alien sea could very well host an eternal tempest.

With his quest, he might well have doomed them all.

Dragon shape was lonely.

Toinette hadn't mentioned that to Erik when she'd spoken of her preference for a ship, but that was another truth: she could speak to nobody in that form, not even other dragons. The oldest had been able to talk mind-to-mind, or so Artair's stories had said, but she was descended too far for that. All the words that tied her to others were gone while she was in dragon form.

In the sky, after a long time in much company, that was sometimes restful for a little while, but too much time with her own thoughts and Toinette grew ill-humored under even the most cheerful circumstances. In the storm-tossed ocean, with her crew staring at her in horror, an hour might have driven her to screaming if not for Erik's presence on the other side of the *Hawk*.

He couldn't speak either. Still, he met her eyes from time to time, his shining almost the same blue-green as the lightning-struck water. More than that, he was present and there, another member of her bloodline. It helped more than she'd ever thought such a thing would, and certainly more than she'd ever admit to him.

They went onward, floating and paddling to stay in place, as the storm shrieked itself out around them. It drowned the voices of the crew, but Toinette didn't mind that. She very much doubted that she wanted to hear anything they were saying just then. She could imagine quite enough.

No matter: if they and she both lived, then they could sort out the rest one way or another. Toinette only prayed that the storm would end soon, that lightning wouldn't hit her or Erik directly—that might kill even one of them—and most of all, that the clouds wouldn't spawn a waterspout. She'd seen one of those once, from a blessedly great distance. For a crippled ship, it would probably be doom.

When the thunder began to grow softer and the lightning less frequent, Toinette feared it was an illusion. Wishful thinking was a flaw she knew well. She watched, not daring to hope too highly, as the waves gradually settled. Lightning became flickers in the clouds once again, fading, then gone. The clouds themselves broke up slowly.

Toinette craned her head back to look at the *Hawk*. The shattered remnants of the mast stabbed into the clearing sky. The rail was broken in several places. God knew what damage the waves and wind had done to the wood. The storm was ending, but it had left them in a bad state indeed.

In time Toinette and Erik both shifted to the side, letting the water take the *Hawk*'s weight once more. Neither moved to change back. Toinette could guess at Erik's reasons. Most resembled her own: it was best to be on hand in case damage became worse with time and the ship started taking on water; transformation took strength that neither of them had; and the crew, who would have to get them back aboard, were all occupied. She couldn't have said whether he had her reluctance to face the men, nor whether it would be easier or harder for him, not having known them as well beforehand.

For a while they floated. The men pulled up the anchor, slow and clanking. The ship drifted forward, but without wind, the tide moved it very slowly. It took only the occasional flex of muscle for Toinette to keep up. The water was cool around her, supporting and sustaining as it had been treacherous not an hour before. She ducked her head as a school of swordfish swam near, bit the pointed bill off one, and swallowed the rest of it whole. Blood and flesh began to take the edge off her weariness almost at once.

She knew that she should go back aboard. The men would want an explanation. They'd need a captain. Erik couldn't supply the second, nor was the first his duty. She, Toinette, had taken these men into her employ, and she would meet their accusations with as much courage as she could manage. She had to.

Sighing, she turned her head upward to look at the deck again. Marcus had just come to the rail. That was well: of all the men, he was probably the most likely to bother pulling her up when she turned back to a woman.

"Captain!" he called, cupping his hands to make his voice louder. Just before changing, Toinette halted in place. "Captain, we think there's land ahead!"

In her exhaustion, she hadn't even thought to look.

Toinette whipped her head around—the motion of her neck sent water splashing upward in a small fountain—and peered out past the horizon. Her third eyelid slid down, focusing her vision and screening out the worst of the sun's glare.

Yes, there was a dark smudge on the horizon, too low and stable to be a cloud bank. Even she could make out nothing more definite at their distance, but she nodded her head rapidly—enough of a sign for Marcus, judging from the short cheer above her.

Erik seemed to have understood as well, for he caught her eye from across the ship's prow and nodded, jerking his head toward the shape. Toinette waved a wing slowly across the water, eliciting another nod: they'd float for a while, regaining their strength and letting the current move them.

When the tide did shift, she and Erik came closer to the ship. They didn't take the full weight of it again, but they pushed it toward the land, making up as much as they could for the lack of sail. Such interludes were thankfully short. The sea itself seemed to be with them, for which Toinette sent up a prayer or seven of thanksgiving.

The dark shape in the distance became an island perhaps ten miles long. Cliffs took shape, and the twisted forms of wind-stunted evergreen trees atop them. As the *Hawk* drew closer yet, Toinette could see the long, tan line of the beach.

Plenty of rocks studded the sand. They were large enough for her to spot even at a distance, which meant there were likely to be more in the water as they approached. At the speed the *Hawk* was going, even running aground was likely to leave all the men standing; still, Toinette wanted to keep the ship as whole as she could. Hope spawned hope, and she had begun to think of repairs.

Such thoughts kept her going. All else was beginning to fail. Even a dragon's strength ended, and food could only do so much. Her outstretched wings ached. The side where she pushed the *Hawk* was alternately numb and burning. Her vision blurred every few minutes, and she had to blink it back to clarity again.

Just a little longer.

Toinette lost herself in purpose and sense. The smell of blood still mingled with salt, but she didn't wonder whose, or how badly injured they might be. The water was cold. The wind was colder, and the glare of the setting sun brought no warmth with its red light. Birds, returned after the departing storm, called far overhead.

She spotted the first of the rocks and leaned her weight into the ship, pushing it sideways. Erik caught on quickly and helped her. They seemed to move like people in a dream, slow and drifting, with no feeling that they'd actually get anywhere.

Truly, it was a surprise when the *Hawk* came to rest on sand. Toinette couldn't stretch her mind around it for a little while.

The ship had stopped moving.

She let go of its weight, sighing in relief, and swam forward. A few strokes brought her far enough toward land that her claws touched the ocean's bottom. A few more steps and she was on the beach itself, the sand moist beneath her feet.

They'd done it. They were out of danger. Toinette pushed herself a few more steps, until she was far enough up the beach to escape the incoming tide. Then she collapsed, stretched full-length on the sand.

Later, she would explain things to her crew. If they wanted to slit her throat in the meantime, that would be too bad, but right then she couldn't make herself care enough to stay awake.

EIGHT

WHEN ERIK WOKE, THE SKY WAS DARK AGAIN. THIS TIME THE stars shone through it and a crescent moon hovered over-head. He followed familiar constellations with relief: ratio-nality said they weren't likely to have traveled beyond the skies he knew, but after the day he'd had, he still welcomed the reassurance of the Pleiades and Cassiopeia.

Following Toinette's lead, as she knew her crew better than he did, Erik had lain down beside her and slept with-out changing form. After he came to full wakefulness, he stretched and allowed himself to slip back into a man's shape. This time it went as quickly and painlessly as the change normally did.

A month on ship had ensured that magic recognized all his clothing as a part of him, and thus he was still dressed as a human. He was glad of it. Modesty aside, the night air was cool and damp, and the sand rockier than he'd have wanted to walk without boots.

He smelled smoke and turned to follow the odor. Several yards off, the sailors had built a fire between two of the largest rocks. They sat huddled around it, small fragile shapes against the empty night.

"Only six," said Toinette's voice from behind him.

Erik turned back toward her. She was human again as well, bright hair loosed from its moorings and straggling over her shoulders, rumpled red wool clinging to her figure. The gold sparks in her eyes might have been reflections of the firelight, and her face was expressionless.

"Yes," said Erik after a quick count.

"You saw more than I did in the storm. Do you know who didn't make it?"

"Gervase." That image stood out in Erik's mind. From experience, he knew it would stay there a while yet. "The mast."

"He didn't drown," she said with a bitter and exhausted mirth. "You could argue that the earring was worth its price, couldn't you? Who else?"

"Yakob fell badly when the ship tilted. Broke his neck. Emrich went overboard. I only heard that after, when it was too late." Erik spoke bluntly, as he'd learned to do in war. He didn't think Toinette would welcome either gentleness or hesitation.

She nodded, lips pressed together, and crossed herself. "It was a good thought," she said eventually, "transforming. Might have saved the rest of us."

"I'd no way of knowing it would work."

"Comes a point when you've no way of knowing that about anything." She made an attempt at gathering up the untidy mass of her hair, realized it was futile, and let it spill down her back again. "I should go speak to them. You can come too, or not, as you wish."

"I'll join you," Erik said. "If you think it'll help rather than hinder."

"That point I mentioned?" She quirked her mouth up on one side in a half smile. "We're still at it. Come on, then."

Wet sand made for unsteady footing. Toinette grumbled, but only half-heartedly. Keeping her balance was a distraction. Looking down at her feet meant less time watching the faces that had turned toward her as she approached, looking from her to Erik.

She wasn't sure whether or not she was glad to have him there. Allies were good. Witnesses, if the conversation went badly, were not, most particularly witnesses who'd seen her when she'd been fifteen, filthy, and desperate. If this ended with Erik feeling sorry for her, she thought she might fly off then and there, no matter that she had no notion of where she was going.

The waves washed steadily against the sand. The fire crackled, burning shades of blue and lavender: driftwood. Pretty as the flames were, they cast all the crew in an eerie, ghostly light. Perhaps that was good. Perhaps it would make them feel on more equal footing.

Toinette cleared her throat. "Well," she said, hands clasped behind her back as if she were a girl again and facing her tutor. Reciting Latin would have been easier. "You saw."

"That we did," Marcus answered, his voice and eyes both expressionless. "You're dragons."

"We're people," said Toinette, "who turn into dragons. Sometimes."

"How?" asked Sence.

In every pair of narrowed eyes lurked the shadow of a horned figure. "Blood."

"Inheritance," Erik said at her shoulder. "It goes back generations." Toinette thought of the other meanings *blood* could have, and gave him a grateful look.

"We made no pacts," she said, holding her open hands in front of her. "As best I know, my soul's intact. I go to mass as often as any of you"—at that she heard a couple of the men, including Marcus, chuckle, and a few, including Raoul, look down at the ground—"and if you'd like

me to recite Scripture, I could likely manage a few lines
at least."

"Here," said Samuel, getting to his feet and holding out
one closed hand. It took a moment for Toinette to make
out the rosary dangling from it, jet beads glimmering in the
witch light of the fire. "Hold this and say the Ave Maria. A
creature of the devil couldn't do that."

Asking how many of Satan's creatures he'd tried it on
probably would not help at that juncture. Toinette closed
her fist tightly around the silver cross. "*Ave Maria, gratia
plena...*" she began.

It had been a long time since her last mass. The words
came clumsily to her, but the prayer helped in more ways
than one. By the end, Toinette felt the tight knot of her
sorrow ease, and though their predicament weighed on her,
the guilt no longer felt like a barbed hook in her insides.
The lessened suspicion on the men's faces was probably a
good part of that relief too.

She opened her hand and turned it over, letting the men
all see her palm. Transforming had healed her palm of the
scrapes from her final desperate struggle with the wheel,
and neither cross nor beads had left any mark.

The crew looked with the gravity of men buying horses
or weighing accounts. Sence was the first to nod.

"Are you relations?" asked Franz. "If you're both...if
this is blood."

"Lord, no!" said Erik, quickly enough that Toinette
lifted her eyebrows, wondering if he feared contaminating
the MacAlasdair name by association with her. "Or only
distant ones if we are. More than third cousins, likely."

"I don't know who my father was," Toinette added
briskly. If the truth was to come out, it might as well all
come out—or almost all. "What I heard of him doesn't

resemble any of Erik's kin. So. Now we all know. And we're all here."

"That," said Marcus with a sigh, "we are indeed."

"Wherever that may be," said John.

All of them turned to Erik, who hesitated and shrugged. "This *might* be the island I was seeking." He looked up at the stars, frowning, then shook his head. "I believe it is the right place, but I can't read the sky as well as you can. My map…was with the rest of my belongings," he added, looking back over his shoulder at the bulk of the landed ship.

"We'll salvage tomorrow. The light'll be better then. No need to go in with torches and set it all on fire," Marcus said.

Wordlessly, the men moved to open a place for Toinette and Erik. The gesture went further toward calming Toinette than speech ever would have, and Raoul helped by handing over a small tin box. "We did get out a little of the food."

It was dried bread and salt beef, with a skin of warm wine going around for drink, but Toinette relished it. So did Erik, by his expression and the way he ate. Usually the size of prey they took in dragon form would have kept them full for a while, but occasionally snatched fish hadn't been nearly enough fuel for the effort Toinette had put in that day. Her muscles were already making their objections known.

"It's too dark to build any shelters," Marcus said. "But we've all slept rough before, and it's not likely to rain again." Indeed, the sky above them was clear enough to count every star, and the wind blew warmly from the east.

"Any creatures out yonder?" Erik waved a hand to the dark bulk of the forest.

"None that we've seen or heard, save birds. It's likely our fire will scare most beasts away. All the same, we'll keep watch. There's enough of us that no man will have to lose more than an hour or two of sleep," Marcus replied.

"Nor do we have to be up at dawn," Toinette put in. She stretched her feet out toward the fire, enjoying the heat on her damp boots. When dragon shape recognized her clothing as part of her, the garments stayed in the same condition from one human moment to the next: wonderful for avoiding further damage, but it did very little toward drying out wet clothes. "Well, I don't mind taking the midnight shift, if it's not claimed. I'm a few hours ahead of you men as it is."

"Oh," said Franz. "John's taking that. We've given them all out."

"Didn't know when you'd wake up, did we? And anyhow, the two of you have exerted yourself far more than the rest of us did today. Best that you get a full night of it. We'll work out more arrangements come the morning." Marcus gave her a quick smile. He might have intended it to be reassuring, or apologetic, or both.

There were even odds of him being sincere about the reasons. Even if those weren't *all* the reasons, the men had planned the watches before Toinette had given her explanation and proved that she wasn't in league with Satan, at least so far as rosaries could determine. It was important to keep such things in mind, particularly when she was in a melancholy humor to begin with.

She made herself give her normal smile, breezy and matter-of-fact. "I'll never say no to an extra night of sleep, Marcus. You know that."

They let the fire burn. The man keeping watch would guard it too, and they needed a balance to the cold sand beneath them.

After the planning, the conversation turned desultory, with long pauses that grew longer. It was too late and everyone was too tired to talk of the men they'd lost or the uncertainty of their future, but anything else would have been hideously incongruous. A few at a time, the men lay down and sought the release of sleep.

In time, only Sence, Erik, and Toinette were left sitting at the fire, all three of them silent. Unfamiliar night birds called in the forest behind them. The stars were quiet overhead. Taken out of context, the scene might have been a very peaceful one.

"Have you enough wood?" Erik asked.

Sence jerked his chin at a pile off in the shadows. "We gathered it earlier. Should last until morning, or near enough."

"Good," Erik said. "Then I'm off as well. Wake me if there's need."

He lay down on the sand. Even with the sleep he'd gotten earlier and his less-than-comfortable bedding, fatigue soon stole over his body, weighing down bones and eyelids alike. Sleep itself didn't come for a while, though: not until he heard Toinette's voice muttering her own good night, and felt the disruption in the breeze as she stretched herself out on the land. She lay beside him, though several feet away, and he heard her slow, steady breathing.

If she was asleep, she'd been quick about it. If not, she feigned well. Either way, the sound sent Erik off too, pulling him down into slumber as into the sea itself.

NINE

Daylight, food, and a full night of sleep worked no miracles. They were still stranded on an island in the middle of nowhere, and three good men were still dead. Toinette couldn't exactly be cheerful under those circumstances, certainly not less than a day afterward. After eating, she did feel that she could see the world without a hazy veil across it and move about without her limbs weighing twice what they should have. That would suffice.

What she could see of the island by day was a strip of sandy beach that curved around in a crescent shape. Cliffs rose stark, gray, and forbidding a half mile or so up the shore, and trees, mostly pines and birches, grew atop them. The rocks on the beach were smooth, well worn by the water. The form of the ship at rest might have been just another one, larger and oddly shaped.

"We should salvage what we can from the *Hawk*," Toinette said after the mostly silent meal. "It'll be easier to repair the less we have aboard, and we'll want food and bedding close to hand, if there's any undamaged. And"— she glanced toward the mast—"we'll want to give Gervase and Yakob a decent burial."

Heads around the fire nodded, Sence's particularly strongly at the last statement.

Erik added, as if it was a commonplace suggestion, "The two of us could get the cargo off in our other forms, aye? At least once we've got it onto the deck—pluck it off while we're in the water, and swim it over."

"I expect so," said Toinette slowly, watching the faces of her men.

"At that," Marcus said, "you could overfly the island. It'd be well to know how the rest of the land lies, and a sight easier than getting up those cliffs." He waved a hand in their direction. "We'll see about making shelters in the meantime. There were some chunks of driftwood too large to burn, and I thought I saw a few likely rocks further up the beach."

"There's sense in that," Toinette replied.

Marcus rolled his eyes at her. "Sound a bit less startled when you say so, Captain, if you would?"

It was the first joke he'd made to her since the storm. She laughed, and the air took the sound strangely—but perhaps any air would have seemed to do so just then. "Humility is a virtue, haven't you heard?"

"I've enough virtue as it is. Best not to overdo it."

This time, the men's laughter joined Toinette's. The morning got a bit better. There was no need to explain that she'd sounded startled not by Marcus's idea but because he'd been so willing to voice it.

"Best begin, then," she said. "Erik?"

"As my lady commands."

"Whoever your lady is," Toinette said, "I suspect she has considerably less sand in her boots."

They went off a little way to transform, as much to spare the men the sight as to avoid putting the fire out. Still Toinette thought that some of the crew were watching, Marcus and Samuel most notably among them.

Between her arrival at Castle MacAlasdair and the storm the previous day, she'd never transformed in front of anyone but other dragon-blooded. In the storm she'd had no time to think. She felt naked now, only mere nudity had never bothered her so much.

Stop being a simpering maiden, she told herself. *Pretend they're not around.*

Toinette closed her eyes and clenched her teeth. Briefly she feared that awkwardness would hinder her change, but it went as swiftly and smoothly as ever. Dragon form had always come easily to her—too easily in her youth.

As soon as the change was stable, she leapt into the air, circling upward. The air currents were unfamiliar and, she soon learned, treacherous. She found herself frantically beating her wings for altitude one minute, while in the next, a headwind would force her backward. Damnably odd weather, though who knew what normal was like in this part of the world?

She wouldn't have wanted to try to fly out, even if there hadn't been the men to consider. It was as much as she could do to get enough height for a view of the island.

It spread out wider after the cliffs. The rough crescent stayed the same over all, but they'd certainly landed on the inner edge. The rest was a dark mass of forest. Occasionally, birds flew up above it—ravens and gulls, mostly, from what Toinette could see—but the trees were too dense for her to make out more life. They were too dense for her to try landing there too.

To her side, the sound of vast wings alerted her to Erik's presence. She turned and saw him there, looking much as she remembered him from their youth: sky-blue, with eyes that glowed a bit like Saint Elmo's fire as it normally appeared, and more square than sinuous. With her black scales nearby, as Moiread had observed once, they put an audience in mind of a summer thunderstorm.

He seemed to be having as much trouble staying aloft as she did, and showed no more inclination to land. Toinette wasn't mean enough to find that satisfying, but she would admit that she would have felt worse if the wind hadn't been giving him any trouble.

Drifting down toward the beach again, she did see that one end wound up the cliffs and into the forest. It wasn't much of a path, but it would be better than trying to climb the cliffs themselves, and they would likely need to go up there. Repairing the *Hawk* would take more than driftwood; also, there might be food that wasn't fish. In dragon form, Toinette didn't see the appeal of vegetation, but she knew humans needed it.

She landed on the sand with a lightness that pleased her: the satisfaction of knowing her body still worked well, after she'd put it through a trial or five. The small pleasure sustained her through the next few minutes, when she shifted and walked up to rejoin the men. They were rising from around the fire and forming small groups under Marcus's direction. Past them, the *Hawk* sat dark in the water, maimed and still. Toinette tried not to hear her say *You failed*.

"We'll retrieve the bodies first," she said, "then the supplies."

"What are the usual rites? When someone dies at sea, that is?"

"You pick the best ways to make conversation."

Erik shrugged. "I just didn't know if I should be doing something. War—" He spread his hands. "When we had time and a priest, we might have buried the men where they lay, or taken them home if they were noble."

Less than a hundred years back, it would have been *mos Teutonicus* for a good many noblemen: boiling the flesh off the bones, as a skeleton packed lighter and cleaner than a whole body. Cathal had told stories about seeing such things on Crusade, but one of the last few popes had forbidden the practice before Erik had been to war.

"Over the side for us, generally, and pay for masses later," said Toinette. "You can't keep a dead body on a ship. We've got enough land for burial here, but…" She shrugged. "No priest. Hard luck for them, but they won't be the first, and if they go to Purgatory for it, they'll have company enough."

"Aye," said Erik, "right you are."

In the plague years, thousands had gone to Saint Peter unshriven and buried without rites, many without even their own plot to lie in. They'd died too fast for the priests—who'd been dying themselves. God would hopefully understand. Granted, God had presumably sent the plague in the first place, but Erik was no priest and that was not a road he wanted to go too far down.

Morbid thoughts weighed on a man's mind. As he followed Toinette up the *Hawk*'s gangplank, Erik thought it took more effort than it should have, as though the island was trying to tug him back down and he had to fight it with every step.

Don't make a fuss, lad, he told himself. *You're weary, that's all, and distressed.*

The sight that met his eyes when he reached the deck hardly eased his mind. Gervase, or what was left of him, lay crushed under the broken mast. One arm was flung up and out to the side, as though he could have shielded himself. He had no face any longer, but the gold earring shone up from the red mess on the deck.

"Holy Mary, aid us," said Toinette. She shook her head and closed her eyes.

Erik put a hand on her arm. "I'm truly sorry," he said. "I know he'd been with you a long time."

"Years, yes," she said, and neither of them bothered specifying *long for a mortal*. Toinette spoke hoarsely. "They say worse things happen at sea. This is one of them."

"That it is, lass."

Toinette drew her thumb and forefinger across her closed eyelids, tracing the copper fans of her lashes before pinching the bridge of her nose. "We can make shrouds out of the sailcloth. There's enough left whole, and spare below for getting back."

Separating cloth from mast was a tiresome, sweaty business, and a grim one as well, as it meant working around Gervase's body. Both Toinette and Erik were silent while they worked, and then while they carefully wrapped the shroud. Anything else would have seemed an affront to the dead man.

The cloth was almost an affront itself: damp, grimy, and clumsily cut at the edges, as belt daggers were not made for that sort of work. It *was* thick enough that the off-white didn't turn red immediately, for which, Erik thought, God be praised.

Toinette worked quickly, with steady hands and set lips. Once Erik opened his mouth to say that she didn't need to do this, that she could go back to shore and rest, but he stopped himself. The girl he'd known would have blackened his eye for such a suggestion. The woman had likely learned better manners, but even if she accepted, Erik doubted she'd do so happily.

Instead, when they'd tucked in every fold that they could, he straightened up and asked, "Would you rather take him back while I go below and get Yakob, or the other way 'round? I don't think there's any need for both of us."

"No," Toinette said slowly. "Best for one of us to stay up here while the other's below. If the ship's taken more damage than we can see from here, and the deck collapses, whoever's below will want someone close at hand."

"Ah," said Erik, considering that prospect. "We could each likely scream loud enough to be heard from shore, but I take your point. Above or below, then?"

"I'll wait here," said Toinette.

As Erik descended into the hold, he saw her clasp her hands behind her back and stare out across the water.

TEN

"GRANT THIS MERCY, O LORD, WE BESEECH THEE, TO THY SERvant departed," Marcus spoke in clumsy Latin, Erik having told him the words only minutes before. For a burial, the rite was rather a farce. Whatever God thought about the dragon-blooded, the men would have found it unsettling if one of them had spoken the prayers, but they were the only ones who knew Latin.

The compromise was undignified. Then again, there was seldom dignity in death.

Erik stood and listened as Marcus continued. "That he may not receive in punishment the requital of his deeds who in desire did keep Thy will, and as the true faith here united him to the company of the faithful, so may Thy mercy unite him above to the choirs of angels. Through Jesus Christ our Lord. Amen."

In dragon form, Toinette and Erik had dug the holes: simple work enough. The men filled them in though, as seemed more proper, and set a crude driftwood cross atop each of the graves.

Sence, of all the men, wept openly: quiet, but without shame. The others hung their heads, blinked tears away with some pretense of disguise, or simply stared in silent grief. Only some had known the dead men well, but their deaths were a reminder to all of what had passed—and the uncertainty in which they all now found themselves.

Toinette stared straight ahead, her arms folded under her breasts. She'd taken her blue gown out of the ship and donned it before the burial. It was damp, but whole and free of sand. She'd also brushed her hair and bound it severely back with string. Bare of that softening influence, her face was stark, her lips a knife edge. The angles of her shoulders and elbows and jaw all spoke of pain.

Standing barely inches from her, Erik longed to offer her comfort, but dared not even touch her arm as he'd done on the *Hawk*. Even if she'd welcome the contact at another time, it might do more harm than good in front of her crew.

"May his soul and the souls of all the faithful departed through the mercy of God rest in peace," said Marcus. He stepped back, dropping his once-folded hands to his sides.

They all lingered for a while, in the same awkward silence that attended funerals everywhere. The Eternal had touched that place and the people gathered there, if only for a time; taking up worldly duties felt alien, as a familiar house did on returning after long travel. One walked around then, looking at furnishings, until the sound of feet on that particular floor became familiar once again. With burials, there was that time of shifting, of clearing throats and looking from one to another.

"Franz has found a few rocks we could move for one side of a shelter." Samuel was the one to finally speak. "And the cliffs could be the other wall. The lot of us could likely shift them."

"Do what you can while we're getting the supplies," Toinette said, and the thickness in her voice vanished gradually as she spoke. "If there's need, we can—" She waved a hand in the air.

"Yes, Captain," said Samuel.

"Good work, all of you."

That got smiles. A few of them were guilty, and others turned that way quickly. Erik knew that part of things too.

He'd been present at a great many funerals. Eventually, unless they shut themselves away from the world entirely and early, all the dragon-blooded were.

"Two holes in the hull," Toinette said. She spoke aloud, more for her own benefit than for Erik's, though he stood on the deck beside her and listened. "Too small and too high for risk just now, but nothing I'd want to go to sea with. Broken railing in places. And the mast, of course."

"Can you repair it?"

"I'm no shipbuilder, but—yes. We can. It'll be clumsy work, but it'll likely hold together until we reach a civilized port." She glanced over at Erik, and tried her best to phrase what came next gently. "You know we can't go onward."

He was silent. Toinette braced herself to make her case: sharp words, hard facts, the lives of her crew. She'd marshaled almost all of her forces by the time Erik spoke, only to have them scattered by what he said. "We may not have to. The island's in the right position, as near as I can tell."

"You think the Templars landed here?"

"If they landed anywhere. If they existed at all. I'll know more when I can look around the island, but—aye, if this isn't it, then we'll not find it this trip. Even Artair would say we've done more than enough in service of this mission."

"That does indeed absolve us of everything." Toinette turned to the hatch. "The supplies won't be growing legs any time soon."

They both needed to go below this time: corpses were easier to carry than barrels. Toinette went first down the ladder after an awkward pause when she realized that Erik was letting her go ahead on account of her skirts. His voice drifted down to her along with his feet. "I would think that you'd look on him more kindly, considering."

Toinette stopped, hands on a barrel of dried peas. "Thank you," she said. "I'd almost forgotten I was a poor relation—other than the relation part."

The hold was dim, but dragon-blooded saw well enough in the dark that she knew Erik had the good grace to flush. "I'm sorry," he said. "I didn't mean that as it came out."

"As it happens," Toinette went on, pushing the barrel over to the bottom of the ladder, "I'm quite grateful for what he did. I'd have come without the debt, but it did weigh in my thinking. I believe he's a good man. Good men still act in their own interests first. You were always surprised by that. Take hold of the top and pull. I'll push from below."

Between the two of them, the barrel wasn't heavy, only awkward. Neither of them spoke until they'd gotten it onto the deck; it took too much concentration to keep the thing steady. An injury wouldn't kill one of them, nor render them unfit for work as long as it would a human, but having one's foot broken was far from a holiday.

They went silently down into the hold again. Toinette pushed a splintered crate to the side and stepped around its contents—formerly dried bread and now neither dry nor bread in any real sense. She picked her way around the floor and pushed another crate out, this one holding salt beef.

Erik was standing at the bottom of the ladder. "I wasn't always surprised," he said. "I knew there was evil in the world."

"Yes, but...you always seemed to expect more from people. You called Artair heartless once yourself."

"Did I?" Slowly his face changed from half-friendly

argument into something more fraught, his eyes darkening and a slow smile coming to his mouth. "Ah. Aye, I did, once."

That recollection might have been a mistake, Toinette thought. She wasn't thinking of their argument any longer. She was remembering herself at sixteen, and the lanky golden-haired boy who'd taken umbrage to sending her away. She was remembering the feel of his mouth against hers, urgent and seeking. Toinette had hoped the kiss would be better than those she'd known when she'd barely come to womanhood, the attentions of spotty youths and old drunks who'd taken a bastard girl for fair game.

She hadn't realized how *much* better it could be until she'd kissed Erik. And he'd been an untried youth then, and her own practice scarce and largely unwilling.

"You were very much the young knight, as I remember," she said, her voice low and sensual.

"I tried. Though there are those who'd say I failed that time."

"Best pay no attention to small minds. Besides, I gave you little choice in the matter. Assaulted your purity, mayhap." Toinette met his eyes, which shone in the darkness of the hold, and let her mouth curve up in a teasing smile.

"Hardly an assault," he said huskily.

"So speaks the warrior. Of course, I know little of such things." She stepped toward him, letting her hips sway. "No surprise I didn't do it right. If I were to have a demonstration of the proper way, now—"

Then he grabbed her—*had* grabbed her, really, for she didn't realize he was going to move until she was crushed against his broad chest, with one of his hands at the small of her back and the other tilting her face up toward his. Erik took her mouth with bruising force, not asking for a response but drawing one as the moon draws the tides.

Desire made Toinette's head swim. Opening to Erik, urging him on with lips and tongue, she clung to his shoulders just to stay upright, until he shoved her back against the wall of the hold. Then her hands were free to roam. She could dig into his back with her nails, or cup his arse, or snake one hand around to the thick bulge in his hose, tracing fingers down the side to make Erik's breath hitch.

He was none so bad at leaving her breathless either: rough, yes, but in a way she welcomed. The hard pressure of his hands at her breasts was just what Toinette needed then, like the weight of his body pinning her to the wall and the scrape of his unshaven jawline against the tender hollow of her neck. When he pinched her nipples through her gown, she cried out into the silence of the hold.

"God's wounds, you undo me," he muttered against her neck, the words short bursts of heat. His hands left her breasts, slapped hers away from his cock, and Toinette could feel him struggling with the laces of his hose.

As she reached for her skirts, the boat swayed. A creak from above heralded a shower of sawdust, as well as a larger chunk of wood that hit Erik between the eyes.

"*Mannaggia!*" Toinette swore in the Italian of her birthplace. Erik kept his silence, but he pulled back, rubbing at his forehead.

However the wood might have wounded him, it had punctured their embrace like a dagger in a wineskin, and lust drained rapidly. "We can't," Erik said, panting. "We'll no' be safe staying here so long."

Toinette thought about asking him how long he thought it would take, but restrained herself. His eyes were still glazed, and warmth lingered between her legs. Teasing was asking for trouble. "There's that. And if the ceiling does fall on us, best we look respectable when the men come to our rescue."

"Aye." He turned away to take hold of the crate. Toinette made no immediate move to follow him, though she did let her eyes linger on his tented hose. Her nipples ached for his touch, and her sex felt nigh as damp as the waves that lapped against the hull.

When she did move, she grabbed the other end of the crate and was glad of the strain on her muscles. Hard work was the cure for lust. So she'd always heard, and so she prayed would be the case.

ELEVEN

WHATEVER THE MERITS OF HARD WORK, THERE WAS MORE THAN enough to go around.

They dragged the barrels and crates of supplies up the shore and stacked them against the cliffs. The night guards had specific instructions to keep an eye on them against the predations of either animals or gluttons. They'd about a fortnight's worth left of beef, bread, and turnips. Dried peas and cheese had taken more of a blow. Toinette estimated a few days there, carefully rationed. Yet the men had already caught a fish or two, and John thought he'd seen mussels off the shore. Rations were not their only option.

As usual, water was going to be the problem.

Their supplies, mixed with wine, would last roughly a month—but it would take a month to get back, perhaps longer. To aid in conservation, the ruined sailcloth that hadn't become shrouds, as well as the fabric of the dead men's sleeping pallets, became rain collectors: pierced and tied to sticks, they formed small basins around the camp.

After clearing out the *Hawk*, helping place wood and stones, wrestling with stakes and ropes, and digging out a pit for the fire, all on short rations, Toinette was at least able to push her awareness of Erik to the back of her mind. She slept by the fire at night with the dreamlessness of exhaustion and later a sense of satisfaction with work that progressed well.

Rain would have found them in good shape after the first day. Driftwood and rocks had let them form a cozy sort of artificial cave against the cliffs, with enough space and air in it for a fire pit. Toinette and Erik had gotten the hide sacks off the *Hawk*, so there was bedding, although the dry sand was pleasant enough for most.

Rain would have been fine—if it happened. Toinette knew from long experience not to expect it; counting on the weather was only slightly more foolish than counting on men.

The trees on the island were tall and thick above the cliffs. She very much doubted that they depended entirely on rain.

"I'll wager there's a spring up there," she said to Marcus on the morning of the third day, "and I say we should go and find it, or at any rate the stream it births. We'll need to get wood for the repairs, and half a damned tree for a new mast, and I'd not mind fresh meat for dinner. Squirrel or rabbit would do."

"Well," said Marcus, "at any rate it's not likely *you'll* be dinner. Take a few of the men. I didn't see you sprouting extra eyes in your other shape, and you might need hands."

Since the first few revelations, he seemed to have taken Toinette's dragon form as he did any other piece of news: factoring it into calculations of risk and reward, mentioning it as he might have done a wounded shoulder or a good following wind. Toinette had no idea what his actual feelings might be. She would have felt like a gawky stripling asking, and so she was simply glad for the practicality.

"Best leave m'lord here with us," he added. "Should aught go amiss, you'll want reserves, or we protection."

It was a wise suggestion. Nothing about Marcus's expression, nor his tone, suggested any more than that. Still Toinette wondered. The two of them had been friends for many years.

The only real response either way was not to ask, to believe that he'd had nothing behind his words but what lay on the surface. Even with friends, Toinette had learned, it didn't do to look too deeply.

"Right," she said. "We'll sort the men accordingly too." If she could pretend that Erik was another of them, or just one more asset to be used where he'd do the most good, it would relieve her mind immensely—not to mention taking the strain off other parts.

Toinette took Raoul, Sence, and John up the cliff with her. Going with the new men was less strained than it might have been. She had far less of their previous behavior to look back on, and so far fewer changes, or possible changes, to raise questions in her mind.

They trooped up the steep path from the beach, walking two by two. None of them spoke. All kept their eyes open and their hands on their swords. Just before the outing, Toinette had taken her belt dagger and slashed the skirt of her blue gown up to her knees. If any of the men took it amiss, they hadn't let her know by word or act—and most of the old hands had seen women in far less regardless. Her lower legs felt terribly exposed, but she'd be damned if she'd spend the whole journey tripping and getting caught on brambles out of modesty that was frankly laughable on her at any rate.

She'd also taken Gervase's sword before they'd buried him. Again, it had been only practical—but it felt worse than the short skirt did.

The trail was white and rocky at the start. As they climbed farther up, they began having to push their way past brambles and duck under low-hanging branches. The plants pressed in on either side. They were a darker green than those Toinette had seen in Italy and elsewhere, more like those that had lined the Scottish hillside. She even made out the pale-pink flowers of herb Robert springing from the mass of green, along with darker pink blossoms she'd never seen before.

Shortly after they reached the top of the cliff, Raoul grunted in recognition and held up his hand. The party paused for him to bend and pull up a broad-leafed plant, wincing as he did so, and sniff at it. "Nettles, Captain," he said. "We can eat them, if we boil them first—or even if we don't, if we're desperate enough."

"I'll feel a bit like a goat," said John.

"You should always," Sence told him, half in jest.

"If it wasn't for sailing home," Toinette put in, "I'd trade any of the lot of you for a good nanny in milk right now. But I'm glad to know of the nettles, Raoul. We'll come back and get more later, when we've gloves and bags. Meantime, keep an eye out for anything else we can eat, all of you."

"How much do you think we'll need?" John asked. "That is, how long d'ye think we'll be here?"

"No longer than we can help it, but I've no notion how long that'll be." She saw their faces as she spoke and half wished she could have brought herself to lie to them. "And we'll have a journey ahead of us when we do go. Best have the stores as full as we can, no?"

With those more or less encouraging words, the best Toinette could do, they went on. An occasional rustling in the undergrowth suggested small animals or birds, but none broke from cover. Toinette tried not to think of roast partridge.

"We can get the bows from the ship and come back," Sence said after the second time.

"Or set traps," said Raoul.

"Both, likely," said Toinette, "and if there are birds, we can find their nests."

John chuckled. "I did that plenty as a boy. Was always running off from chores for it too, and getting my hide tanned as often as not. And now look at me."

"Wouldn't your tutor be surprised?" Raoul said.

"Old Father Henry? Oh, he always knew I'd come to no good."

"We haven't yet," said Sence.

"Indeed," said Toinette. "Think of the stories we can tell when we return." She stopped and looked around, searching for the glint of light on water. Nothing met her eye, but she was hopeful. "The place couldn't get this green on rain alone," she said, half to herself. "We can dig a well, if we truly must."

"Can you dowse?" Sence asked.

Toinette shook her head. If the magic for finding water did exist, it was a peasant's art, like healing stock or taking off warts. Artair's instruction to his kin, even his ward, had concerned loftier matters—or martial ones. It seemed rather a pity now.

"We'll trust to Providence," she said. "If we must."

"If you can fly," asked Samuel, sharpening a slim driftwood stake, "why did you bother with a ship in the first place?"

"Even birds need to land." Erik leaned back on his elbows and looked out to sea. The day was cloudless and the horizon a misty band of pale blue above the darker waves. He couldn't see a trace of land anywhere. "We're not albatrosses, not even close. It takes strength to get us aloft and keep us there. More than most birds, I'd reckon, though I doubt any man's made a study of it."

"Ah." The other man's brown eyes lit with curiosity. Here, Erik thought, was one who might have been a scholar had his birth allowed as much. "What's the furthest you can fly?"

"That'd depend on the winds," Erik said.

After the first bustle of activity, the remaining camp had settled into near idleness in Toinette's absence. Marcus and Franz fished, though Erik suspected that they might be drowsing in the process. He and Samuel were keeping watch, whittling spears for fishing and cooking, and talking. The men spoke to him more easily now. For all the revelation of his nature, the wreck had stripped away a few of the boundaries rank and payment implied.

Turning the stake in his own hand and scraping the wood with the knife, he thought it over. "I spent a whole day aloft once. I was young, and one of my cousins had dared me to do it. Could barely move for the next week." He chuckled with the memory. "My uncle gave me no sympathy at all. The chambermaids, on the other hand…"

He and Samuel laughed together. "I tried to ride my father's best stallion once," said the other man, teeth flashing white in his dark face, "by way of impressing the goldsmith's daughter. I was lucky to get away with only bruises. Dad said, if Leviathan had left me able to sit down that night, *he* wouldn't have—which was more than a bit embarrassing at sixteen."

"Your father owned many horses?"

"Sold them. My older brother does now—or last I was in port long enough to see him. I was trained in that too, but—" He shrugged.

"Never liked the beasts overmuch?" Erik asked.

Samuel nodded. "Too temperamental. Too messy. Fine mounts for noblemen, of course," he added hastily.

Erik laughed. "You needn't fear to give offense. We're not much for riding when we can avoid it. Few horses can abide us calmly."

"Ah," Samuel said, and scraped away a bit more at the stake. "Stands to reason, that does. They're damned panicky beasts at the best of times. Now, going to trade them was likely what gave me the taste for the road—it just took a different form. I remember my first sight of the ocean. Went on forever, it did, and could take me anywhere."

"Not quite mild-mannered itself," Erik pointed out, gesturing around them.

"No. But it smells better."

"Were you always with Toinette?"

"Nay, I ran away—more than fifteen years gone now." Samuel scratched his head with the slow gesture and the startled look of a man finding that time tallied up faster than he'd expected. It was an expression long familiar to Erik, on mortal and dragon-blooded face alike. None of them could ever keep up. "I've been five with the Captain. I'll say, I knew she was an odd sort of a woman, but I never thought anything like—" He waved his hands, heedless of knife and spear alike, in an inarticulate gesture.

"Hard to think of it," said Erik, "until you know it's possible. That's probably true of a good many things."

"Mmm. Do you know each other? Even when you don't know each other, that is?"

"Not mostly, I'd think," said Erik. "There are signs: often we've odd-colored eyes even as men, and fire won't burn us, and we live a long time. But you'd have to wait around a long while for the last, plenty of mortals have strange eyes, and you can't go around shoving people's hands into the hearth on suspicion. And then, we're not the only uncanny creatures in the world."

Samuel cast his eyes down to the rosary looped through his belt. "*Are* there demons?" he asked.

"Oh, aye," said Erik. "I've never seen one, but a few of my cousins have fought them. Nasty things, from the stories they told me. Not so likely to trouble most folk, though, save those that anger a wizard of great power and no morals. Generally they've got to be called up."

That news looked to calm Samuel a trifle. Erik wished he could have been more certain; he'd only a few stories to go on. It was true that most men went their whole lives without seeing more demons than came out of a wineskin, but that was in the known world, with the Church and magic like Artair's to hold the fabric of it together.

Erik suddenly became aware of how much water surrounded the island, and how few people were alive on it. For Samuel's sake, he repressed the urge to shudder, or to cross himself.

TWELVE

"WE DIDN'T FIND THE SPRING YET," SAID TOINETTE, SEATING herself on a rock. "But there's a stream up there that'll do nicely. Means we can bathe too, so long as we do it downstream of where we get water."

"Couldn't you bathe in the ocean?" Erik stacked another piece of driftwood onto the fire.

Samuel, assisting him, shook his head. "Salt itches. Surprised you haven't noticed."

"I've been trying not to feel too keenly." Erik didn't look at Toinette when he said it. He hadn't meant lust when he spoke, but it was all of a piece, in a way: the damp sand for a bed, the dried salt on his skin, the restless urges that they hadn't the solitude to satisfy. Best, he thought, to avoid dwelling on any of it.

"We'll drink what we brought first," Marcus said from the other side of the fire pit. "It'll go stale, else. Should we cast off, we can refill our casks then."

"Water and food," said Franz. "Fortune is with us."

John hastily knocked on the nearest piece of driftwood, glaring at his companion. While Erik didn't bother with the glare, he was glad he'd been touching wood already, and his sympathy was with the Englishman. *Call no man lucky until he's dead*, his mother's people said. They meant it as philosophy, but given everything, speaking of their fortune did feel like tempting it.

"We can go back and set snares in the morning," Toinette said, pulling off one of her boots. Accomplishing this task meant stretching out one long, muscular leg, and Erik couldn't take his eyes from her tawny skin, nor the way her butchered skirt fell back above her knee. He bent forward quickly, glad of the excuse building the woodpile offered. He was no stripling, but he didn't entirely trust his self-control where his body was concerned.

"Means I'll be going out again," Raoul said, "or should."

"You can have two days down on the beach after. It's not my fault you've got certain valuable skills," Toinette said. Her other boot thumped onto the sand.

"Rewards of knowledge," said Marcus cheerfully. "That's why I've never tried to be an expert in anything."

"Oh, is that why?" asked Samuel, to general laughter and a mock growl from Marcus.

Erik stepped back from the fire pit. "We can add more if you think it wise," he said, addressing himself to Marcus and Toinette alike, "but I think my part of this is done— unless you'd like me to light the fire."

"*No*," Sence said straightaway.

The others—whether they'd seen the teasing lift of Erik's eyebrows or simply were relieved that Sence had spoken and relieved them of the need—laughed again. Toinette's voice was the last to join in, considerably behind the others, and her chuckle was brief and subdued.

Erik glanced over his shoulder. Toinette was sitting on the rock, slim, bare ankles crossed in front of her. Her eyes were unreadable as she watched him, but when she saw him looking, she shrugged and grinned. "Don't start volunteering, or they'll ask me to do it. Besides, we take up enough room as it is."

Neither joke was very funny, and she looked more tired than amused. It had been a long few days, longer for her—perhaps that was all, but perhaps not. Erik might have asked, had they the privacy for such a conversation, but he wasn't sure she'd have told him the truth even then.

The water closed over Erik's head: darkness, salt, ice. He'd learned to swim as a child, by way of his father throwing him into a lake. The dragon-blooded didn't drown easily, yet the mortal part of him had shrieked in terror at the time, until instinct had fired his limbs. That had been calm water, in summer, and nothing to the raging ocean in the storm.

He gathered himself for the change of shapes, a vague familiarity dancing in the back of his head. The change was second nature, literally, but he thought he'd been in just such circumstances before. Erik brushed the thought away, as a distraction at a time of need, and concentrated harder on the power in the center of his chest, calling it forth to sweep over his body.

It didn't answer.

Always the shift had come at his call. The difficulty, in youth or at times of great strain, was control, not summoning. Yet now when Erik bent his will toward it, the power slipped away, draining into the ocean's chill. He remained two-legged, wingless, fragile, and mortal. Waves slapped at his face as he paddled frantically, and the water forced itself into his nose and mouth with a persistence even the sea had never possessed before. He coughed frantically, the salt burning his tissues while the water scorched his lungs.

Inside his nostrils, the water had a smell beyond salt and seaweed, one he couldn't place. Even as the thought struck him, sharp ridges closed around his calf.

Erik kicked instinctively, and with all his strength, but the grip was strong. He looked down, through water grown

suddenly and horribly clear, and screamed without caring
about either witnesses or waves.

All the dead waited below the water. Soldiers in rusting
chain stood by priests black and disfigured with plague,
rotting while they yet lived. Erik's grandfather watched
with dead white eyes in an age-withered face, white mus-
taches floating above his missing jaw.

The hand around Erik's ankle led to the arm that had
been the only part of Gervase left truly whole. The body
beyond it was a shambling horror, meat sculpted into a
rough man-shape with chunks of bone sticking out haphaz-
ardly. The gold earring shone beside the eyeless, mouthless
oval where the face would have been.

Around him, a voice came sliding through the water,
and he didn't know whether it was from the dead or the sea.
This, it slobbered. *This waits*.

Even after he opened his eyes, saw the dying fire in
front of him, and felt the sand beneath his fingers, the voice
lingered in his mind.

"Captain." John's face was pale above her, his hand heavier
on her shoulder than he would ever have dared without fear
behind the touch. "There's somewhat happening, Captain.
I can't understand it."

Toinette dragged herself up the long, steep tunnel to
wakefulness, leaving an unpleasant stew of half-formed
images. She never truly remembered her dreams, and she'd
likely be glad of that. The impression of worms eating a
human tongue lingered for a heartbeat before she shook it
off, turning her attention to the waking world.

The fire in the cave burned low. Around it, sleeping men
stirred fitfully. Peaceful nights were likely hard to come

by all around, once exhaustion had given way to memory. Toinette knuckled sleep out of her eyes and got to her feet. "Show me," she said, keeping her voice low.

Barefoot, sword in one hand, she followed him out of the cave. Outside, waves lapped against the shore, calm and steady, and the sky above was clear. Still, when John gestured and Toinette turned to face the cliffs, she could no longer see the stars above the trees.

Gray-green light flickered over the forest instead. Toinette watched as it curled upward into vague tendriled shapes, flickering and fading and vanishing only to rise anew from the treetops, branching into the sky as if it were lightning in reverse.

"By God and all the saints." She didn't have to remember to lower her voice. The breath to raise it had gone out of her, leaving her winded and dizzy as she stared upward. The sword hung from her hand, a motionless, alien weight.

Toinette had sailed for a long time, and wandered before that. She'd seen red tides on the beach and blue fire wreathing ships, men who walked barefoot over hot coals and beasts out of a drunkard's legends. The light above the trees was nothing that she'd ever even heard of.

"There's more," said John, and gestured. "Watch the trees."

When the next flash of light came, Toinette saw what he meant. The night was calm. A faint breeze stirred from time to time, but it wasn't enough to lift a strand of her hair. Despite that, the trees on the cliff thrashed as if in a gale. Their tops stood out against the light, malformed fingers clawing up toward a goal Toinette could not know and did not want to imagine.

"Earthquake?" she asked, but doubtfully. The sand beneath her feet was as stable as any ground she'd ever trod, nor did it seem likely that the island could shake so violently not a mile from her while remaining solid where she stood.

"I looked to the cliffs before I woke you, Captain," John said. "No stones are falling. Not even a pebble. I thought perhaps to climb the path and see what happened above, but—"

"No," said Toinette.

The answer came more hastily to her lips than she could have explained. In all the scene before her, she could find no direct threat. Light and the motion of trees were nothing to harm a man. Yet, watching, she felt her hackles rise and her gut twist in an unease she'd never felt from storms or pirates.

From the relief on John's face, he shared her sentiments. "It's a foul night, Captain."

"It is," she said, and again could not have said why. Typically she used the term for storms, or at least the sort of rain that made everything stink of wet wool at best. The air was peaceful, dry, even warm. Toinette would almost have preferred sleet falling sideways. "Plenty of time to go up in the day. No sense breaking our necks on fallen logs, to start with."

"Aye," said John, and grimaced, but there was a hint of relief in it. Toinette had named a good solid reason for staying below. Now they could pretend that the other possibilities didn't exist, or not speak of them, which would do almost as well. He sat back down on the wide rock outside the cave. "I'll, ah, just wait out my watch, then. Sorry to wake you."

"Don't be," said Toinette. "You did right. In fact"—she glanced up at the sky again—"I'll wait with you, if you don't mind."

"I'd be glad of it. Best two of us are awake—in case the earth does shake or there is a storm coming up."

"My thoughts exactly," said Toinette. "And, you know, it may be just that. The cliffs may simply keep the wind and the lightning off us, and the landscape can play funny tricks on a man."

She didn't know if either of them truly believed her, but she was glad to have said it. Nor did she particularly want to reveal her other reason for staying awake: that she didn't much like the prospect of sleep just then.

Toinette settled herself down onto the rock by John. As with all of the men save Raoul and Sence, they'd spent nights enough just so in the past, when the horizon looked threatening or there was unrest in port. Trouble was nothing new. You stayed quiet, you stayed awake, and you kept a hand on the hilt of your sword.

If that hilt was less comfort than it ever had been, John didn't speak of it. Therefore, Toinette thought, there was no reason for her to broach the subject.

THIRTEEN

COME THE MORNING, TOINETTE GATHERED THE OTHERS AND told them. Better that they hear it from her, and all together, than that the story spread from man to man and grow distorted in the telling.

She laid the matter out with all the calm she'd learned in her life. She spoke of northern lights, desert mirages, and rings around the moon, and of how she'd seen it rain on one side of a street and leave the other dry. "There could have been a storm up there we didn't get down here," she said.

In daylight, with the trees calm against clear blue sky, Toinette could believe herself more easily. No matter that she'd seen no clouds; the light might have obscured them. And if the light hadn't looked like any lightning she'd ever seen, well, neither had she ever been in this part of the world before. Doubtless a sandstorm had seemed demonic to the first man caught on its edges.

The men listened uneasily. All looked almost as tired as Toinette felt, including Erik, who'd not taken a watch the night before. "If you think it nothing, Captain," Samuel asked, "why tell us?"

It was a good question, and a fair one. She could cheerfully have kicked him for asking. "So that you'll not wake the rest of us if it happens while you're watching tonight," Toinette shot back, and regretted it when she saw John wince. She added, "And because caution's not wrong. It might be nothing, it's *likely* nothing, but we've no way of knowing. The world is often stranger than we think."

"Even we," said Erik.

Toinette added him to her list of people she could have struck. It was *not* the moment, if one ever existed, to remind the men of their nature. She cleared her throat and lifted her chin. "And we'll need to go back up there as long as we stay on this island. It's wise to know the place as well as we can."

"We'll leave soon, though, yes?" Raoul asked.

"As soon as we repair the ship and replace the stores. We'll get the wood for the first today. Perhaps I should go back up the cliffs with you, in that case. Erik won't know how to choose for a mast."

"But Marcus will," said Erik, "and I vow I'll abide by his decision."

Toinette's instinct was to contradict, and none too kindly: *Will he know from the air, fool?* She bit it back. No human shipwright could choose from the air, and yet they picked masts well enough. Marcus knew more of such arts than she did, in truth. It wasn't Erik's fault that she'd slept poorly the night before.

Settle yourself. Let your mind guide your tongue, not your temper.

"As we planned it last night, then," she said. "We'll keep a watch here. If you do find trouble, send a man back—don't come yourself."

As yet, they'd not seen signs of anything intelligent enough to lay an ambush, but it never helped to be careless. One man running back through terrain he knew even slightly would be better than the group's best protector abandoning them with the unknown ahead.

As Toinette thought about that, she realized the other reason for her irritation: a cover for relief. She shouldn't have been glad of the excuse not to enter the forest again, but she couldn't deny that she was.

Light or no light, Erik welcomed the distance from the water. The sea had never held much terror for him, or no more than for any other man, but this morning he couldn't look at it without thinking of his dream.

This waits.

He'd broken his fast only perfunctorily, swallowing bread and washing it down with overwatered wine out of the knowledge that his body required the fuel, not any real appetite. The task ahead became a welcome distraction.

They went further than Toinette and her party had gone before, taking advantage of the trail the others had broken for them and then following the stream inward. Briars tore at their clothing, until Erik loosed his sword and began to chop them out of the way. Doubtless it would dull the edge, but he wasn't inclined to care. He had other weapons at his disposal if he needed to fight.

"You could change," said Franz. "Burn a path for us."

"Set the whole island afire too," Marcus snorted. "Fool."

The man had never been overly gentle in speech, but that was sharper than Erik had heard him. By Franz's look of wounded surprise, he wasn't used to it either, but Marcus's rank throttled whatever reply he might have made down to a sound in his throat and a sullen turn of his mouth.

"I could crush a path," said Erik. "And I'd not feel the briars so much. If you'd not mind." He gestured to the other three.

"If it gets us through this hell quicker, you can turn into whatever you desire," said Marcus.

Franz and Samuel didn't answer, but neither looked likely to run away, nor to attack him at the change, and Erik took that for assent. He took a few paces forward, finding a more-or-less open area along the stream.

"Wait—" Samuel held up an open hand. "When you're a dragon, can you hear us? And understand?"

"Aye. I can't speak, but I know everything I do as a man. Language too."

"Ah. It's good to know, in case."

Marcus nodded. "I'd rather you didn't blink back and forth like a firefly just so I could point out a likely tree, for one. Now…" He waved one hand in rapid circles: *Get on with it.*

Shifting was itself reassuring. After his impotence in the dream, Erik relished the feeling of the power rising at his command and reshaping him when he released it. As his hands became claws and skin transformed into scales, he knew a vast sense of relief: *That truly wasn't real, thank God.*

He'd never had the Sight, nor even managed much in the way of scrying when he'd gone through the rites for it under Artair's teaching—but one never knew. Prophetic dreams chose unlikely people at times, as both the Scriptures and the lore of his family had recorded. Erik had no wish to be one of those instances, particularly not for such a dream as he'd had.

It was a dream, and he was the dragon, a creature of eternity and thus of the moment. His senses sharpened, save for touch. He smelled squirrel in the trees, hare and wildcats elsewhere, and the smoke from the fire on the beach. There were scents he didn't recognize too, including the trace of one on the eastern wind, cold and gelatinous like worms stranded on rock after a rain.

Erik snorted in disgust and bent his head away. The stream ran north. He forged his way forward, taking savage delight in the way plants crushed beneath his claws and branches snapped against the weight of his chest. The larger of the trees could stand against him, but not most of them.

The men followed at his heels, small chattering creatures. He could hear bits of their conversation, but cared little for either the words themselves or the sense behind them. Talking served men well. He had other purposes.

Up they went, following the stream. The shallow rise of the hills was nothing to Erik, though he'd not have wanted to try flying with the forest so thick around him. He didn't know whether he could have cleared the treetops without his wings getting entangled. As it was, he held them upright by significant effort and knew that the muscles of his back would ache before the day was out. It was an ache worth having, though, to forge a path and clear his head both.

When they finally found the spring, flowing from a crack between two huge mossy rocks, Erik was the first to take a deep drink. He found the water cool and sweeter than any he could call to mind. Of course, memory was different in dragon shape, and he'd spent weeks drinking stale water from casks, then slogged his way through the forest, but whatever rot might take place on the other side of the island, it hadn't found purchase near the spring.

After he quenched his thirst, he swung his great body aside, letting the men drink and fill their waterskins. The forest around him was cool and green, the earth gave easily under his feet, and birdsong filled the air. No deer or hare would stay in a dragon's presence, but the birds seemed to realize that they were too small to be prey and circled near Erik's head without much fear.

From below him, Marcus cleared his throat. "That tree," he said, gesturing to one of the nearby pines, "would do well."

The pine in question was smaller than some of its fellows, manageable rather than goliath, but like them it grew straight, not even branching until halfway up its length. Even Erik could see the potential there for the mast. He nodded his head, slowly enough that the humans would get the message without the force of the gesture knocking them over.

"Just don't bring it down on our heads," muttered John. "If you can manage it."

The sun was warm, the sound of the waves constant and soothing, and Toinette was tired. She didn't let herself fall entirely asleep; strictly speaking, she was on watch. They'd had no threat during the day yet, though—no threat, in truth, in the two days they'd been on the island—and so she did relax, lying back against a rock with half-closed eyes. When Jehan had lived, she'd spent a good many of her days at sea just so, aware that she might need to act but resting while she waited.

Remembering Jehan, she was glad he'd died before Erik's voyage, and she couldn't feel shame for the gladness. He would have been no more likely to survive than the others—less, as he'd been older than half of them when Toinette had first met him—and she doubted she could have stood the worry for his safety, much less the likelihood that he'd have shunned her once he knew her nature.

The men had reacted better than she'd thought. That was different than—

A shout took her from her thoughts. It was a day for perverse joy, for she almost welcomed the distraction. Sword in hand, she bolted upward from her seat and spun to face the sound.

A ways down the beach, Raoul and Sence had thrown their fishing gear aside and had come to blows of no uncertain sort. Even while Toinette grasped the situation, Sence grabbed Raoul's shoulder, only to catch the other man's fist in his jaw and stagger back.

Toinette didn't run toward them. She strode down the beach, quickly but with as little impression of effort as she could manage to give, and although she was muttering curses half the way there, she raised her voice loud and clear when she addressed the men.

"What in God's holy name do you think you're about, you stupid, poxy sons of whores?"

They stopped. Whether they thought *Captain* or *dragon* when they heard it, Toinette's voice acted like a pail of cold water on the brawlers. For once, she didn't wonder which. She took the silence, set her hands on her hips, and began to curse them out in the many languages of profanity she'd picked up as a child of the streets and a woman of the world.

"He said—" Sence began to defend himself.

"Am I your God-rotted *nurse*, *cabrón*? I don't care if he said he buggered your mother on top of the altar at Easter, you keep your fists to yourself! And you"—she rounded on Raoul—"you keep a civil tongue in your head, and if you can't figure out whether you'll give offense, be *silent*. In case either of you are too dull to count, we've eight men here, one who's not manned a ship." In her anger, she decided the Viking boats didn't count. "And we'll need all of you to get back. Even if you want to die here because of a pissing contest, I don't!"

They stood silent, abashed. Raoul's eye was turning black, and Sence's lip was split.

"Put the word out," she said. "Next man who throws a punch, I'll have his hands bound behind him for a day. He can eat off the ground like a dog."

With that, she strode back off down the beach, relishing the thud of every footstep in the sand.

FOURTEEN

DRAGON SHAPE HAD ITS OWN SOCIAL ADVANTAGES. ERIK DIDN'T try to get airborne while carrying the pine tree, but he did fall behind the others, and heard little of their conversation as they took the cleared path back. He was glad of it: by the time they got to the beach, bickering had broken out into full-on argument at least once that he'd witnessed, and probably a few more times when he hadn't been paying attention.

When he saw Sence and Raoul, he realized that he'd been lucky his group had kept themselves only to words. The notion did nothing to improve his mood.

He was stranded with a throng of idiot humans and a woman he couldn't have. Despite the unfamiliar territory, the odd lights, and the foul smell, flying off to the other side of the island had a sudden intense appeal.

Duty won out over impulse: duty to Artair, to the men he'd hired, and to Toinette, though he knew she wouldn't be happy to hear that. The most self-indulgence he could manage was taking the pine a little way off from the others and remaining in dragon form while he broke off the remaining branches.

The destruction didn't lift his mood immediately, but he did feel better while it was going on. Men periodically carried away the discarded wood, stacking the larger branches for later use and putting the others on the fire. None attempted to speak with Erik. They had that much sense.

As the scent of pine filled the air, mixing with the salt

and reminding Erik of winter evenings when he was a boy, his thoughts became less prickly. The crew did the best they could—and they'd all had an uneasy night, not to mention being under considerable strain. Expecting sainthood was a fool's game under such circumstances. He hadn't precisely been in a meek and mild humor himself.

He turned back into a man with no more thoughts of desertion, and one who no longer found the society around him a burden. Conveniently, the others seemed to have drawn back their spines as well. He noticed Sence offering Raoul a few quiet words as the food went around the camp-fire, and Raoul replying with a sheepish look and a shrug.

Likely it was no wonder. They'd a mast, and tools from the ship carried in case of just such an occasion. Finishing it would take some days' work, as Toinette observed after dinner, but they were one step closer to leaving the island. That was a prospect to brighten any man's outlook.

The wood might truly have helped too. Thinking back, Erik remembered the smell of pine at the castle in the depths of winter, when confinement and lack of light tended to make all within most fractious. He knew not if that had been mere chance, knowledge that Artair hadn't seen fit to pass on, or the lore of some old man in the for-ester's employ.

As with many things, Erik took the results gladly and without questions—particularly so that night, when he slept long, heavily, and without dreaming.

Trimming the mast and patching the holes in the *Hawk* was enough occupation for ten men, had they been able to devote such numbers to the task. Mast or no mast, how-ever, they needed food and water, so Toinette led Franz and Raoul back up the cliff the next day. All three carried sacks that they'd roughly made from the cast-off fabric of Toinette's skirt and the scraps of sailcloth left over from the shrouds. They half filled them with nettles on the way to the spring, drank and bathed, and then pressed onward, hoping to see signs of deer or at least rabbit.

Signs of the Templars or their magic would be good too, Toinette supposed. Having been stranded for Artair's goals, she would find it a trifle more satisfying if the whole ordeal proved to have been for *some* purpose.

That didn't keep her from thinking highly uncharitable things about men and nations as she pushed her way through the forest. She was developing a fine list of objects of ire, in fact: the undergrowth, the game that would spook at the scent of a dragon and thus meant she couldn't simply change shape and barge through as Erik had done, Erik for getting to take the easy route (*except for carrying a tree*, said her conscience, and she told it to be quiet), the sun for making her sweat when she'd just bathed, nettles for stinging so damned much, and herself for not bringing thick gloves on the voyage.

She'd been in a decent mood on waking, but as they'd gotten further up the path, the day had gotten worse. Strictly speaking, it *hadn't*; they'd done quite well. That was annoying too, that discomfort should so mar her moments of triumph.

Oh, aye, Toinette told herself, as she and Moiread had mocked each other back in their girlhood, *and your martyr's crown is surely a wee bit tight, isn't it?*

She grinned, despite her mood, and in her amusement she almost missed the flicker of movement from the corner of her eye. If Franz hadn't shouted, she would never have seen it.

To the east, through the trees, metal glinted in the sunlight and then vanished into shade.

"Hallo!" Franz shouted. "Hallo, you there!" Nobody responded. "It was a man, Captain! A man in mail, I think. I saw his face just an instant. Come on, then. He must not have heard us. He can't be going very fast in this, not in armor. Hallo!" he called again, starting to run. "We're friends!"

They might *not* be. Toinette would have reminded Franz of pirates and cannibals, had he given her longer. With more warning, she would have grabbed him by the neck like a youth and made him listen.

But he was running too fast for that, bolting off into the forest with a speed Toinette hadn't expected.

She only had time to think *Dammit, what is* wrong *with everyone?*

Then she dropped her sack of nettles and broke into a run too. The smell of crushed plants rose up to meet her; her own heartbeat grew loud in her ears. She could hear Raoul close behind her too, keeping pace well enough for a new man.

Undergrowth tangled Toinette's feet, slowing her further, and she had to dodge around trees—many big enough to have been obstacles for her dragon form, let alone her human one. Her saving grace was that Franz did too. So should have the man he was chasing, but when Franz finally stopped, the phantom was nowhere in sight. Toinette and her men stood on a sparse trail, one whose presence did make her hopeful about deer—or even elk, by the way the plants on it grew—but which showed no sign of a human presence.

"Gone," said Franz, panting. "But…I swear I saw him."

"So did I," Raoul put in.

"Oh, and I did too, or close enough," Toinette replied

testily. "If it was a vision, we're all going mad, for we're never saints. Hush a moment, both of you, and we'll look for tracks—assuming the good knight's friends aren't hiding behind the trees with bows at the ready."

She sniffed the air as they looked around, as quietly as she could manage while still getting what scent she could as a human. Cool earth and broken plants overwhelmed most else. For all she could tell, they were the first people to ever pass down the trail.

"There's nothing here," Raoul said. He'd been kneeling to examine the dirt and moss; he got to his feet with a frown. "Could be the plants are just too thick to show footprints, but—well, look." He gestured at the trail ahead. "None of the branches are broken."

"A man running away wouldn't have dodged them," Franz agreed.

All three of them stood still. "It might," Toinette said slowly, "have been a bit like a mirage."

"Not a desert," said Franz.

"No, but we don't know this land." Toinette didn't sound convincing to herself. The men looked more doubtful yet. "If not, then—"

She trailed off. None of them wanted to say the words aloud, not alone in the forest. They'd come a ways from the spring, Toinette noticed then: a pink-and-white vine she hadn't seen before climbed up many of the trees around them, and fewer birds sang overhead, although that might have just been a result of the racket she and the men had made.

"We should go back," she began to say, thinking of retrieving the nettles before other creatures got to them. Not *many* things were desperate enough to eat nettles, but the island might have goats—and the thought made her stomach growl.

Naturally, that was the moment when the vines detached themselves from their trees and lunged.

The vines were as strong as any man, and they'd struck from surprise. Toinette yelled like a kicked cat as they yanked her backward into a tree, which struck the back of her head with a loud *thwack* and a burst of pain that left her cross-eyed for a few moments.

Thinner vines crept around the tree, opened fleshy pink spots, and pressed them against Toinette's exposed skin. The edges of those spots were sharp. Her blood started flowing at once, and the vines pulsed, drinking it down. She screamed again, as much in revulsion as pain, and heard Raoul and Franz crying out as well, their voices baritone counterpart to hers.

Struggling did little good. When Toinette managed to get a hand free and draw her sword, the vines swiftly wrapped around her arm again, hindering her motion. She wasn't strong enough to break free of all of them at once, and little less would be sufficient.

Bugger this, she thought, and transformed.

The smell of sundered plants was strong and sickly sweet. They snapped around her without any real effort on her part; her sheer mass was force enough. Toinette slammed a hind leg contemptuously into the tree behind her and swung her weight forward to address the plants preying on her men.

Fire, alas, was too likely to catch Raoul or Franz, but her claws were sharp, and she could put considerable muscle behind them. *Hold damned still*, she thought at Franz, and swiped through the vines as carefully as she could manage in a hurry. He was in one piece when he bolted from the tree and over to her side, and Toinette didn't notice any serious wounds.

Good enough. Another slash freed Raoul. Toinette didn't wait for him to run, but plucked him up by the collar with her teeth and deposited him onto her back.

Now fire would work. As the wounded plants writhed, she drew a long breath and called forth flame, careful to keep it controlled despite her rage. She didn't want to set the whole forest ablaze—or likely wouldn't, when she'd calmed down and had a meal.

It had been a long time since Toinette had used fire on anything. Containing it was a bit of a struggle at first, but she managed to keep the flame narrow, crushing it out with a forefoot as soon as the blood-drinking plants had blackened and crumbled. They writhed as they died. She was glad of it.

Franz and Raoul stayed silent, frozen. While she was killing the plants, Toinette took no notice of it. She would have expected such a reaction to either her or the situation. Only after she transformed again did she realize that they were both staring in the same direction and see the shine of metal against a familiar yellow-white.

In the course of stamping out the fire, she'd dug up the earth around the trees considerably. Four skeletal fingers now rose from one of the churned patches. The silver ring on one was tarnished, but Toinette could still make out the narrow-armed cross of the Knights Templar.

FIFTEEN

"Devils," said Franz. "This place is cursed."

"Because of the plants?" Samuel shook his head. "Lions don't make a plain cursed, nor wolves a forest. Not unless the whole world's cursed."

"It's not just the plants." John poked at the fire, sending up a brief fountain of sparks. "The lights. The storm. The shape in the forest. 'Tis uncanny. And now dead men."

"There are plenty of dead men in England and France," said Marcus, punctuating the sentence by pulling a section of fish off his skewer and popping it into his mouth.

"Aye," said Raoul, "but Templars? Who's to say that the stories of devil worship weren't right?"

The eight of them sat eating. The flames crackled merrily, lighting and warming the makeshift cave, and the smell of cooked fish in the air was appealing, but neither lifted the tension that hung thick as storm clouds. Ever since Toinette's party had stumbled back to camp, white-faced and wide-eyed, the evening had been an uneasy one.

The description of the plants had been revolting, but, to Erik, no more fearsome than tales of any other predator. The ocean had sharks; the road had brigands; a wise man traveled armed and in groups. He, being not entirely a man, had never worried much about either. The hand with its ring—that was a different matter.

Aye, but Templars?

He met Toinette's eyes across the fire. The flame illuminated the gold specks in them and cast shadows across her narrow face. Like him, she'd largely kept silent, letting the men talk. Erik wished he could have read her expression better, and he knew there was cowardice in that desire.

He'd hired the *Hawk* and her crew. A man had a duty to those who served him, and that meant facing their displeasure.

"One of the stories does seem true," he said, against the waves and the burning wood. "That is, the one that brought us here. And so—"

"—the one about the treasure might be?" Raoul's young face shifted, interest not replacing the fear but surely tempering it.

He was young. Around him, the other men showed more mixed reactions. Franz and John looked skeptical, Samuel thoughtful, and Sence blank as usual. Marcus stroked his chin, frowning, but Erik didn't know whether in disapproval or simple calculation.

Toinette said nothing and rolled her eyes.

"If the danger *is* too great," Erik said, trying to pretend that her reaction didn't sting, "we can call off now."

"Easier ways to earn a coin," said Franz.

"Are there?" asked Marcus. "We're here as it is. We'd chance no more dire weather by staying a few days longer than we would if we left now. And we've not *truly* met with any more danger than we did in Damascus, say," he said to Franz, "nor that time in Cadiz with the guildsman. What's threatened us so far? A few plants that we've the means to fight off."

"And *ghosts*," John put in, shaking his head.

"*A* ghost," said Marcus. "Perhaps."

"One or a thousand, what matter?" Franz's pallor had taken on a gray-green tinge, and he swallowed again before he spoke. "It was there. It vanished. We found the body. What else could it be but a phantom?"

"And as I hear, if you hadn't been fool enough to run off after a man you'd barely glimpsed," said Samuel, "you'd have been at no more risk than you are now."

"You'd have done the same," said John. "That girl in Medina—"

"Was flesh and blood, thank you."

Before the argument could pull them too far off course, Toinette raised an interrupting hand. "There's some truth there," she said. Her voice was calm and considered, her face as blank as that on a statue of Justice. "Let's say that the island *is* haunted. It'd be far from the first place. That doesn't mean it's any more dangerous than it was before, if we're careful. Hurl a brick in Paris, and you'll hit two men who've seen ghosts and lived to tell the tale. Frequently."

"And how many of those really saw anything more than the moon past the bottom of a wine cup?" Marcus asked. "If ghosts *are* here, I'd not want to judge the real ones by tavern stories."

If this sudden shift in the wind bothered Toinette, or even surprised her, she didn't let it show. "When you have enough stories," she said, "they might start to add up."

"Maybe the ghost is gone now," said Raoul. "We found his body, didn't we?"

"His hand," said Marcus.

"Still, if we're going by stories, sometimes that's all they want."

Another moment of silent thought fell over the assembled men. Marcus tossed a pinecone into the fire, where it popped merrily. Erik ate more fish and tried to keep his eyes from seeking Toinette's face. He already knew he'd see nothing promising there.

"What if they're guarding the treasure?" Samuel asked. "They didn't want it taken then. Why would they now?"

"Doesn't matter what they want," said Sence. "We're not goose girls to fear a shape and a voice. Show me a ghost that can hold a sword. Then I'll worry."

"And if they're not ghosts?" Franz asked.

"Then we're worrying over nothing," said Marcus. "Aren't we?"

"You forget devils," said Franz.

The fire seemed to dim at the word, and the waves outside grow louder. Men looked uneasily at one another; even Marcus let out a quick and uneasy breath. "I signed on to risk my body," said Raoul slowly. "My soul's different."

Sence's dark eyes flashed. "And you think that's in anyone's hands save yours and God's? As it always has been?" he asked, lifting his head suddenly to stare around the fire. His upper lip curled back over his white teeth. "Fear is one thing, folly is one thing, but surely we need not progress to blasphemy as well!"

"But the devil—" Franz began.

"—has no power you don't give him. Or are you a Cathar of a sudden? If we are here, it's the will of God—either to chastise us for our sins or for some higher purpose of His. Trust, and stop your whining."

"Surprisingly devout, that man," said Erik. He and Toinette sat on the shore, watching the waves come in and listening to the men's voices in the background. "Surprisingly well-educated too."

"Don't know that he's right, though."

"You didn't contradict him."

Toinette shrugged. "Why would I? What he said worked." She gave Erik a sidelong glance and added tersely, "For the present."

"I have a mission. Would you have me abandon it now, when I know I'm on the right path?"

"You know *a* Templar was here. You've no idea whether he's one of those who fled, whether he brought any treasure with him, or whether the treasure, if it exists, is still here." Feeling the need to be fair even when annoyed, she pursed her lips and conceded, "Not that I've seen much sign of people between that poor bastard and us."

After finding the hand, they'd dug around the roots of the trees just to be certain. More bones had turned up, though not all—the man hadn't lain that deep, and the island likely held scavengers enough—but no treasure. Without the *visio dei*—the vision of the spirit world—they couldn't be certain the ring wasn't magic, but it didn't feel that way, and nothing had happened when Erik grimaced, apologized to the owner, and put it on.

The moonlight turned Erik's hair silver and danced in his eyes. Toinette wished she didn't notice such things when the two of them were arguing—or about to argue. "And what's the harm," Erik asked, the Scots burr low in his voice, "of staying a wee bit longer to make certain one way or another? We've food enough, and wood, and water. Are you wanting to get back to anything at home?"

"No," she said, ire rising at the open skepticism of his tone. "Though I might, for all you know of the subject."

"You told me otherwise yourself."

"I said no husband living, and you know I've no children. There are other ties." Toinette let him sit with that a moment, resisting the urge to toss her hair. It was tied up, anyhow. When Erik had frowned and looked out across the ocean again, either taking the point or choosing not to think about it, she went on. "But the weather gets worse the later we get in the year, in case you've been too busy with your *missions* to notice. I'd rather not recover from a storm and then sail into the teeth of another."

Erik shook his head. "Marcus said another few days won't make a difference."

"And he's likely right," said Toinette, "which is why I didn't speak out then. But that forest is thick, Erik, and the island's not too small. A week or two *will* lengthen our odds of getting back safely. And you didn't think to ask."

"I said we could call off now."

Toinette snorted, not caring how unladylike—or indeed how draconic—it sounded. "Any page who's taken a dare knows *that's* not the same thing. And you weren't over-quick to say it."

"Well, then," Erik said, turning toward her and spreading his hands, "do you think your men are but boys, to be drawn into unwise action by the slant of a few words and a delay in speaking? I thought you trusted them more."

The barb struck. Toinette looked down at her knees, and at the ragged red hem just below them. Her face was probably approaching the same color. Sitting with a mortal man, she'd have found the dark reassuring; she knew too well that like her, Erik could see in the dark. Damn him.

In their youth, they might have come to blows. Civilized rules about fighting women didn't apply to the dragon-blooded, and brawling was of less account when broken bones would heal within a day or two. In front of the men, Toinette wouldn't call him out, as much as it would relieve her feelings.

"It doesn't matter whether it worked or not," she settled for saying, clipping her speech to sound as remote and adult as she could, as she did when haggling with employers or disciplining her crew. "It matters that you tried. Or that you didn't think *not* to try."

Erik sighed. "Men live with danger every day. Mortal men die every day. These men signed on for it willingly."

"They didn't know it would come to this," Toinette said, biting back more angry words about the other things he'd said. She got to her feet and shook sand sharply from her dress, not caring where it went. "You have a week. I'll help. But when the week's over, we leave. If we meet with anything worse than the plants, we leave. I'm not sacrificing another man to Artair's pride."

"It's—" Erik started to object hotly.

"It's *all* pride, as far as I'm concerned. Kings and crowns and banners—it's all pride, it's all stupid, and none of it's worth a drop of my men's blood."

She stalked off toward the end of the beach, away from Erik and the fire both. It *was* true that nothing on the island so far could really harm her, and she didn't think she could be around anyone for a few hours. Not safely.

SIXTEEN

Two silver coins glinted up from the dark stump where the old mast had been. One came from Spain, the other from England, but Erik suspected they'd both serve their purpose just as well, even if his MacAlasdair side scoffed at the notion of good luck coming from anything with Edward Longshanks's crowned head on it. Silver was silver for magical purposes. Surely it would be so for more abstract luck as well.

God knew they needed it. The week wasn't half over, but he'd seen no other signs of the Templars, much less their treasure. Flying over the island revealed little, as the trees were too thick to see through, and he could only hack his way through the forest for so long before coming to the end of his strength. Duty required him not to exhaust himself completely, lest another storm or an unexpected attack require him to defend the men, or the *Hawk*'s repairs require more might.

He knew Toinette would expect as much too, although she didn't say it to him. As strained as affairs might be between the two of them, she trusted him to know his work, much as Erik had faith that she looked diligently for the Templars on her days in the forest and put her back into clearing a path. They might not talk often, but they were both old enough to recognize the need for cooperation despite that, and to manage it.

Erik did miss her joking, her sidelong smiles, and the occasional glance that recognized their mutual heritage and background, the things that set them a little apart from the others. Since the argument, she'd been a woman purely of business with him, reporting the day's tasks and results, asking necessary questions, and otherwise keeping her silence. He couldn't have called it *sulking*, as she was cordial enough when they did need to speak, but he felt the difference and was himself inclined to resent it.

He tried to be understanding: if she didn't understand a man's duty to his lord and kin, well, she'd never had either, nor a country and a people to guard against conquerors. Still, when she stood on the *Hawk*'s deck and cast her eyes quickly over him, just as she might have done one of her men—or a part of her ship—Erik nodded once in reply and thought *I can be as distant as you, my lady*.

God would doubtless hold him to account for such petty spite someday, but God would hold him to account for any number of other sins first.

Erik shifted easily, like swirling a cloak around his shoulders. The mast lay in front of him, now as well-shaped and worked as the crew's efforts and tools could make it. None were experts in shipbuilding, yet most had learned enough through the years. He took hold of it gently, for one in his form, held it in his foreclaws, and made the necessary adjustments so that the weight balanced.

Strength wasn't everything. He'd learned that in his youth. Misjudging weight could break rather than transport, and could leave even a dragon injured.

He was just as careful when he took flight, making certain that the wind from his wings would harm neither the assembled sailors nor the *Hawk*. Even at their fiercest, dragons weren't as strong as a storm, but they were much more focused. Artair had explained many ways to use flight itself as a weapon; in time, Erik had employed a few of them and seen the results. They didn't stand out in his memory with quite the grisly detail as others, especially those of flame, but he would much prefer to avoid creating them again, particularly on men who were his allies.

Slowly he circled around the *Hawk*'s deck, righting the mast and bringing it closer until it fit into the top of the stump, covering the silver coins there. Then Erik hovered in midair above the ship, holding both himself and the mast steady. He did have to beat his wings rapidly to manage that. On the deck, Toinette's hair escaped its bindings and streamed copper into the blue sky, while the shorter crops of the men only ruffled, as did the water below.

Marcus put a hand on the mast and felt the joining, then stepped back and assessed the angle. "Good," he said to Toinette and Erik alike.

Toinette nodded, then turned to the men. "Ropes and pegs now. Quick as we can. He can't hold that for very long."

The man's pride in Erik bridled. Yet the dragon was foremost: it was a creature of instinct and fact, with no thought for pride or shame in human eyes. What Toinette said was true. Already his muscles were aching from the effort of hovering in the air, so that his weight might not break or swamp the ship. The sooner he could stop, the happier he'd be, and so he was more grateful to Toinette than annoyed with her for mentioning it.

She was in action alongside her men too, catching and tossing coils of rope, tying huge, firm knots in the compli-cated configurations of line that would bind the new mast to the deck, and not hesitating for a heartbeat about any of it. The remnants of her blue skirt danced around her slim legs in the wind, as if they wished to become part of the sky they so resembled.

Within the dragon, Erik the man watched and, despite his irritation, couldn't help but admire her. Her legs surely caught the eye, but her unhesitating competence drew the mind and the heart to attention.

Despite the physical relief, it was almost a pity when Marcus stepped back, eyed the rigging, and declared the process done—for now. "Let go," he added to Erik, "but make ready to catch the thing in case we've fouled up somewhere."

"Your faith is inspiring," said Toinette, flashing the grin of a woman who knew she had nothing to fear from the results of her work.

And indeed, when Erik gingerly loosed his hold and backwinged a little, the mast stayed well in place. The ropes rippled a little, adjusting to the new weight, but held firm.

"Good!" Toinette said, and clapped her hands once together. "Get the crew aboard. The tide's with us. We'll go once 'round the island, and see how she does with the open air and the current. Stay in your shape, if you would," she added to Erik, with a more friendly countenance than she'd shown for a while. As he remembered, joy at success made her forget her resentments. "We may need your aid yet."

As the crew climbed onto the *Hawk* and made ready to cast off, Erik took the chance to rest on the beach, catching his breath and stretching out the muscles of his back and wings. The sand was warm and pleasantly rough against his scales; the sun beat on his shoulders while a fresh breeze blew from the east. If not for the possible task near at hand, he could have easily fallen asleep.

He did close his eyes, intending only to rest them for a short time, while the noises of the men casting off went on around him. They fell into a rhythm, irregular but there and soothing after its own fashion. It was pleasant to hear work when his was complete for the time being.

The splashing of the boat in the water and the snap of the sail came next, then an unexpected groan from many throats. Distant, but audible to one in dragon's form, he heard Toinette's voice: "Wind's shifted. Bad luck, but we've had worse. Shift sail, and we'll tack into it."

Odd, Erik thought, muddled though his mind was by both sleep and form. He hadn't felt any change in the wind. The sea could be strange like that.

A shout went up from the ship: despair, not triumph. Erik opened his eyes, afraid that the mast had snapped—though he thought he'd have heard that—or that the wood covering the holes had come off. What he saw instead was the *Hawk* sitting only a few yards out to sea, its sail pinned back against the mast by a wind going precisely the wrong direction. Men stood with their heads turned upward, staring at the sail and babbling, until Toinette raised her hands and yelled for quiet.

This time, the wind carried off many of her words, but Erik could see her gesture. The men went to work accordingly, hauling on ropes and turning wheels. The *Hawk* shifted in the water, the sail angled to catch the wind, and she began making headway toward the open sea—

And then, abruptly, the wind reversed itself, pushing the ship back toward the island.

Erik heard oaths in many languages. Some were angry. Most were scared. He caught a glimpse of Marcus facing down one of the other men, and of Toinette shaking her head, shoulders stiff. "…God-cursed *breeze* keep us here," he heard her say, and then she raised her voice to call him.

Even if she hadn't, he'd have known what she was about when she jumped over the rail and transformed.

After the restful warmth of the beach, the cold water was an unpleasant shock back to wakefulness. Erik hissed his displeasure, sending steam curling up above the waves, much to the apparent alarm of Raoul and John. *The sooner you do this, the sooner you can be back ashore*, he told himself, and swam out to the *Hawk*, taking a position on the opposite side from Toinette.

The men furled the sail, that the wind might not be a hindrance to the dragons' efforts, and then Toinette and Erik began to push.

By rights, the undertaking should have been far easier than it had been on the night of the storm. For one thing, the tide was with them. For another, they were both in much better condition. Erik, for all he'd been doing that morning, hadn't been struggling to rope down cargo in the midst of a storm, nor holding the ship steady through a gale. They'd had many nights of rest and many meals at least as good as they'd managed on shipboard. It shouldn't have taken them much time at all to find a good angle for the wind, nor to push the *Hawk* out far enough to find a fair current.

Yet the island pulled.

Erik thought the feeling began as soon as he started pushing the *Hawk*, but thinking back, it might have happened earlier. Had the water honestly been that cold and unwelcoming, his muscles so resistant? Or had he explained the weighty feeling in his limbs using the first tools that came to hand? He couldn't be certain.

Whichever the case was, the true situation quickly became clear. Force like a team of oxen, slow but stubborn, tugged Erik backward toward the island, growing greater the harder he struggled with legs, wings, and tail. That alone he might have broken through, but the island drew the ship backward as well, and the weight of it took him along. Panting, he raised his head to look around and found that they were no farther from land than they'd ever been.

Around him, the tide kept running carelessly out to sea. Neither the *Hawk* nor his body seemed to recognize that—nor, when he met her gaze around the ship's hull, did Toinette's frame. She was panting as much as him, her eyes glassy from the struggle.

The alarm on deck when the wind changed was nothing to the hubbub now. One of the men was screaming. One was simply uttering steady denials. Others were shouting suggestions, or perhaps only shouting. Erik couldn't make out many words.

Eventually Marcus's voice rose above the din. "*Enough!*" He strode to the railing and shouted over. "Take us back. No use in keeping on right now."

SEVENTEEN

"*WHAT* IS OUT THERE?" MARCUS FLUNG A HAND OUT TOWARD the waves. They rolled in as calmly as ever, giving no sign of the disruption of Nature itself not far beyond the line where they broke. "You're the uncanny one, you and my lord. You tell me, Captain."

Toinette had barely managed to resume her human form before finding Marcus in front of her, demanding answers. If disembarking from the *Hawk* hadn't taken time, she likely wouldn't have managed that much. She'd seen wrath in his face before, but never directed at her.

The sarcasm that laced both syllables of *my lord* and the glance he bent on Erik were fully acidic, but it was the uninflected phrase beforehand that truly stung. *You're the uncanny one*. Marcus likely hadn't even been trying to insult her.

"I don't know," she said. "It's magic. It must be, but..." She whispered the words of invocation, but as in the storm, her vision didn't shift at all. "But I can't see it. The spirits of vision don't answer me here. I couldn't tell you why or how this works."

At the end, she felt her voice cracking alarmingly, and cleared her throat. Losing control of herself wouldn't help anything. She looked at the man who'd been her closest companion for ten years, watched him regard her as he might a horse trader of dubious honesty, and waited.

"Nor could I," said Erik. His thick burr, stronger than usual, fell into the empty gulf between Toinette and Marcus. "I'd guess it's verra powerful indeed. Salt water washes away magic, as a rule. That's likely why the waves are no' drawn to the island all the time, but keep their normal tides. For the spell to work on us, and on the *Hawk*, it'd be a mighty thing."

"Did you know about this when you hired us? Any of it?" Marcus asked. His eyes lashed over Erik, then snapped back across Toinette's face. "Did *you*?"

"*No*," she snarled back. It was so easy to fall into anger, even when she knew she aimed at the wrong target entirely. "I'd never have come if I did. And I surely wouldn't have brought anyone else."

"I'd no notion," Erik said, and clasped one hand over his heart. "I swear it. By God, and Mary, and by any of the saints you choose."

The crew were largely off the *Hawk* now, and heading toward the three of them. "…doomed, I tell you," Franz was muttering in a broken voice, and many of the men were quiet, listening to him. Sence didn't look to be, but his face was stony, even more so as he looked at Toinette.

She couldn't let herself flinch. That, she knew, would have begun the end of things between her and her crew, if there was anything left to save there.

Marcus looked over his shoulder, then shook his head. "You'd both best go," he said to Toinette and Erik. "Find a safe place and stay away for a few hours. I think I'll have calmed them down by sunset, but it'll be far easier if you're not here."

Once again, he likely didn't mean anything by what he said.

Erik and Toinette went warily up the path from the beach, weapons close at hand. Nothing accosted them, and that was truly no surprise—no creature they'd seen on the island was large enough to harm a man, let alone inclined to do so. Keeping watch gave them a mission, though, and an excuse for walking a while in silence.

Mostly silence. Toinette stomped along as though she were twice her weight. For his part, Erik took a certain delight in the feeling of sticks breaking under his feet— the joy of destruction, yes, but also the chance to hurt the island, if only a minor and dead part of it. *Had* an animal come out of the underbrush, he knew it wouldn't have fared well at all.

At the top of the cliffs, by the spring, they finally stopped, Toinette first. Still without speaking, she knelt and dipped her face in the water, then lifted her head and drank deeply. Erik imitated her, to his satisfaction. He'd done thirsty work that day, and fear had a way of drying a man's mouth.

He *was* afraid, and in his own mind he could say as much. He'd fought and killed men and beasts; he'd heard of and could imagine doing the same with wizards or demons, though it was a more daunting prospect; but the magic of the island was different. "If we only knew where it *came* from…" he muttered, and only realized he'd spoken aloud when Toinette gave him a long look.

"Yes," she said eventually, but her voice was flat. There was an absence in her eyes as well, and Erik would have much preferred the fury.

That gave him an idea—not one that would get them free of the island, but one that might at least salve their minds. "Come on, then," he said, getting to his feet and stretching.

Toinette blinked. "Hmm? Come on and what?"

"Like the old days," he said. "Two falls out of three wins. Or whoever cries off first." He saw realization dawn and smiled for the first time that day: a predator's grin, as he pushed his argument forward. "You've been wanting to do this for days, and you know it."

With the years separating them from their youth, Erik had thought he might have a little more persuading to do. Toinette had become a woman, and women's society frowned on brawling. She'd captained a ship and learned to control her temper. For a moment he faced her in the shadow-dappled clearing, birds singing around them, and tried to come up with further arguments.

Then she kicked him in the knee.

Oh yes.

It had been decades since Toinette had fought with another dragon-blooded. She'd forgotten how appealing it was: as heady and easy to lose herself as in any life-or-death battle, but without the risk of death for her men, and with no need at all to hold back. When Erik staggered from her kick to the knee, she grinned.

Toinette didn't stop when he recovered himself and used his angle to land an excellent upward punch to her stomach. Though the blow knocked the breath out of her, there was a satisfaction in the impact—even in the pain. This was real. This was solid. She could feel it, with nothing ephemeral or confusing, and she could hit back.

She did. A fist to the jaw left Erik shaking his head. Toinette tried to follow up by sweeping a foot at his ankles, but he pivoted away, stepping nimbly over a fallen branch, and then used the momentum to come back at her with a boot to the thigh.

Ow. Damn.

That one might bruise. She almost laughed aloud. Then

she darted back into the fray, throwing an uppercut that landed on Erik's shoulder.

Before she could pull back, though, he grabbed her wrist, then turned his body with a fluid strength that Toinette admired even as it pulled her weight off-center. Mortal bones might have broken; hers held, but she went flying over Erik's head to land in a patch of grass, tucking her head just in time to miss a tree trunk.

Erik followed up swiftly. Before Toinette could get to her feet, he was kneeling above her, one broad hand holding down each of her shoulders. He was smiling too. One lip was bloody from her fist, but that only made him look wilder—and more handsome. "One fall for you," he growled. "Surrender?"

"Piss off," said Toinette, and whipped her head upward toward his nose.

Erik dodged just in time, but the effort of doing so shifted his weight. Toinette shoved him off and backward; twigs snapped beneath his body. She rolled up to her feet, shifted to fighting stance, and waited.

As she'd thought he might, Erik charged her, shoulder first. If he'd taken Toinette square on, he might have won then—he weighed more, in human form, and was at least somewhat stronger—but she sidestepped neatly, grabbed the hair at the back of his head, and yanked. At the same time, she slammed her lower leg into the backs of his knees. The combination took him over backward.

It was her turn to pin him, and she didn't bugger about with hands on shoulders. She dropped to her knees on Erik's chest, sending the air out of *him* for a change. "Second," she hissed, "goes to me."

"Pulling hair," he said, gasping to get his breath back. "Typical woman. Scratch my face next?"

"If I was truly being womanly, you'd have had a knee in your stones by now."

"Aye," he said, and smiled again. "You've aged past that, have you not?"

"No," said Toinette. Looking down into his eyes, feeling the muscles in his chest straining under her palms, smelling his clean masculine sweat, she knew why she hadn't gone near his groin. It would have been her second target in any other fight—second only because men were quick to defend that location, unless she distracted them with pain elsewhere first—but she'd wanted Erik uninjured in that regard.

She lunged forward. He raised his head at the same moment, and their mouths met with heat and force. All the vital energy of their fight changed in an instant, finding different channels, but the transformation was incomplete. Still they struggled against each other, warring for control with lips and tongues.

Toinette stretched herself out atop the hard length of Erik's tall body. Her breasts flattened against his chest with exquisite friction. The pressure bordered on pain; she welcomed the bright heat of that edge, the clarity of the sensation. A knee on either side of Erik's hips held her stable and let her feel his cock hardening between them, tenting the cloth of his hose and pushing against her mound.

Clothing was a very stupid idea.

She would have done something about it, but that would have meant releasing Erik, and she didn't trust him not to take advantage of that. As she'd shifted position, he'd snaked a hand up and around her neck, his fingers long, forceful, and nearer her jugular than Toinette would have permitted from anyone else, particularly anyone whose nails could become claws with a thought.

With Erik, the contact sent tendrils of humming desire down through her body, hardening her nipples and spiraling inward to her sex. She made no move to shake his hand away. When he pressed her head down, crushing her mouth against his, the hint of pain only went well with the pleasure, a sharp wine with a rich meal.

Yet she had no wish to surrender. The fight was half the fun.

Toinette dug her fingers into Erik's shoulders, hard enough for him to feel the nails even through his shirt. At the same time, she pulled back: not enough to stop kissing him—she didn't want to do *that*—but far enough to bite his lower lip. She did no damage, but she wasn't *entirely* gentle either.

The sound he made was as close to a growl as human lungs could manage. Erik's hips flexed upward, hard and sudden and involuntary, driving his erection between his stomach and Toinette's. As the heat in her own sex spread outward, she wondered if she could drive him over the edge still clothed. The thought made her pulse with arousal—and, at the same time, chuckle low in her throat.

Erik was the one to pull back this time. "Oh no, lass," he said hoarsely. Sweat was beginning to glisten at his temples, darkening his golden hair, and his eyes were almost all pupil, but he had enough confidence to smile up at her again. "You're not winning this one."

Then, with a quick twist of his arms, he rolled them both over.

EIGHTEEN

At last Toinette was where Erik had wanted her for weeks. She writhed beneath him, full breasts heaving as she panted, hips twisting with a power that belied their slim outlines, but he had her. Unnatural strength was one thing, but strength and size still weighed in the balance, particularly in human form—and just then, neither of them wanted to be anything else.

She was no easy prey, though. Almost as soon as her back hit the ground, she was whipping a hand up toward Erik's head. Whether she meant to claw his face, gain leverage to reverse their positions again, or just pull him down for another kiss, it didn't matter in the end. He caught her wrist in one hand, grabbed the other, and pulled her arms up over her head.

That the new position tilted her long neck back and thrust her breasts forward hadn't been his prime objective, but it was a very gratifying development, and one that made him even happier with the difference in their sizes. That difference let him hold Toinette's wrists firmly captive while he palmed her breasts with his free hand, pinching the stiff nipples through the fabric of her gown as she called him obscene names in a breathless voice that only made his cock harder.

Careful not to loosen his hold, he bent his head and took one rigid peak into his mouth, lashing it with his tongue and then biting lightly. Toinette's hoarse moan filled his ears as he moved to the other breast. Her arms went limp; if

Erik had been less wary, he might have let go then, but one hand was enough to thrust beneath the ruins of her skirt.

"Best idea you've ever had," he said, punctuating the words with more rough kisses to her breasts, roaming up to where her neckline bared skin. "Never wear long skirts again."

Toinette opened her dark eyes to glare at him. "I'll wear what I like, devil take you." Both words and glare lacked some of the force they might have had, since her face was flushed with desire and her hands on his shoulders urged him back to his attentions.

He didn't comply. "You've the *taking* right, pretty girl. But you're wrong about who'll do it to whom." Beneath her skirt, her thighs were sleek and strong—and she squeezed them together at the first intrusion of his hand, as proper as any novice. "Stubborn, are ye no'?"

Toinette laughed, eyes gleaming and hair spread out on the ground like a glorious cloud. "If that's a surprise, you're duller than I thought."

Erik bit her neck for that—not to her displeasure, judging by the way she hissed and arched—and lunged forward, prying her legs apart with knees and hand alike. With a mortal woman, he would never have dared, would have stopped at the first sign of anything that might be taken as reluctance, but this was Toinette, fighting him only because the fight itself was worth something.

It cast her arousal in its own light too. When Erik's fingers reached the cleft between her legs and found it wet enough to dampen her thighs, he added the sin of pride to that of lust. "Eager," he murmured against Toinette's neck. "You can't tell me otherwise now."

"Neither can you," she said, and canted her hips so that her thigh rubbed against his cock, a slow, hard grind that had Erik seeing stars and biting his own lip for some measure of self-control.

Every instinct told him to move, to rut blindly against Toinette for the short time it would take to satisfy himself. Barely he gained mastery, long enough to undo the laces of his hose with a clumsy hand. "Hold still," he growled.

For once, Toinette did as he told her. He thrust inside her, sudden and rough. The way she caught her breath made him pause for an instant—she was no virgin, of course, and she'd been giving every sign of enjoying their roughness, though he didn't doubt that even she had limits—but in that instant she'd wrapped her legs around his thighs and risen up to meet him.

"Well?" she gasped, a challenge and a demand.

Erik met it eagerly, drawing back only to plunge forward with the same savage motion. This time he kissed her, delighting in the parallel heat of her mouth and body, the strength with which she responded, the sting of her nails raking down his back, and the pressure of her thighs at his waist. There was no time for subtlety, no will for restraint, only lust as elemental and unslacking as the storm had been at its height.

Even with his mouth on hers, Toinette was crying out before long, making desperate guttural noises that rose in pitch as her hips pumped frantically against Erik's. He cupped her arse in his hands to hold her against him and drive deeper, faster, until finally Toinette bowed her back and screamed, inner muscles clenching over and over again around his cock.

Had Erik needed further sensation to find his own climax, that would have easily done it. As it was, he had only to let go for pleasure to twist its way upward from his bollocks, pulsing outward in a lightning strike of ecstasy that hit over and over again.

Slowly the world settled back into its expected form

around him, and Erik looked down into Toinette's pleasure-hazed eyes. As long as the moment had been in arriving, he couldn't quite believe it had finally happened—and in such a way—but neither could he regret any detail.

"Do you think they heard us?" Erik asked, glancing over one naked shoulder toward the path that led to the beach.

Toinette stopped combing pine needles out of her hair and shrugged a nonchalance she wanted to feel. "Doubt it," she said, and meant *that*. "You didn't hear us when we were fighting the plants, and we were louder."

"You were further away."

"Not that much further." Actually, they'd stopped a good distance from the gravesite—neither of them being fool enough to spar, let alone swive, where blood-drinking vines might still be lurking—but sound often carried further than people thought. "They're likely making noise enough of their own, and we don't hear *that*."

Erik smiled, distinctly smug. "We werena' paying very much attention, were we?"

Undeniably, he had a point. Toinette couldn't even reprove him on the grounds of overconfidence, especially when his smile still retained a trace of sensuality and the afternoon light slanted alternate patches of brightness and shadow over his muscular chest, giving the crisp hair there an even more intense glow.

"No," she said, going back to her hair. The pine needles were legion. That only supported Erik's argument that Toinette hadn't noticed any of them insinuating themselves. "But it doesn't matter. Mortal hearing's far shorter than either—and it wouldn't distinguish the sounds we were making from, say, animals crashing around."

"Not too far off, at that."

"Speak for yourself," she said. "And most men take their shirt off *before* bedding a woman. Just a piece of helpful advice for your future."

Erik shrugged. The muscles in his back rippled, a sight that commanded Toinette's attention almost long enough for her to miss his response. "I was hot," he said, "and you hardly gave me time."

"Hmm," she said. Since she'd not bothered with her dress except to let Erik hike up the skirt, she had no real response, save for bending down to find the cord she'd used to bind up her hair. In so doing, she missed Erik tying his hose—a pity, both to miss it and that it happened. The soreness around her ribs gave her an idea. "They'll believe we were sparring, if we tell them. Especially with your lip. If they did hear anything, which they didn't."

"You know a great deal about mortal hearing."

"I know how to pretend it's the only kind I have." The cord was broken. Of course. Toinette sighed and shook out the remains of her skirt. "If your senses are too good, people think you're odd."

"I suppose they might," said Erik, sounding as though the thought had never occurred to him. "My whole family is odd, if you ask their villagers—either at Loch Arach or my father's keep."

"Yes," she said, "I heard. A few times, in my youth. Never seems to do your people any harm." Toinette fought to keep bitterness out of her voice.

It was an easier struggle than it had been at other times. As Erik had perhaps intended, at least where the sparring was concerned, everything that they'd done in the clearing had helped. Toinette had lost herself in the moment, in pain and pleasure and the mix of both. Action had burned off her nervous energy and broken her mind out of the sharklike circles in which it had been moving.

"Anyhow," she said, "if they do know what happened, what does it matter? They know everything else now."

Toinette tossed her hair back as she spoke and thrust out her jaw. She could speak boldly enough, as though she didn't wonder what further doubts such knowledge might cause among her crew. She could go halfway to convincing herself.

Yet, when they returned to the beach, she took care to stand some ways apart from Erik.

The men fell silent at their approach. Samuel looked to have been silent already: he sat on a rock, staring out across the ocean at the setting sun. Sence and Marcus, building the fire, likewise probably hadn't been talking, knowing Sence, and Franz was crouched by their shelter, rosary moving steadily and slowly between his fingers. His lips stopped moving as he looked up, but that was all. John kept cleaning fish, but Raoul, to whom he'd been talking, let both knife and flesh dangle from his hands.

Toinette had gone most of her life without being the object of uneasy stares. It had happened twice in the last week, and it felt no easier than it had at thirteen. As she'd learned to do, she kept her head up, her shoulders back, and her hands dangling loosely at her sides, badly as she wanted to do otherwise—cover her neck, for instance. She doubted that Erik had left any marks, and surely he hadn't left any that would stand out in the dim light of early evening, but she couldn't be certain.

All of the crew were alive. Except mayhap Franz and Samuel, all of them seemed capable of keeping on with the tasks that would let them stay that way. None had attacked her.

One had to start somewhere.

Toinette started by standing and waiting, with the last light of the sun coming down over her shoulder and the waves washing up the beach. She stood with empty hands and let the men decide when they would speak to her, if they would speak at all. She didn't look at Erik.

There were such moments: you stood at the wheel and watched the storm, knowing that it would break or not, and you'd weather it or not, and you'd done all you could. Gamblers spoke of letting the dice fall, and riders—which Toinette had never been—of letting the horse have its head. At times, any action but waiting could only hurt your cause.

Her stomach rolled. She felt sweat collecting under her arms and behind her knees. Nobody could see any of that, so it didn't matter. She thanked God for fifty years' practice not being sick.

"What do we do now?" Sence asked. At first, a human voice sounded almost alien, and the words might have been Greek. But he went on, asking without panic or complaint, simply acknowledging that the future hadn't vanished, only changed. "Do we live out our lives here?"

"We eat first," said Marcus, and bent a gimlet eye on Raoul. "If we're not too busy gawping to get the food ready, that is. I told you: it's better to make plans with everyone who might have knowledge, and it's better still to make them on a full stomach."

"Can we help with the fire, then?" Erik asked.

Sence shook his head. "Just about done, m'lord. Best sit down."

Toinette was glad he'd suggested it. She wouldn't have liked having to ask, and she wasn't at all sure how long her knees would hold her.

NINETEEN

THE FISH WAS GOOD, SILVER-WHITE AND FLAKY, AND IF BOILED nettles weren't precisely what Erik would have chosen as a dish to go with it, hunger did not leave him inclined to be picky. Eating occupied both his mouth and hands, so that he didn't fall into the temptation to fidget, nor to talk only to hear his own voice.

In time, as the food vanished and the process of digesting perforce calmed the men slightly, Marcus sat forward. The fire leapt up, and his bearded, angular face looked saturnine in its glow. Yet the men turned to him without hesitation. Even Franz had roused himself from his endless prayers long enough to eat, and now his eyes stayed on Marcus, not on his rosary nor darting nervously from side to side.

"It seems to me," said Marcus, "that we can split our problems in two. Half is what to do right now, and that's best planning like we'll be here through winter, at best." His voice was calm and dry: businesslike. When none of the men spoke out, he continued. "We'll need better shelter. Could be we should move higher up the cliffs. We'll need a good pile of wood and stores of food. We'll start with all of those tomorrow. Prepare for the worst, yes?"

"Then what's the best?" Samuel asked. "Do you think we've a chance of getting home?"

Marcus shrugged. "If there is one, I don't know it. I wouldn't. That's where I'll give you the wheel, Captain," he said and, with a quick gesture to Toinette, sat back.

Her face in shadow was like a statue in a long-forgotten temple, all hint of feeling drowned in deep contemplation. Idly her hand played with the ragged hem of her skirt, winding a loose red thread around her finger again and again. "I'd not give anyone false hope," she said, her voice slow and measured. "I've seen nothing like this before, nor heard of it. Nor have I fooled with magic for"—she hesitated before bringing out the words—"for longer than any of you has been alive. I wouldn't be the one I chose to fight it. Yet I was trained, and Erik more, and from what I do know, most spells *can* be broken."

Only then did Toinette turn her head, asking Erik to speak with a gesture very like Marcus's. He wondered briefly if she was aware of the imitation, then answered her unasked question. "Aye," he said. "It may be a matter of raw power, or the right set of circumstances. We've no way of knowing yet—but there is a chance."

"How *can* we know, then?" Samuel asked.

"Toinette and I—and any of you who wish to learn magic, to some degree—can start learning more tomorrow. We've magical ways, scrying and that, but," he added, remembering how little the *visio dei* had worked before, "the best way forward may be on this earth."

Across the fire, Sence waited for him to elaborate, while John watched with narrow eyes and asked, "Why?"

"Magic needs a point of attachment to the mortal world. An anchor, if you will," he added, knowing his audience. Long ago, Artair had spoken of flames and wicks, but water worked as well as fire for metaphors. "Often that's a person, but I doubt there's anyone but us living on this island." Recognizing the possibilities in *that* statement, several of the men crossed themselves. Erik went on quickly. "It's most likely that the spell's bound to an object—it might be a place, but that's a sight harder."

"And if it's the whole island?" John asked, his eyes narrow.

"Then our task is even easier, in some ways."

"Breaking strain," Toinette put in. "Or more room for holes, maybe. Size isn't always the best defense—you remember that time in Rome, John, and that little wretch with the knife?"

John winced and put a protective hand to his thigh. His face changed briefly too, in a way that spoke of more than thought and remembered pain. Toinette was again his captain, the woman who'd been in Rome with him and likely fought in whatever brawl they spoke of. For a little while, he forgot *dragon* and *Scot* and *They brought us here*.

As when she'd imitated Marcus's gesture, Erik wondered if Toinette had intended just that.

"No use wondering," Marcus said. "We'll find out, and we'll work from there. Tomorrow morning I'll say who's for building and who's for food. We'll need you two as well, should we have to go further into the forest, but for now best that you figure out what's happening here."

"That it is," said Toinette.

She made no objection, Erik noticed, to the way her first mate seemed to have taken command. He spoke without waiting for orders, and with no sense of deference. Perhaps it was always so between them in times of crisis—they had known each other for many years—but it stood out to Erik now as it hadn't before.

They had no privacy for him to ask her thoughts, nor did he think she'd welcome the question. He wanted to put an arm across her shoulders, to offer comfort, but he knew that it would likely only make matters worse. Instead he sat and stared at the fire, one of a silent crowd.

Blearily, Toinette rubbed her eyes and glared into the purple light of early morning. She'd slept poorly the night before, the day's events collecting into a ball of weariness that squatted in her stomach and refused to transmute to actual sleep for hours. When she finally had drowsed, she'd woken often.

In time, she'd remembered the feel of Erik's body atop hers, his cock deep inside her and his face as he lost himself in pleasure. That had helped—sensation, even remembered sensation, had been strong enough for a distraction—but facing him in the morning, across a circle in the sand, Toinette squirmed inside. Fun was fun, but finding its memory comforting was a step too far.

"The hour of the Moon," she said, "is too damned early."

"Have a word wi' the spheres about it, then," Erik said, his accent speaking of his own lack of sleep.

Had matters been less urgent, Toinette would have suggested simply putting off the scrying for a while: the hour of the Moon came around a few times a day. She couldn't have justified the delay in this case, though, not to herself and not to the men. There were few of them awake yet, but Samuel and John both sat watching nearby.

"You take the shapes," Erik said, passing her a thin pine branch. "I'll write the letters, and the men can light the candles. Such as they are."

Artair's training had involved lambskin, bronze, and beeswax candles. On the island, they had sticks and sand, with tapers of wine-soaked firewood and sailcloth as rough torches. In theory, Toinette thought, spells would work regardless. The right elemental correspondences were what mattered most, and the right inscriptions. She hoped *most* was *enough*, and also that Erik remembered the inscriptions.

Yet the process came back to her as any childhood skill would. Walking slowly around, she drew the inner circle, then the five-pointed star, leaving herself in the middle. Samuel and John planted a torch at each compass point. The smell of burning began to fill the air.

Erik chanted as he wrote the sigils, speaking the name of each. At first the words sounded normal; as he went on, they developed echoes that sounds shouldn't have had on the beach. When he stepped into the circle and wrote the last word, his voice was like a hum of bees.

The lines in the sand slowly filled with blue light. That light rose up around them and then shifted, splitting into lines that reconfigured themselves, midair, to form a net. A word in ancient Aramaic from Toinette and Erik's throats alike cast that net outward. It grew on the way, though the inner circle stayed around them.

Through it, in a wall of images around her, Toinette saw the island flick by. She recognized the tall pines and the brush, even the burnt area where they'd found the plants, though it was all faintly blurred and colored with the more extreme shades of magic. The spell didn't pause to look at the scenery: it *sought*, as a good hound might do. Magical power left her, a bit at a time, to form the "leash."

Then it stopped. Rather, it *was* stopped. A shock ran through Toinette. She remembered the feeling from falls in her youth. It reverberated up the lines of power and into her. She felt no pain, not exactly, but a momentary whirl-wind of sensation. Darkness was part of it—so too was cold—and a thin, whining howl wormed through her mind.

The spell tried to seek further, but to no avail. If there was a way around the thing blocking it, or a path through it, both required more strength than even she and Erik had together. Toinette raised her hands, drew her power back, and spoke the Latin words that would end the spell. After a syllable or two, she heard Erik join her.

They collapsed as it faded, both of them dropping bonelessly to the sand. This was the bad side of magic, the aftermath that left the magician wearier than three days of fighting and sicker than three of drinking—although it was far from the worst. Toinette knew that, even as she struggled to make her stomach behave. Scrying spells *usually* didn't backfire violently, from what Artair had told her, but she was glad not to have touched off one of those rare occasions.

She *thought* her eyes would grow back over time if necessary, but she wasn't sure. Organs were tricky.

"Here." A voice spoke above her. Toinette didn't open her eyes, lest vision make her spew the previous night's fish along the sand, but she placed the speaker: human, male, English, and therefore John. When she didn't move, he put a tentative hand under her chin. "Drink this."

She smelled watered wine, with a bit of honey in it, and sipped slowly. The first swallow left her sitting rigid on the sand, convinced that all her willpower would go to waste—and then her stomach shuddered and righted itself. She drank more quickly and, when she was done, tried to focus her sore eyes on John. "Thank you. How did you know?"

He shrugged. "The Scotsman"—a glance over at Erik, who was finishing his own drink with Samuel in attendance, a fact that made Toinette feel better—"said last night that you might feel sick after. Wine with honey helped my Elsie when she was carrying. So I thought—" Another shrug. "Didn't expect it *this* bad, though."

"Me neither." Toinette wiped her lips. The wine did help, though her stomach twisted again at the mention of John's wife—and his children. She at least had nobody waiting for her return. "The thing that's keeping us here doesn't want to be found."

"You saw nothing, then?" asked Samuel.

Erik shook his head. "Not nothing. Only nothing definite. We got into the forest, past the Templars' bodies. And maybe those should be our next try."

"Grave-robbing." Samuel shook his head. "Unsettling."

"What isn't?" John asked. "I'd dig up my own grandmother if it meant getting off this rock."

"Besides," said Toinette, "it's not actually a grave, is it?"

As justifications for necromancy went, she knew, that was very thin.

TWENTY

Necromancy had to wait.

Toinette and Erik spent most of the morning either asleep or otherwise flat on their backs. Once Toinette woke long enough to see Erik's face, only a short distance away, and to smell the warm scent of his body. A dim flicker of lust stirred even then, a quick spark in a body that had no fuel left to catch. More disturbing was the urge to roll over and lie against him, not out of passion but to enjoy his warmth and solidity.

She stayed where she was, closed her eyes again, and was unconscious before too much longer.

She was her own woman, and he was Artair's man. Lust was acceptable, a working partnership necessary and even pleasant in its way, but comfort was a dragon-sized step too far. Artair acted for his own good and that of his people—and Toinette didn't know that she counted. She knew that her crew almost certainly didn't. Erik was his agent; she could trust him, but not depend on him.

Not that she could, or should, depend on anyone else.

In a few hours, she was more or less herself again, capable of walking and speaking like a normal human being, and even of helping to gather wood and build the evening's fire. The muscles were quick to recover.

"All the same, best were we to wait a day or two before trying with the bones," Erik said. The two of them and Marcus were chopping up nettles and crumbling stale bread. They'd mix the result with water and boil it for a kind of pottage. It worked well enough, though passing the pot around got a bit awkward. "The soul hurts more than the body with magic, and what we face is formidable—if merely scrying on it took that much out of us, breaking a spell could be quite the task. And I'm sorely out of practice: I was always more squire than scholar." He had the chivalry not to mention how rusty Toinette's skills were. "Best to go in as hale as we can."

"You'd know," said Marcus, though he cast a quick glance at Toinette first, getting her small nod before he spoke. It was a relief to see that, though he talked to her less than he had and often spoke to the crew without consulting her first. The men might look to other mortals before her or Erik. She'd expected as much, and the pain was endurable. Petty as it might be, she thought it would have hurt more if they'd preferred him.

"Meantime, there's the, ah, winter quarters," she said. Keeping her mind on things she could do; that was often the key. "Plenty to do there. And if I remember rightly, some lifting and digging is often what's wanted the day after."

Marcus gave her a bland look that, in a companion of more than ten years, said more than an illustrated breviary: *It's what* you *want,* you mean, right now.

He was right, of course, though not necessarily about the timing. Toinette mostly wanted to eat and follow that with more sleep. She was biding her time until she could manage either. After that, yes, she'd want to get her hands dirty with practical things. And she wanted to work alongside the men, where they'd be doing the same task and neither clumsy words nor awkward glances would be necessary.

"Have you a place in mind?" Erik asked, breaking the silence.

"Not yet," Marcus replied. "You've already done a bit of clearing up where you fought the plants," he said, glancing in Toinette's direction, "so that might not be a bad spot, if we can be sure there aren't any remaining."

"Found something," said Raoul, stepping through into the shelter. In one hand he held a long brown root, twisted and knobbled into rings. "We dug up a sort of a sunflower while we were pulling more nettles. We've never seen the like, but I thought one of you might know if it'd be any good to eat."

Marcus took the tuber in one hand, sniffed at it, and shrugged. "The Ottomans make a tea out of something similar, I think. Or something that looks similar. I've never been one for knowing plants."

"I'll try it," Erik said. When Marcus and Raoul peered at him, he grinned. "Oh, I didn't mention: it's damned hard to poison us. Fatally, that is. We're wonderful bodyguards that way. My cousin Moiread met her husband when she drank some ale meant for him that had hemlock in it, I think, or perhaps arsenic."

"Wonderful," said Toinette. "Very romantic."

Erik continued, ignoring her. "I'll try a bit, and if I don't feel wretched, you'll know you can most likely eat the thing."

"Well, all right, m'lord," said Raoul. "If you're certain."

"May as well be useful," said Erik.

Toinette swept her chopped nettles into the pot, careful to get all of them. She had no way of knowing if Marcus and Raoul were staring at her now, nor, she told herself, should they have any reason to be. They'd had plenty of reminders that she wasn't human; what was one more?

Raw, the root tasted a bit like nuts, a bit savory, and quite starchy. "Probably better cooked," Erik said, "but so far edible enough. Talk to me again in the morning."

"I thought," said Raoul, "it'd be another bit of food for the winter, if it's not poison. And it looks to be the kind of thing that'd keep well."

"That it does," said Marcus. "If m'lord here doesn't have a bad night of it, we can harvest more when we go to start clearing land. Two birds with one stone—or three, if we're lucky enough to catch one." He chuckled at his own joke, then added in Erik and Toinette's direction, "Four, if you do want to try anything with the Templars. Rings and bones are all there, aren't they?"

"They are," said Toinette thoughtfully, the first time she'd spoken for a little while. "And I think we should get all of them up. Whatever else we do, we can bury those men properly while we're at it."

"We don't have a priest," said Raoul. "But neither did we for our men."

Toinette nodded. "Happens often enough, doesn't it? We could bury them next to our crew, get a proper little graveyard going."

"If there's more than one," Marcus said, "we might have to guess at whose bones are whose. And they might be a bit incomplete—but come the Judgment, I hear that'll all be sorted."

"God will figure it out, I assume." Toinette leaned backward and took in Marcus and Raoul with a look. "In the meantime, our job's to live like civilized men."

The glint in her eyes, and the line of her jaw, dared anyone to point out any reason she might not qualify.

After Erik passed an uneventful night, a day of clearing, cutting, and digging resulted in a small circle of bare earth, a pile of felled trees to one side, and the bones of three men. *Most* of the bones: there were three skulls and six hands, but only five feet, and nobody was quite sure about anything else. "Scavengers," said Samuel.

"That didn't get killed themselves?" Toinette asked.

"Not if they're small enough—rats, say. Or the vines might sleep after a kill. Or only eat men." He touched the burnt remnant of one of the vines and shook his head. "Truly, there are many strange beings in this world. I'd say it was a pity to kill the plants without learning more, if they weren't so deadly."

"Natural philosophy can wait until nothing's trying to drink my blood, thank you," said Marcus.

They found two more Templar rings with the hands, as well as a rusty chain shirt, two swords in crumbling scabbards, and the remnants of a boot top. "They must have been taken by surprise," Toinette said. "Only one of them had time to draw steel."

"Poor souls," said Raoul.

Toinette remembered the quick strength of the vines. The Templars had been fewer, and none of them dragon-blooded. The fight would have been over quickly; God willing, they would have died quickly too. She shuddered.

Yauuuw.

The sound came from behind her: a low, scratching whisper that was almost a voice. *You* as a drunk or a foreigner might pronounce it, but with a hollowness that neither wine nor unfamiliarity could explain. Toinette turned, nails already starting to extend.

The forest stood empty before her. The treetops swayed in the faint breeze, leaves and needles rustling. Had that been what she'd heard? It must have been.

Wind hadn't sounded like *that* before.

"Captain?" Samuel asked. "Did you hear—"

He left off before he could name what. He stood tense, his nostrils flared, frowning into the forest.

"I thought I did," she said, hiding her hands behind her back until she could get her claws safely away, "but I see nothing."

"Nor I," said Marcus.

"Likely we're all on edge," said Toinette.

"But," said Raoul, frowning, "is this a wise place to build? Meaning no disrespect," he added toward both Toinette and Marcus, "but if men died here, mightn't they take it amiss? And if"—he gestured toward the forest—"if that sound was real, what is it?"

"It's a fair question." Not for the first time, Toinette wished that they'd brought a priest along, or that she'd learned more of magic with Artair. She spoke slowly, drawing her thoughts out on the words as thread on a wheel. "But men have died in many houses, and many by violence, and there's plenty live there safely after. We're burying these. With luck, that'll count with them, if their spirits do linger."

"And whatever spell traps us here, it hasn't done anything to harm us yet," Marcus added. "Lights and noises have never yet been deadly. High tides in winter, on an island—I know that danger, and it'll take more than a juggler's trick or two to make me chance it."

In the center of the magical circle, Erik sat facing three skulls. Having Toinette at his side bolstered his courage, but still he was far from easy as he began to speak the incantation. For one, he'd never learned any distinct spell for this. He knew a few ways to break spells, and he'd put this rite together by combining that knowledge with what little he'd learned of the restless dead.

For another, he didn't know that these dead *were* restless, whatever might be the case with their spell. He'd committed a great many sins in his life, repented of a few, and lived well enough with others. Necromancy was new.

His throat was dry as he went on speaking. Each word took an age to form.

Gradually his vision shifted. He rose up above his body, seeing the island from above once again. This time, though, he saw it wrapped in a dense web, the purple-black of plague sores. The furthest tendrils, fading almost to gray, reached far out into the ocean, and Erik knew in that moment that the storm had been no mere freak of weather.

Drawing back to his body and the beach around it, he saw thinner black strands reaching for him and all his companions, wriggling obscenely, and then drawing back from the circle around the fire. Wood or flame or simply the presence of men drawn together to talk and eat like civilized creatures…something kept the web's influence at bay. Erik was glad of it; he knew not precisely what that influence might be, but doubted it was good.

He reached out and put a hand on each of the skulls nearest him, with Toinette doing likewise. Her fingers settled on top of his right hand, slim but callused from the sword and the ship's wheel, and her power linked to his. They would send it through the skulls and punch a hole in the web.

Indeed, the skulls took the power easily. Glowing golden, they rose from the sand and hovered in midair—but nothing else happened. The magic went into them, but the black web of the spell rested unmoving and unharmed around the island.

Briefly, from a farther distance than Erik could truly imagine, he caught the wisp of a feeling from the skull in front of him: regret.

Looking closer, he saw that the black webbing lay only lightly on the skulls, without the inward growth or the strength he would have expected from a true connection. Those bones, in life, might have partaken of the spell, or might have merely been trapped as Erik and his companions were, but they weren't part of it.

There was nothing there that he could use.

TWENTY-ONE

"Now what?" Toinette asked. She would have felt bad pressing Erik on the subject under other circumstances, but the men were watching, she knew they were asking the question in their minds, and it was best she be the one to give it voice.

Even so, she regretted the necessity. Erik looked gray and weary; since Toinette had a headache pounding at her temples and a mouth that tasted like the inside of a boot, she was sympathetic. She thought the spell had been a mite easier on them both than the scrying, which perhaps meant they were getting back into practice, but that was a low bar to clear.

"They didn't cast the spell," Erik said, gesturing to the skulls. "We'll need to find the people who did—or *their* bones."

"That means searching more of the island. Of course." Toinette sighed.

Erik turned toward her, eyes narrowing. "Would you rather be trying to break the spell by ourselves? Wi' nothing to give us an opening?"

"No," she said. Even thinking about it made her headache worse. Nor could she truly accuse Erik of having engineered this, or even of taking pleasure in it. Still, she knew it would be a relief to him if he *could* tell Artair he'd looked as well as he possibly could. No sworn knight would lightly break off his mission, after all, and even escaping from a haunted island might count as light enough to trouble a man. Despite her angry words before they'd realized they were trapped—it seemed a lifetime ago now—she couldn't fault the mission itself, either. With Balliol's invasion, it had become clear that the English were acting out of vengeance now, and she could blame no man or country for wanting protection from that.

Toinette wanted to spit, and cleared her throat instead. "Same as before, then. We each take a day to go forward and a day to help build, or fish, or whatever's needed."

"Aye. I'll take first," said Erik, settling back into weary resignation. "Tomorrow."

"Tomorrow. First we'll have the burials." Toinette looked back at John and Samuel. They'd briefly been studying the landscape intently, as men did in proximity to an argument they wanted no part of, and the realization made her wince. She hid it with a smile and felt every muscle involved. "Think of it this way: the further in we go, the better chance we have of finding food besides nettles and roots and fish."

"Do you think there might be a deer or two in there?" Samuel asked. "I've seen a few tracks that made me think so, but they were old."

"If there was one, there might be more," said Toinette. "I've seen squirrels enough that it'll be worth getting good with a stone again."

John blinked. "Were you once?"

"Once," she said, only then realizing what weariness had led her to let slip. Before the island, that would have dismayed her. Since the men had seen her change into a dragon, it was harder to care. "I wasn't a rich girl when I made the trip to Scotland. I walked a lot of it—and would have gotten taken up for poaching a time or two, likely, if I hadn't been quick on my feet."

"You and Raoul both, ay?" John grinned.

"The sea takes all sorts. You know that. But I was never *caught*." Toinette felt Erik looking at her, shrugged, and stood. "And if you gentlemen will excuse me, I'm going to try to sleep this off."

She wouldn't be around them when she was tired enough to speak of the animals she'd *truly* learned to kill with stones, nor of the myriad other ways she'd earned daily bread as a girl, nor yet of the household she'd earned for. They knew enough of her past, Erik especially.

Another three graves sprouted on the beach, and Erik thought of trinities. Father, Son, and Holy Ghost; morning, noon, and night; land, sea, and air; and what would the dead men have been? Gervase, Yakob, and Emrich: the joyful, the hard-working, and the quiet, he supposed, though he'd known none of them well. He knew nothing of the three Templars they buried now, save that they'd come to the island and died, and that they'd not cast the spell of imprisonment.

Would they—had they—disputed with their fellows about it? Had their deaths come about that way? Or had they died before the spell, with only circumstance leaving them so unconnected?

If there was a way of knowing, he didn't have it. His training had been scant on ghosts.

Marcus's Latin was getting better. He didn't stumble over the phrasing at all when conducting his second funeral. God willing, that wouldn't come up again—Erik thought of trinities once more, and sent up a silent prayer of aversion.

Around him, the men bowed their heads in more vocal prayer, and he joined them. Most of their Latin was off,

too--they didn't stumble, but the responses were too quick,
the words jumbled together, as with all forms learned out
of habit without knowledge behind them. Samuel's and
Sence's were a shade more precise. Franz's weren't, but
he looked the better as he said them, losing some of the
haunted look that had been in his eyes ever since they'd
discovered the spell.

Toinette, who had been trained better, who had at least
learned Latin, slurred her responses anyhow, just as her
crew did. She kept her head bent and her hands folded
neatly in front of her. Her slashed dress said otherwise,
but the posture was that of a respectable and pious merchant's wife.

Of course, at the end, she stepped forward to take one
of the shovels and the image shattered—but there had been
that moment. And Erik, filling in one of the graves himself,
watched her and wondered if she knew she was trying, and
how hard she was trying, and why.

The groups had divided further. Marcus and Samuel stayed
in relative safety on the beach, fishing and drying what
they caught; Erik led John, Sence, and Raoul further into
the forest, seeking any object that might anchor the spell;
and in the clearing, Toinette and Franz hacked notches
into pine logs. It was sweaty, exhausting work, but it was
simple physical labor, with the clean scent of pine rising in
the air as they cut, and Toinette gave thanks for it, much as
she disliked the cause.

After cutting notches, they laid the first logs out in a
rectangle, fitting them together at the corners. The next
layer went on top, and so on: with two of them working,
they could produce a cabin twice as tall as a man, and one

that could fit all of them inside. It would be a bit close, but Toinette had seen farmers and poor city folk alike living in less space—and the more people inside, the warmer it would be come winter.

The walls were halfway done when Franz caught his breath and narrowed his eyes. Toinette worried that he'd seen another image, or was about to go all odd and prayerful again, but he actually looked both calculating and hopeful. "Captain," he whispered, slowly reaching for the small bow on his back, "I think there's a deer nearby."

Almost immediately she could taste venison, and her mouth watered. And when she tried, she *could* smell the animal, though long habit kept her from saying as much: a shade muskier than the deer she remembered in Loch Arach, but it had been a long time since she'd hunted in the wilderness. "Go slowly," she whispered back. "Remember this place is tricky."

She hated to remind him and see the sudden fear in his face, but she would have hated more to see him die.

As Franz slowly walked forward, moving upwind with an arrow fitted to his bow, Toinette trailed behind. Even in human form, the scent of the dragon-blooded was generally enough to scare herd animals. It was hard to find a horse that would tolerate her, and the time in Morocco when she'd tried to ride a camel had become a running joke with Marcus and others of her crew.

She still thought she should have just eaten the creature.

Up ahead, the brush rustled, making far more noise than any normal deer or even a man would have caused. Franz stopped and raised his bow. Toinette put a hand to her sword, in case what came through *wasn't* a deer.

They were both right.

Slowly, a long brown head with a pouched jaw pushed

its way into view. It paused to shake massive flat antlers free from the surrounding trees and bit a shoot off a branch. Then the creature stepped forward, and Toinette stifled the urge to whistle. Its body was a bit like a deer's in general shape—four long legs, a stubby tail, no claws or wings— but at the shoulder it was almost as tall as she was in dragon form, and the rest of it was proportional.

While she stared, gape-mouthed, Franz had no such moment of disbelief. He drew and shot quickly, sending an arrow deep into the creature's neck.

It turned. Toinette briefly thought she saw surprise in its small dark eyes, but the shot was a clean one, and the arrow had sunk deep. The beast made a low grunting noise, then its legs sagged sideways and it fell, several small plants snapping beneath its dying weight. Its ribs heaved up and down a few times. Then all was still.

Toinette swore, quietly and in Italian, and stared back and forth between the creature and Franz. "You win the prize for archery. And for quick thinking. What in God's name do you think that is?"

"Elk, that is," said Franz, surprised but in no way uncertain. "With my grandfather I used to hunt them, though it was rare for us to catch one, and dangerous to try without many men and dogs."

"I'd think so."

"But I thought, here there are many more dangers, and we'll need food. The meat keeps well. And you're here."

Toinette blinked, and smiled before she realized she was doing it. She'd known Franz for many years, long enough to tell that he was being sincere. She cleared her throat. "Well. Nicely done. That should set people's minds at ease a bit about food, and it'll make a damned fine change from fish."

"That it will," said Franz. He knelt, clasped his hands together quickly, and said a brief prayer in German. Toinette caught the name of Saint Hubert, patron of hunters, and she echoed Franz's "Amen," though the rest of the prayer was unfamiliar and her German spotty at best and mostly fit for taverns.

"I think our plans for today just shifted a touch," she said, when he stood up again. "Do you know how to clean this thing? And can you tell me how to assist you?"

"Gladly so," said Franz.

They were moving forward. It wasn't in the direction Toinette would have liked, and she had to admit that it might not be for a long time, if ever, but it was forward all the same. She took comfort in that.

TWENTY-TWO

"WIND'S IN THE WEST," SAID ERIK. IT FELT GOOD ON HIS FACE: a fresh breeze after the close, clammy scent of the far forest. He and John stood on the edge of the cliff, looking out to sea and waiting for Toinette and Raoul to join them. "Autumn soon."

He didn't expect the other man to answer, not in more than a grunt or a dispassionate *mmm*. John took instruction well enough, but he'd never sought Erik out, nor started conversations. As far as Erik knew, the Englishman was as hostile as he'd been the first day aboard.

Therefore, when John spoke, thoughtfully and at length, it took a moment for the actual words to take shape in Erik's mind: "The harvest will be coming on well, back home."

"Aye. I'd give much for a ripe apple, or a loaf of fresh bread."

John actually smiled. "It's bread I miss when I'm away. That and my wife, of course."

"You're a good man to say it, and rare."

"She's a patient woman." John looked from the sea and the clear sky to Erik. "You don't know the thing you're here after, do you? Not in any specific."

"No."

"But you're hoping it'll give your lord power."

"My land, rather."

"Your side, let's say." John rubbed at his beard. "If you do get back, say, and the treasure's as powerful as all that, what do you imagine you'll do with it? What would your lot do if they won, and could keep on? Would David take London?"

Shades of Artair came back to him, and easy words died in Erik's throat. "I'd think not," he said after a long time had seemed to pass. It was the best he could manage. "We didn't before. I'd say we'd settle back to the borders we'd had. The men I led are tired of war. So am I."

"Kings don't tire so easily as other men."

"Yours didn't, that's for certain," Erik replied hotly.

"Well—" John began to respond in similar temper, and Erik had to admire him in that moment. Not many would speak that way to a dragon, no matter how provoked. Nor did he think it was fear that stopped John's tongue, but a wiser, more worldly emotion. "No. No, and there's not much honor in what he did, in the end. But honor's for your sort. For me, I want to know that my home will be safe, and my family."

"I think they will. From us, at any rate. A king will find it hard to fight a war if his lords are against it, and mine wishes no more fighting than I do. We'll claim our own again, and that'll be an end of it."

"And if you're wrong about your lord?"

"Then I'll do my best to change his mind," Erik said, though he winced inwardly at the notion of trying to change Artair's course once he'd set it. "This thing, if it exists, might keep our sons from killing each other. That's my hope."

John nodded slowly, then as slowly asked, "Do you have any?"

"No. It's…difficult, for us, with mortals."

"I keep dreaming of mine," said John. "Not good dreams."

"I don't think anyone has good dreams here."

Darkness, death, and a voice: "This is what waits."

His answers echoed, hollow: "This is a nightmare. We made it. You can show me all the corpses you want; I know this is a dream."

"Dreams speak truth. You know this."

"Not all dreams are prophecy, and not all prophecy is fixed. Go away."

"You can't stop it. You are one."

"I'm not alone."

"They break. They fear. They run."

"Who are you?"

"She cares for herself. For her pets. She would turn on you to save them. She will."

"*What* are you?"

"This is what waits."

"We'll set a circle of protection around the camp," Toinette said, filling waterskins, "and another at the cabin when we come up for the winter. Erik says that should keep out anything uncanny, though it won't go very far."

"What is it, this magic that you're doing?" Franz asked, the gray light of the cloudy day making his solemn face even graver.

"Calling on angels," Samuel said before Toinette could. "So nothing that should alarm you too much."

"No, I didn't think… I don't think you would traffic with demons," Franz said with an apologetic look at Toinette. "Do they reply?"

"Not in so many words," said Toinette. "If the spell works, that's an answer. Actions speak loudest and all."

In motions that had long become reflex, they drew strings tight and knotted them, tied the skins to their belts, and stood. Franz looked off into the woods. "You will laugh," he said, "but I swear it... I hear voices."

"I won't laugh," said Toinette. "I've heard a few of my own."

"And I," said Samuel. "In the wind, at night?"

"And my dreams," said Franz.

"Aye," Toinette agreed. "What do yours say?"

"I can't remember my dreams, never could," Samuel said, "and I'm glad for that. I've not heard many words from the waking ones. 'You,' maybe."

"And '*nichts*.' That's 'nothing' in English. That they speak different languages is new."

"Or we hear different," said Toinette.

"You have nobody," said the voice from around her.

"Pigshit. If I had *nobody*, I'd not have a horrible voice in my dreams, would I?"

"You have nobody. I am nobody. I am nothing. You are nothing."

"Go to Hell."

"Hell waits for you."

"Now you're a priest?"

"You are damned. You know this. They know this. They all know."

"Piss off."

"They fear you. They hate you. Every smile is a lie."

"I don't believe you."

"He serves his master. You are no kin. He has his task."

"Go away."

"They let you live for fear. Nothing more. You're not their captain. Never were. All a lie."

"Go. Away."

"No woman. No human. No soul."

"*Go away.*"

"Damned. Monster. Devil. Misbred."

"*Go away!*"

TWENTY-THREE

SHE WOKE IN THE COLD, DAMP DARKNESS THAT HAD MARKED ALL of her nights for a month. Overhead, the sky was flickering sickly green. The voice still echoed in her head: *Monster. Devil.* Toinette stared across the sand at nothing and held still.

The men slept in the shelter. She and Erik slept outside, each off to one side: sentries, harder to kill than most of the crew. Toinette had volunteered shortly after she and Erik had returned. Nobody had spoken against the idea.

Turning her head, she could make out the figure on real sentry watch: Raoul, that night. He still looked hale enough. As she watched, he scratched the back of his head. All was, if not ever well, as well as the island got.

It was a dream. Go back to sleep.

When she closed her eyes, she saw the faces again: Jehan, Gervase, the man she'd stabbed in Mecklenburg, the bodies from plague carts, her mother. The dead lips spoke again, their writhing splashed in paintings across her mind.

"Shit," she muttered, and got to her feet.

Quiet as she was, Raoul was alert—good lad—and turned to meet her eyes. "Captain?"

"Can't sleep. Walking a bit." She saw the recognition in his eyes. None of them were sleeping easily of late. *That* was just what a crew already wound wire-tense needed, but there was nothing to do about it. They needed the wine to make the water good. "Don't mind me."

"Yes, Captain," he said, and turned back to his duty: still obedient, still earnest, as though that would save him.

They all made their own armor. Sence's was his faith, John's and Samuel's magic, hers... She wished she knew. Duty usually sufficed; duty was a damned poor fabric when she kept suspecting they'd be better off without her.

She walked. She tried not to look at the sky, and failed.

Erik slept behind a semicircle of rocks, shielded from the wind. Halfway there, Toinette realized her destination, shrugged, and kept on. Making sure he was safe would do as well as anything else for a task.

She suspected that seeing him might calm her too, but she didn't want to dwell on that.

By the time she reached the ring of stones, she knew that Erik's sleep wasn't easy either. The sound of his body tossing back and forth came in unsteady counterpoint to his frantic breathing. When Toinette did stand above him and look down, she saw his brow wet with sweat and his eyes moving frantically beneath their lids.

She knelt and put a hand on his shoulder.

Instantly his hand clamped around her wrist in a bruising grip. He was half up off the ground, grabbing her by the shoulder, before he fully woke; then Erik froze, his wide eyes staring into hers, his mouth stilled mid-oath.

"Do you see the dead too?" she whispered.

"...aye," he said, coming back to her from a long and horrible way off. Toinette knew the path he walked. She gently eased her wrist out of his hand and helped him sit up.

"I hate this place," she said.

"Aye." He sounded more certain about that, and less surprised. Slowly he gathered himself, wiped his brow, let out a breath: the steps of reasserting himself as a man and the world as less horrible than it was in his dreams. She knew that well too. It was what had driven her to find him, after a month when she'd avoided being alone in his company.

"Bear in mind," she went on, keeping her voice quiet but knowing how welcome a voice speaking rationally would have been to her, "I've been in some wretched hives. Place up north where we all had bad meat—I never thought I'd hate anywhere more. And yet, there's this. The world just keeps surprising me."

"It's…enterprising that way."

"Would you like some water?"

"I'd like strong drink. Otherwise…" He shrugged. Moonlight picked out the muscles of his shoulders beneath his unlaced shirt. "No need. Thank you for waking me. I didn't cry out, did I? Disturb you?"

"No. I had the same problem. I thought…" It sounded stupid, now that she came to say it, but she'd learned that the only cure for sounding stupid was to keep going. "I thought a walk might do me good. And I wanted to be sure nothing had made off with you in the night."

"Don't trust your sentries?" he asked with a semblance of his usual grin.

"Four eyes are always better than two." She pushed back her hair, aware suddenly that she'd probably been thrashing around in her sleep fully as much as Erik had been, and that she'd not even tried to mend her appearance. "Or maybe I just wanted company that didn't have to keep watch."

"Oh?" He lifted his eyebrows, and the way he smiled let her know exactly how he was interpreting what she'd said.

Toinette opened her mouth, starting to protest that she hadn't meant it *that* way—but then, why not? They were away from everyone else's view, neither of them were on sentry duty, and the beach had always been fairly peaceful regardless, and there was nothing like sport to make you know that you were alive and not, say, in a nightmare den of underwater talking corpses.

She leaned forward and kissed him. She was better at that motion than she'd been when they'd been young. It was easy for her mouth to settle atop his, to curl one hand around the back of Erik's neck as she let her breasts graze against his chest. His arms slid around her with far more grace than before, and the splay of his hands on her back was unhurried, without pressure. They were old enough to be smooth now, when anger and despair didn't drive them.

Slowly Toinette learned his mouth, the fluid glide of his tongue against hers, the way his fingers slowly clenched, dragging themselves across her lower back. She thrilled to the hitch in his breath and leaned further toward him. In time she'd have to shift position—hers was already unstable, her weight balanced half on Erik's shoulders and half on one knee—but the very precariousness was interesting, a factor to work around and to lend unexpected pressure.

He skimmed the side of her breast with his fingers, brought them up in a tingling line to her collarbone, and finally cupped her chin as he pulled away.

"You'll have to be verra quiet, you know," he whispered, his voice like thick velvet. "Do you think you can do that this time?"

"Do you?" she asked, while even the question brought her sex to pulsing heat.

Erik's fingers tightened. "I asked you."

Arousal was a slow twist in her gut, a tightness in her chest. "Then," Toinette said softly and from her throat but in no way uncertain, "I'll be quiet. There's no man born can make me cry out if I set my mind against it."

His eyes flared. "We'll see, won't we? Stand up."

Toinette could have told him to go to hell. She could have ignored him. She considered doing both, but the order itself made her shiver with sensation. She wanted to obey.

The idea wasn't entirely new to her. She'd heard stories enough. She'd spent a few nights drinking with whores, while her men enjoyed themselves, and heard of bishops who liked to be whipped and lords who enjoyed being slaves for an evening. Yet her own liaisons had never been so complicated, and this was *Erik*, and she was actually blushing as she got to her feet.

That only made her more excited.

Putting a hand to her hip, she cocked her head and looked back down at him. "So, then?"

"Take off your gown," he said, no less authoritative for whispering.

She wanted to undress smoothly, without any of the frantic scrambling that had happened last time. She almost managed it, though as with any gown, there was an awkward moment when her head was covered with fabric. Then she dropped the fabric to the ground and stood, feeling the night air cool against her naked body.

Erik's gaze was almost warm enough to make up for it. He sat spellbound, looking first at her bare breasts and then down over her belly to the tuft of hair between her thighs. The uncanny light spilled across them both, and Toinette could have done without it since it made her look as though she was underwater. Still, it let her see the stark desire on Erik's face, and the thick ridge rising from his lap, and for that she'd almost forgive it.

The silence was rich and shortly unbearable, the anticipation too drawn out for her willpower. "If I were mortal, I'd be freezing right now," she said, by way of something *to* say.

She'd expected that to break the mood. Instead, Erik chuckled, shaking his head, and stood up. "But you're not, are you? Stand still." He slipped around behind her, his breath hot on her neck as he ran his fingers over her hard nipples. "No, it's no' chill behind this."

The touch, light as it was, was wonderful agony. Toinette leaned back, thrusting her breasts toward Erik's hands, seeking the solid heat of his body behind her.

He allowed the contact for a heartbeat. Then he stepped back and his fingers closed harder on her breasts, pinching. "Did I no' say stand still?"

"I—" She struggled to keep her voice even. The pain was small sparks, feeding the fire within. "Didn't realize how still you meant."

"And now you do. No moving. You can talk, but that's all."

His hands eased again. He cupped her breasts lightly, then slid his fingers down over her ribs to her waist, all the while placing brief kisses along her neck. Toinette drew a ragged breath. "And if I don't obey?"

Erik laughed again, a hot vibration against the juncture of her neck and shoulder. "Then I stop."

"There are times," she said, "that I hate you. You know that."

"Is this one of them?"

The breeze wound between her parted thighs, caressing slick flesh only enough to tease: no substitute for anything Erik might offer. He stepped closer, pressing his cock against the cleft of her arse, bringing his hands back to fondle her breasts. Toinette's only comfort was hearing the unsteady sound of his breathing. "Not quite," she said.

"Mmm," he said, a pretense at thoughtfulness that his voice was too husky to quite sustain. "Good girl."

Finally, too slowly, he wound his fingers through the curls around her sex. Toinette closed her eyes, relishing both the touch and the way his hips thrust forward as her wetness provoked his lust, trying not to move or cry out.

The challenge became a near impossibility. Erik stroked slowly along her cleft, alternating between a tantalizingly light touch and a pressure so firm it would have been painful had she been less excited. His thumb rubbed lightly at the center of her pleasure, then danced away again.

She thought of every oath she knew, in every language. That didn't work. Once Erik slid two fingers inside her and began pumping, rubbing his cock against her in time with each stroke, not even biting her lip helped. The sound from her throat was stifled, as best she could manage, but Toinette couldn't have denied that it was a whimper.

"Not so quiet as all that," he whispered into her ear. His teeth closed on her earlobe, and he pulled his hands back at the same time.

Toinette hissed in frustration. Despite the edict, she half turned, looking over her shoulder into Erik's eyes. "Will you stop now?" she taunted him. "Truly?"

"Only change the rules," he replied, and grabbed her by one hip. He'd been reaching to undo his hose, Toinette realized then. When he pulled her back against him, his cock slid between her thighs, thick and hot against her, *almost* what she needed. She flexed her hips, and the friction made both of them growl.

"No," said Erik, and the hand on her hip was punishingly strong. "On your knees now."

She knelt, quickly enough that she squirmed inwardly at the memory. The sand was soft under her knees, then under her elbows—she knew what he was telling her, and she wanted no delay.

Delay she had nonetheless. Erik covered her with his body, one hand holding the dripping head of his sex just at the entrance to hers. His breath came quickly on her neck, and when Toinette turned her head, she could see his pulse pounding in his throat, but he didn't enter her.

She lifted her eyebrows and shot him a challenging look. The sport was a thrilling one. She didn't even mind— entirely—if he won that round, but she'd not take the fall without a fight. "I could just go take care of myself, you know. It's no *greater* sin than fornication."

"No greater sin," said Erik, and the presence at her cleft slid slowly along, working her open and then stopping, "but no' nearly so satisfying, is it, lass? You canna' tell me your hand feels like this."

Toinette closed her eyes, dug her fingers into the sand. Despite Erik's words, she knew he was close to breaking—but the ache between her legs was too much, her body too desperate.

"God. *Please*, Erik," she whispered.

Saying the words was itself treacherously exciting; the long slow thrust that followed sent starbursts exploding behind her eyes; and best of all was Erik's groan, mingling lust and relief and telling her that he'd been in as much blissful torment as she.

Slowly, deeply, he moved within her. She'd been on the edge before; now her whole body went rigid with need.

Leaning down, Erik brushed her hair away from her neck and whispered in her ear, his rhythm never ceasing. "Almost there, aye? Let me feel it—that's good—yes, oh Christ, yes."

His voice fell into a shattered snarl as Toinette's climax began. In the midst of her pleasure, she felt him speed up, felt the bursts of warmth within her, adding to her passion—and was thankful that, at the end, he slipped a hand over her mouth. She surely *would* have been heard, otherwise.

TWENTY-FOUR

THE AFTERMATH OF CONGRESS HAD USUALLY BEEN AWKWARD for Erik. Always he felt he should speak; never had he known what to say; and with his urges satisfied, the women he'd been with had all seemed increasingly young. In time, he'd found it less trouble to satisfy lust himself or, *in extremis*, to confine his attentions to whores.

Had he tried to predict the moments after with Toinette, he'd have hoped, at best, for the same briskness he'd been used to. After their coupling in the forest, that had seemed most likely.

Then, not long after he came back to himself, Erik felt her stretch beneath him and laugh, quiet of necessity but unmistakably content. "First pine needles and now sand," she said, shaking her head so that more of her hair fell around her neck. "I think I'll be frightened to seduce you again, lest we end up on hot coals. Get up, will you?"

The request, which wasn't really a request, made her sound very much like the girl he'd grown up with. One could see that at times: bits of the past blending into the present, ripples in metal showing the hammer strokes. It was rare to find it in one of his own race, rarer in one so close to his own age.

Pulling reluctantly out of Toinette's body and away, Erik ran a hand down her back. "Next time," he said, "I'll make sure to have at least a blanket."

"Extravagant promises like that will turn a girl's head."

"Only the best," he said. They repositioned themselves

to sit facing each other, though not before Erik had re-donned his hose and Toinette her gown. There were good reasons for that, but it was still a disappointment to see her smooth body disappear beneath the cloth. "And would you really say you seduced me?"

"Well, it can't be the other way around. You were only sitting there," she retorted.

Erik grinned. "I sit very appealingly."

"I'm sure I'm not the first woman to think so."

"You'd not believe me if I said you were. Here…" She was trying to comb out her hair. "Let me."

"What do you know about women's hair?" Still, Toinette sat in front of him and obligingly bent her head.

Erik ran his fingers through the strands, gently separating tangles. Without a comb, he could only do so much, but at least he could keep it from plaguing her too badly, and keep touching her in the bargain. "It's not so different from brushing dogs, is it?" he joked, and got a rude noise in response. "And you just said you thought me *quite* adept with women."

"I didn't say 'adept.' I just think I have good taste."

"And I thank you." Erik had done rather well when he wanted to—though he didn't doubt that was as much due to rank and wealth as to his looks or manners. Most lords his apparent age had left a trail of bastards behind them, after all.

The thought made him pause. He studied Toinette's hair, slipped a lock back into place, and then asked, "You couldn't be with child, could you? I—"

"No," she replied, not laughing but not sounding distressed either. Her voice was quite matter-of-fact. "It doesn't take the rites with two of us, but it's still a matter of will."

"Oh." He sighed with relief. "How do you know?"

"Agnes told me. I was fourteen, or a little younger."

"Agnes?" He remembered Artair's elder daughter: studious and refined, the first and totally unreachable object of his infatuation. He couldn't imagine talking with her about childbearing, and particularly not how to prevent it.

Toinette chuckled, a dry undertone to her voice. "She was being helpful. And she wanted me to know that *she* knew that *I* knew."

He was too tired to follow. "Hmm?"

"If I'd had it in mind to trap one of you into marriage by 'accident.' She wanted me to know that I wouldn't fool anyone. Or, I wouldn't fool her—or probably Artair, though I hate to think about *that* conversation—and she'd open any of the boys' eyes that needed it."

"God's bones."

"In her place, I might have done the same. And it *was* helpful information, wasn't it? It means neither of us have to worry—not about *that*, at any rate."

"No." Erik withdrew his hands, having done everything he could with her hair. He was no courtier, to know any real tricks, and just then he felt ashamed to be touching her, imposing on her in the guise of help.

"Which is just as well, as the list was getting long." Toinette got to her feet again. "And speaking of worries, I suppose I'd best go get some sleep, if we're to face the rest of ours."

"Aye," said Erik. He looked up at her, wanting to say more and unable to think of what. "Thank you for waking me" was what he finally settled on, and it didn't feel like nearly enough.

"Ugh," said Toinette, slashing brambles away to either side of her. "Nature is awful even when it's not haunted."

"You've known that as long as I've known *you*," said Marcus.

"I didn't say I was surprised, did I?"

The sea and sky had their own dangers, but she liked them well enough. Hunting at Loch Arach had been similar, but plodding along on a ground full of insects and clinging plants had Toinette swearing almost every step of the way, if only in her mind. She'd not spent much time wandering the wilderness since her journey to Loch Arach more than a century before, and then she'd mostly been walking on roads.

While they searched, they couldn't even stay completely on what few game paths there were, or follow the more level and less overgrown ground beside the stream. Beasts were born and died, even ground shifted with the years, and so they went over the unexplored ground with slowness that made Toinette want to tear her hair out.

Marcus, never much fonder of the wild than she, surveyed the undergrowth with narrowed eyes. "These aren't drinking our blood," he said, his voice immediately undermining any attempt to look on the bright side. So did his next word: "Yet."

"I'd almost rather they tried," said Toinette. "A fight's at least exciting. Do you see anything to the east, Sence?"

"A large tree. Larger than most around here."

"And that's saying a fair bit," said Toinette, although in justice most of the trees on the island were a bit stunted by wind: not runts by any means, but not the towering sort she remembered from Scotland.

"I could climb it," Sence said, turning to look back at them. He made the suggestion without any of the enthusiasm Raoul would have shown, nor Samuel's curiosity, but also without John's reluctance. The tree was there. He could climb it. That was a thing that could happen. "It might give us a better view, but still further under the other trees than you could manage flying."

"Not a bad notion at all," Marcus replied, then looked at Toinette and added, "Unless you want to do it. I'm too old."

Falling might not be as much of a danger for her, but on the other hand... "I can't climb trees," she said. "Never learned. I could try to learn now."

"It'd take too long," said Sence. "Just help get us over there. I'll do the rest."

The plants were hell on the edge of her sword. The search parties spent time every evening with whetstones, and that night would be no different. None of them had come prepared to hack through forests. Toinette did hack, and swear, until she and the others arrived, sweaty and scratched, at the base of a tall pine. Its scent distracted Toinette from the worst of her bad mood, and she took Sence's weapons with good cheer.

He grabbed the tree and quickly started up, so adeptly that Toinette raised her eyebrows. "And where did you come from?"

"The sea," he said. "I'd imagine any of us could manage this—it's better than the mast."

"Ah," said Toinette, making a rueful face. "Hadn't thought of that." She'd never learned *that* skill either. Coming on as the captain's wife, then becoming captain herself, had meant skipping much of what common sailors learned. She knew the theory, but had scant practice. Nor had she ever been tempted. If she'd wanted heights, there was always the sky.

"You were always a city wench," said Marcus. He picked up a spray of needles and began picking it apart.

"And you weren't? Leaving aside 'wench,' which I'd be inclined to hold against you otherwise."

"My family's from the country. I know it well enough not to like it. But I can climb a tree, if I need to."

"Why would you need to?"

"Apples. Birds' nests. Bears." At Toinette's skeptical look, he admitted, "Not actually bears. But I liked the notion that I *could* get away from one, if I ever had to. It lent my life a note of adventure, until I ran off to sea."

Toinette snorted. "That'd cure a man, sure enough."

"Not entirely, or we'd none of us be here." Marcus glanced upward to where Sence had paused to sit on a branch and rest his arms. "I'm surprised you never learned at your uncle's."

"I was too old. And he wasn't my uncle. He's Erik's. No relation."

"Ah, yes," said Marcus. "It'd be rather awkward if he were, wouldn't it?"

"How do you mean?" Toinette asked quietly, wondering just how much of the last night's activities might have been overheard.

Marcus shook his head. "I know you, Captain. And it doesn't take a soldier to spot a battlefield. You'd give all the treasure on this island for an hour with him between your legs."

"I—" She felt the blood rush to her face, not at the phrasing but from horror of being discovered. "We haven't found any treasure yet."

"True."

"And it'd… Do the men think so too?"

"I don't know, and I don't care. Nor, I'd guess, do they—or not enough of them that we'd have any trouble reminding them what's their business and what isn't."

Toinette stared at him, not daring to shift her weight lest the ground suddenly tilt under her. "But I brought them here," she said finally, staring at Marcus, "and it was because of Erik."

"Yes," he said, "but neither of you knew this would happen. *We* all knew that it was uncharted waters, and that the world is strange. And besides that, you weren't bedding him when you signed on. I can swear to *that*. Why would it matter if you did now?"

"My judgment—"

"Doesn't get any worse for doing the deed rather than pining over it. I knew you when Jehan was living, remember?" He paused and frowned. "Did he know?"

Toinette sighed. "Not entirely. I told him I aged slowly, and that I couldn't have children. He…had two brothers, both with large broods, or so he said." The memory of that conversation, of Jehan's hands closed around hers and his gentle smile, brought a smile to her own lips even ten years later. "He just wanted me."

"But you loved him." It wasn't a question, and didn't need to be. "And yet I remember you arguing with him time and time again, when you thought you knew what would be best."

"Saint Paul never *would* have approved of me."

"No indeed," Marcus said. "But we all knew that from the start. Love doesn't cloud your judgment, Captain, not when it matters that you have a clear head. I'll tell as much to any man who questions your thinking, and then I'll break his jaw if I must."

Toinette's throat closed. The effort to clear it would have revealed too much of her heart, and so she could only smile her thanks.

"That said," Marcus went on, "best if you not plan on any merriment tonight. We're badly in need of more to take watch."

"And you want us to join? You must be desperate," Toinette managed to joke, though in truth the request touched her nearly as much as Marcus's declaration.

While he laughed, it ended soon, and he studied her for a long moment while Sence made his way down the tree above them. "You don't think much of people, do you?"

"You know that. It's kept me alive."

"Maybe. But love isn't the only sentiment that can twist a mind."

TWENTY-FIVE

AS WITH SO MUCH SINCE HE'D BOARDED THE *HAWK*, ERIK WAS new to night watch. The benefits of rank had meant he'd never had to be sentry, even in times of war, and he'd been a passenger on the ship, not one of the crew. He hadn't balked at Marcus's not-really-request. Every man had to pull his weight, and the dreams weren't letting him sleep very well as it was.

Telling time was hard, as their travel had put the moon and the stars in different places. The flickering green light was back in the sky that night too, and it obscured the stars at times. By the time the sandglass from the ship was half-way empty on Erik's watch, he *thought* it was somewhat past midnight, but he had no way of knowing for sure.

Truly, it didn't matter. His watch would pass when it passed. He'd wake Samuel and then get what sleep he could. When the sun rose, they'd all wake and the day would start. The time of the outside world was unimportant.

Sitting and watching the sea, with the fire's banked embers in the shelter behind him and the witch light in the sky, Erik could easily believe all of the outside world unimportant—even a dream, at times.

It was a more pleasant dream than the ones he had while sleeping. He'd grown almost used to talking corpses, but that in itself was unsettling.

He'd grown almost used to too many things.

The conversation with Marcus came back to him. If they did stay—if they had to stay—then what? Breed themselves like horses and hope to have daughters who could pair with the men? Would they even have the necessary materials for the rites? And wouldn't any resulting families be far inside the lines of consanguinity with each other?

Granted, plenty of noble families ignored the Church's guidelines about cousins; still, Erik didn't like the thought.

The sky flickered green again, the color of rotting flesh, reminding him once more that the past was not only years but miles away. Below it, the shadows stretched out into odd proportions and danced spasmodically along the sand. The sea roared in and out in front of Erik; behind him, the fire was almost dead and even he could make out no sound from the shelter.

His sword hung at his side. In a breath, he could have twenty such swords, not to mention the other advantages of his dragon form.

Sitting alone in the night, he found that such knowledge helped him as little as did prayer.

The cottage stood empty but solid, with mud filling the gaps between logs and small pine branches forming a roof, parting in the middle for a hole to let smoke out. The next task was to stack wood at one end, that there might be enough to sustain them during a blizzard; in time, they'd put stores of food in the same place.

Carrying out such plans still felt like surrender. They might seek a way off the island, but they were all coming to accept that they'd likely be trapped at least through winter, as the weather would cut them off on its own if they broke the spell too late in the year. Even so, Toinette was finding a certain contentment in the hewing, shaping, and stacking of wood, as she did in catching and drying fish or digging roots, and a satisfaction when she watched the stores of food grow or eyed the sturdy cabin walls.

As a city child, she'd had little of that feeling, save for the rare occasions when her message-running and her mother's sewing had actually filled the little leather purse they kept beneath their pillows. She'd come to know it more as a captain, looking with satisfaction over neat account books and well-stocked holds; she'd never spared a thought for whether it was possible in other trades.

Stacking logs while Samuel and Raoul cut, Toinette startled herself with the notion that the clearing wouldn't have been so bad in a normal place. Yes, the woods were uncanny: the voices and their half-formed words hadn't gotten any rarer, and the strange light flickered in the sky every few nights. Her dreams featured crawling corpses, and what they said was no more kind than it ever had been. The island was not a good place.

The clearing might have been a good place, otherwise. With a wide swath of the plants slashed away, burnt, or eaten—or stored to be food or firewood later—the pines and moss-covered stones reminded Toinette of the forests around Loch Arach.

She'd been happy there, due only in part to better room and board. There she'd learned to control her body's deadly potential. There too, for the first and last time in her life, she'd been among people who'd known all of what she was and taken it as not only acceptable but commonplace. Toinette's life since had held its share of joy, but never had there been so little need for concealment.

The first night after she'd left Loch Arach, she'd curled herself up on a flea-ridden inn mattress and wept into her pillow, silently so that she wouldn't wake the other guests. She *had* understood Artair's decision, as she'd told

Erik, just as she'd understood what Agnes had told her and why—but that understanding only deprived her of the comfort that anger would have provided.

Rage against heaven had never much appealed to her, and even if she took a liberal view of her own damnation, God *had* presumably made Artair MacAlasdair a lord, and herself the bastard on his doorstep—not even one of his own get. To blame him for acting accordingly, and soundly by any practical view, was the sort of luxury men like Erik could afford. Toinette never let herself expect anything else.

She'd had years of good food and education. She had skills to be going on with and knowledge of her own powers. *Bless the slack*, she'd told herself. *Don't curse the drop. Everything ends.*

The thought had been less balm than Toinette hoped, but time and the distractions of a new life had eased the ache of parting. She'd learned to be happy despite concealment—it wasn't that difficult—and had put from her mind any chance of finding again the honesty she'd been able to practice at Loch Arach.

Two centuries later, she straightened up with an armful of wood and realized that she *had* found it again, and more. Little else about the situation, or the island itself, was good—but, through force of circumstance, Toinette hadn't needed to bother hiding her nature from anyone since they'd landed.

She leaned against the cabin walls and laughed until Raoul poked his head around the corner. "Captain?"

"I'm fine," she said, though the earnest concern on his young face made her want to keep laughing even as it touched her heart. He *might* have been only worried that she'd run mad and would kill them all, or that she'd need to be taken care of, but his expression said otherwise. "I just… I realized how little I ever thought I'd wind up in a place like this, that's all."

Raoul laughed, nodding and clearly relaxing. The captain wasn't having a hysterical fit, thank God. "*Oui*, I thought I'd taken my last sight of such houses," he said, gesturing to the cabin, "and never that I'd be hunting for food again, or chopping wood. Though here there's no bailiff's wrath to fear—always a hidden blessing, my mother would say."

"I was just thinking along those lines myself," said Toinette. "Not about bailiffs, precisely."

"No," said Raoul, "I'd not imagine you ever feared anything from them."

"Only because I didn't live in the country." She'd hidden from the constables on occasion as a child, though she'd not often resorted to picking pockets. "We're none of us saints. I'm surely not."

"Saints can come from all walks of life, so long as they repent."

"Well—" Toinette began, intending a laughing remark on the subject of repentance, when an immense roar split the air.

She dropped the logs without a moment's more thought and spun toward the source of the noise, sword already drawn. She heard crashing then, and a great deal of it— almost as much as she'd cause in dragon form.

Erik, she thought, and he had led Marcus and Franz northeast, where the noise was coming from. The roar hadn't sounded like him, though: too guttural and somehow too *wet*.

Raoul and Samuel were by her side, Samuel with the ax he'd been using to chop wood and Raoul with his sword.

"Go back," she said to them. "Get everyone on the beach to shelter, and be ready to defend."

"From what?" Samuel asked.

"I don't know. I will soon enough."

TWENTY-SIX

"THE CAPTAIN," OBSERVED JOHN, FOLLOWING ERIK UNDER AN overhanging branch that had looked too much trouble to break, "isn't at all Scottish, is she?"

"No." Erik cut briars out of the way and stomped forward through the more amenable undergrowth. He didn't look back at John when he answered, but kept alert for any sign: the white of old bone, the glint of metal, or more odd-looking plants. "One of yours, in fact. That is, she grew up in London until she came to us."

"We don't have dragons."

Sence, bringing up the rear, snorted. "You know of everything in your nation?"

"We warred with the Scots. If we had dragons, we'd have used them. Although"—John's voice became thoughtful—"if we don't, I wonder that we won the first time. You're hardly new."

"No," Erik said again. Up ahead, one of the pines lining the game path was split, one section curving down over the game trail in a twisted loop. It looked like the aftermath of a storm, with wind or lightning equally likely culprits, but he studied it for a long moment regardless, looking for signs of stranger things.

None came to mind. He marked the place in his memory, for good firewood later if nothing else, and went on in both body and speech. "I've not seen nor heard of Englishmen with our blood, and certainly none fighting on your side. And I think, if there were dragon-blooded in England,

Toinette wouldn't have come to us. You have other forms of magic. Some as deadly."

"The spells you've been teaching us?"

"Some. We spoke often enough with the English wizards before the war, I hear, and traded tips as many a craftsman might. Since then—" He shrugged and swatted at an insect on his neck. "We only know what we've seen in battle. Your folk are more likely to use devices, or things summoned, to strike from afar. Nor do I doubt there's scrying on both sides, though that's always a chancy matter."

"So we've seen." John slashed at the shrubs around him. He always was more set on clearing his trail than Erik, but then, he was human and wounds hurt him more. "You seem ready enough to tell me these matters."

Erik laughed, though he tried to make it come out kindly. "All who could use such knowledge already have it. On both sides."

"And will you be a soldier, of a sudden?" Sence asked. "Even if we do get free of this rock and return before any war meets its end?"

"Doubtful," said John. "But I've a wife and sons to think of, and friends enough who'd fight for my king, whether by will or by levy."

That was always the way of it in war. That was one of the reasons Artair had sent Erik away, and one of the reasons he'd welcomed the mission. He had no good reply to John, so he looked ahead—and saw a flicker of movement, something huge and dark in the brush.

He held up a hand. All three of them went still, and in the silence came the sound of creatures moving toward them: yet a goodly distance away, but large beasts by the way branches snapped beneath their weight. Erik sniffed the air, but the wind was against them, and the presence of men so close muddled his senses.

"String bows," he whispered. They'd seen no signs of wolves or bears, nor yet great cats; the largest beast they'd encountered had been Franz's elk. "This could be a threat or a meal."

Death or dinner came through the forest fast. The trees blocked Erik's view for a long while. He saw dark shapes, easily taller than a man, and he thought there were three of them, though the lines of head and body were yet indistinct. More elk, he thought. With luck, the men would shoot true and they'd have more food stores.

"We'll take the one on the right," Sence whispered behind him. "Likely the others will run when it dies, but best be sure of the kill."

He was right: chasing wounded prey through the forest would be a hardship, and worse when that prey was large and capable of kicking through wood. Erik sighted to the right, an arrow ready, and hoped the smell of him didn't scare the elk off.

They came through from the northeast, knocking small trees down ahead of them, and instantly he realized that *nothing* would scare them off, and eating them would be a horrible idea.

Once they, or their ancestors, had likely been elk, though they had no antlers. They'd changed.

Taller than him at the shoulder, they ran on spindly legs below grotesquely bloated bodies, in which one part often seemed to separate from the next, only to merge back together moments later. White bone stood out in jagged spikes from their backs and sides, and their teeth had out-grown their mouths, protruding through their cheeks.

All of the men loosed arrows at once, acting as much

from horrified instinct as prior plan. All three took the rightmost elk-thing in the chest. It staggered backward and roared, a sound that had in it the slap of rotten meat against earth, but it didn't fall, and the others showed no fear, nor even comprehension.

"Get behind me," said Erik. "Keep shooting."

The change was slower than he would've liked, the trees getting in the way, and as he shook his wings out, one of the creatures slammed into his side. Only a third his size, it nonetheless had weight behind its charge, weight that Erik felt cracking his ribs, and it reared up its head to sink teeth into his wing.

He swiveled his neck backward and returned the favor, closing his jaws around the elk-thing's neck. It was cold in his mouth, not merely as a dead thing might have been but as the depths of the ocean. The taste of it blended rot and a cold, unfamiliar acridness—and the elk was heavy, even heavier than he would have expected from a thing its size. At first he couldn't even pry it away from his body. Yet it wasn't quite there either. His teeth slid through it in places, as though it were air, only to encounter icy meat and jagged bone a short distance away.

When he clawed at the creature, his talons met the same mixture of flesh and nothingness, mingled in no pattern that he could recognize. Meanwhile it kicked sideways at him, far too nimbly, and its sharp hooves sliced through scales and skin alike.

Arrows sang through the air around him. The elk bellowed as the arrows hit, halted, shook themselves, and came forward again. Erik snapped his tail around and whipped the legs out from under one, flung its brother away with a painful flex of neck and claws, and braced himself just as a third hit him in the chest. It reared up on its hind legs; as Erik whipped his head forward, he looked into its face and saw the same pale eyes that had stared at him from the dead in his dream.

He was glad not to be in man's shape then. The dragon form cared less about such things, knew mostly the fight and the present moment. Inside it, Erik, son of Lamorak, marked what he saw and shivered.

There was little time. He slashed out at the creature in front of him, knocking aside seeking, malformed teeth—they looked sharp, but uneven, broken that way rather than the product of any natural growth—and nearly severing its head. It slumped before him, but the wound began almost at once to knit together. Another ran at him again. His mouth tasted of his own blood, which was better than that of the monsters but didn't bode well.

A shape dashed by him, light flashing on drawn steel and copper hair alike. Toinette hit the ground, rolled on one shoulder, and lunged, slicing through the legs of the elk that was coming up on Erik. As it fell, she leapt aside, clumsy on the uneven ground but quick enough to make it back to Erik's side. "Fire," she yelled up at him.

He was already inhaling, using the space and time Toinette had bought him to kindle the force within his chest. Low, he reminded himself. He would have to be low and controlled, with the trees all about him. A forest fire could be as deadly as the creatures they faced.

The last whole elk was charging Erik when he opened his mouth. The thin strand of flame hit it directly in the face. Rather than catching right away, it smoldered, glowing sullenly while the creature roared and shook and Erik didn't let himself pause to pray. Then the fur caught. Yellow-white light blazed up, and the elk crumbled beneath it, while Erik turned the flame on its temporarily fallen companions.

Those two went down more easily, or advance knowledge kept Erik from drawing the time out with worry. He strode forward as soon as the bodies had stopped moving and stomped on the fire, grinding it out beneath his claws. He felt the sparks and the faintly licking flames as he would have felt scratchy wool in man's form, a mild annoyance but nothing to occupy his mind greatly.

When he turned, the fire out, Sence and John were staring at him. Both were silent. Sence's jaw was clenched.

Toinette was standing, panting, with her hands on her hips and her sword dangling at her side. Strands of hair clung to her sweaty face and neck; soot smudged skin and clothes alike. She didn't look at all hurt, for which Erik gave silent thanks, but she looked alternately at him and the men with concern.

Changing back, Erik missed the exchange between them, but John and Toinette were both at his side when his eyes focused again, and Sence had strung another arrow, aiming off at the woods behind them. The elk had trampled a broad trail there.

"We heal fast," said Toinette, "and he's likely had worse. Yes?" she asked Erik, frowning in a way that could be either impatience or concern.

He nodded. He could feel his ribs already beginning to knit together. "I'll bleed for a bit," he said. "And I'll likely not have the use of that wing for weeks. They were magic enough, after their fashion. Such wounds linger."

"*What* was their fashion?" John asked, looking at the piles of ash and bone on the ground and curling his lip. "Demons?"

"I don't know. No demon I've ever heard of, but—" Erik shrugged. "I've not heard of that many."

Toinette eyed the spreading blood on his shirt. "If you

lean against a tree," she said, "do you think you'll hold up while we look at what's left? Don't try to be brave about it."

"I'll last."

It took a long look at him for Toinette to nod. Even when Erik leaned against one of the pines and she knelt to poke at the bones, she kept glancing back over her shoulder, making sure he hadn't swooned—or seeking a distraction from what she found.

From the expression on her face as she stirred the bones with a handy stick, from the way Sence crossed himself and John swallowed convulsively, they were seeing nothing good, even without the flesh that had moved so disturbingly. Erik wished otherwise, but he couldn't truly have claimed to feel the smallest amount of surprise.

Now that it had happened, even the attack felt like it had been coming for a long time, like he'd always known and could never have admitted it.

He wondered what other knowledge he possessed and couldn't face.

TWENTY-SEVEN

DRAGONS' FIRE OUTDID THE HOTTEST FORGES. TRAINED ON A living creature that didn't have dragon's blood, it left very little behind. Looking at the bones of the "elk," Toinette was glad of that.

Fire might have warped, but it wouldn't have twisted bones in the way she was seeing. Spikes grew out of ribs, ridges burst forth from spines, and teeth bred like rabbits, warping the skulls around them with their sheer numbers.

"It couldn't have *lived* like that," said John. He poked gingerly at a skull, using a long branch—none of them wanted to touch the bodies, and Toinette saw no reason to fight that impulse—and shook his head. "How would it have eaten? Or moved, with that mess on its back?"

"Not long," said Sence. "Or well."

Toinette nodded. The beasts would have been in constant pain, if they'd been capable of any feeling. Their charge at Erik looked as much a rush toward death, in that light, as it did any attempt to kill or feed—unless they'd been acting on another's will.

There were...spaces...in the bones: not mere breaks, nor missing chunks, but places where bone had faded and a shadow taken its shape. The stick went through those places, but they obscured the ground behind them. When Toinette reluctantly knelt to eye one femur more closely, she felt a chill in the air around it, far more than wind would have accounted for.

Youuuuu, sighed the trees. Recognition, accusation, or warning?

She straightened up again quickly, for all the good that did. "I'd say we're done here for now. Let's go back."

The others were fast to agree. "I'll help you walk," Sence told Erik. "Best leave the Captain free, in case."

Toinette saw the logic and was glad Sence didn't have to be prompted or persuaded; yet she watched Erik drape an arm around the man and felt a quick pang before telling herself not to be an idiot.

Before they left, she scraped dirt and branches over the bones. They weren't men, much less Christians, to make a grave necessary, but she disliked the idea of leaving them bare to the sky. "And," she rationalized aloud, "that'll make it easier to see if they've been disturbed."

The notion of a creature that would want to disturb them, or of a scavenger desperate enough to eat such leavings, visibly crossed through everyone's mind, leaving lips curled and nostrils flared in disgust. "What were they?" John asked. "Elk, maybe—the females, without antlers—but—"

He trailed off. Erik cleared his throat. "The word we want," he said quietly, "is 'cursed,' I'm thinking."

Around them, the trees—or a voice beyond—kept whispering, noises that were almost words, words that could mean anything. Toinette didn't bother looking to the undergrowth for watchful eyes, though; she didn't think eyes came into the matter at all. The fight and the fire had left her heated, and she was walking, but her flesh was goose-pimpled all the same.

Back at the beach, she and Marcus examined Erik's wounds: Marcus with the eye of a first mate turned make-shift physician at need, Toinette with greater knowledge of how the dragon-blooded hurt and healed. Neither found anything to contradict Erik's initial statement, and they settled for tying a scrap of Toinette's red dress, washed in salt water, around the bleeding wounds. Erik gritted his teeth at the sting of salt, but agreed that it would probably counter most evil spells that might have lingered.

"But you'll tell us if your side turns green or grows horns," she said, resting one palm lightly on his naked shoulder. It was a casual touch, as one man might have given a comrade, but Toinette felt every inch of her skin against his, and glanced around quickly to see who among the men might have noticed.

If any had, they gave no sign. They were *talking*, certain enough, but neither Toinette nor Erik figured largely in the conversation—or, rather, nothing between them did.

"And he truly breathed fire?" Raoul was asking Sence. "What was it like?"

"Like fire." Sence's mouth twitched as he watched his younger companion's face and added eventually, "Brighter than most flame I've seen. A trace bluer."

"And it did kill the…whatever they were?" Samuel asked.

"It did."

They questioned, told stories, and prepared. Nebulous curses and occasional blood-drinking plants had left them stunned, but although none of them was unafraid now, they all seemed a sight less shaken. Toinette knew that Samuel was considering forms of fire already, and ways to have it ready quickly without the need of a dragon; Franz would invoke his saint of hunters again and give thanks for deliverance from prey-turned-predator; John would want to know how many more such creatures they might expect, and what kind of sign they left.

"Thank you," she said to Erik, quietly. "You put yourself between them and harm."

He shrugged, carefully. "They took my pay. I'm their lord until the end of this journey—or, rather, they're my people, and I've obligations in turn. Besides, if we do get free of this place, we'll need a crew for the return trip, no?"

"Very practical of you," said Toinette.

Slowly Erik sat up and pulled his tunic back on, belting it only loosely out of concern for his healing cuts. "If I'm to be practical," he said, "I'll say we must give thought to a few matters, and that right quickly."

As always, the first thought was for defense.

"Fire worked," said Marcus.

"Our fire did. Normal flame…" Erik remembered the slow way the creature had smoldered, even when he'd breathed at it, and could only sigh. "It's worth a try, if you're in need. But I'd not count on it."

"Might a crucifix?" Franz held up his rosary. "Demons abide those not so well, if the stories are true."

"It could," said Toinette carefully. "I don't know."

"They weren't demons, though, were they?" John scratched his chin and looked at Erik. "'Cursed,' you said. Though I don't know the difference."

"I wish I knew it better," Erik replied. He shifted his weight, leaning back against the cave's rock wall and trying to ease the ache of various wounds. His ribs *were* healing; he could feel them, which was a relief but also a distraction, like a swarm of ants beneath his skin. "Demons come here from hell and, I think, save the sort that possess a person, they're not made of the same substance as things here. Those beasts…were, and weren't, in parts. Magic…overgrew bits of them, you might say? Like lichen on a tree. And they warped around it."

He would have to think more about the precise form of that magic, and of that warping, in due course, though he would've preferred to let it remain a mystery.

"Could it change us?" Samuel asked.

"I don't know," said Erik. "I believe—I *hope*—that men with souls and minds would be harder than dumb beasts, where that sort of…twisting…is involved. But it's not a matter I've studied, nor one I've encountered before."

"No point taking chances," Toinette put in. She leaned forward, holding her hands to the fire as she spoke. "Don't go off alone. Don't go running off at all without at least three others, all armed. If you see anything odd, say so. If a beast you don't recognize bites you, or a strange plant scratches you, say that. And we'll not eat any more food we don't know."

"The beach seems all right," Marcus said, "and the woods around the cabin, mostly. If the food or the water from here to there was cursed, we'd have seen it in the plants and the beasts before now."

Toinette nodded. "Likely enough."

"There's magic that can help," Erik said, though he knew he'd have to rack his brains to think of the spells, and he could only pray that he'd remember them all rightly enough to cast and teach. "Spells that can keep a spot of land pure or bless a weapon. Prayer is always good, and pine might be of use. Might have been already," he added, thinking of the black web he'd seen and the way moods shifted when near the fire. "It may be that the trees here keep this place from being as bad as it might be."

He saw speculation in the firelit faces, and then a dreadful curiosity. It was Samuel, of course, who asked the question aloud: "Who, or what, do you think they'd be holding back, then? That is"—Samuel spread his hands, dark skin gleaming in the firelight—"whether it's a curse or a wraith, why would it change those things so? And when did it? And did it send them after us, or did they come of their own? And what of the dreams, and the lights?" He stopped, looked up, and smiled apologetically. "That is perhaps too many questions. But the one at the bottom might be worth considering: How much of what we've seen is an attack, and how much is only…what is?"

"The creatures," Franz said after a few breaths of silence, "the elk, they wouldn't have come after us. The bulls can have tempers, in rut, but the cows and their calves, they would have run. If they were normal."

"Beasts run mad," said Marcus. "Dogs. Even horses. Obviously," he added, raising a hand to quell forthcoming objections, "this was no simple madness, but it could have been alike. If the bull didn't have it—"

"They stay separate, often. The bull we killed maybe sired two of those three, then left. So if they found the curse, or it found them, he wouldn't have been there."

"Poor creatures," said Sence.

The others stared at him, but out of surprise that he'd been the one to say it, not at the sentiment itself. Solitary by habit or no, there was a certain tragedy in the bull's plight: likely the last of his kind on the island, and that due to a force that even men had trouble understanding. His death might have been a mercy as well as a good hunt.

"So," said Samuel, "did the curse, or the curser, change them deliberately? Or did they pick it up, as though it was a worm? It's not as scholarly a question as it might sound—if there's a living man behind this, one who thinks, he'll know we've killed his creatures."

"There is that," said Toinette, putting in the three words the quiet yet profound unease that had settled over the whole company.

"But surely"—Raoul spoke up after a touch too long—"a man would have done more earlier against us. Tried to talk, or to threaten, or to send his minions to attack us before. We've faced nothing until today."

"Nothing save the plants," said Toinette, with a grimace.

Raoul blinked. "Yes," he said, "and—am I wrong, Captain? Both were to the northeast."

The silence shifted, gained potential. "That's where the light comes from too," said John.

"The light comes from over there," Marcus countered, waving his hand in the vague direction of the cliffs. "The last I heard, none of us had seen a source."

"But would you bet against it?" Toinette asked.

"No," said Marcus with no hesitation. "Then we have either a man defending his territory with deadly force, not bothering with any sort of diplomacy, or—"

"—or a cursed land, and perhaps the center of the curse in it," Erik finished. "But either way, we now have a route to follow, and it could be we have signs to seek as well."

TWENTY-EIGHT

Violet light arced, crackling, between Samuel and Toinette, between Toinette and John, between John and Erik, and finally inward, following the channels of the circle into the three swords that stood on end in the center. There, the signs painted on the metal attracted the light, captured it, and held it in twisting sigils of purple fire.

Toinette held her concentration, feeling power running through and out of her like water through a funnel. Another four breaths brought the end, and indeed Erik began the Latin chanting then, thanking and dismissing the forces that had aided them. "…*et non erit*," he concluded, with a severing gesture of one hand. The otherworldly force that had joined the four of them and connected them to powers yet more otherworldly than that vanished. Toinette sat heavily on the sand.

"We did it," said John, with a glance at the swords.

"Aye," said Erik, breathing heavily. "They'll be potent against darkness. For a while yet."

"How long is 'a while yet'?" Samuel asked.

"A year and a day, generally. Or so I remember." He shoved damp hair out of his face. "It's the first time I've done this, ye ken. We haven't often had the need of fighting cursed beasts. I'm only glad I remembered enough of what Artair taught to get it right."

Samuel cocked his head, birdlike, and asked, "Did you all learn magic?"

"All of us that Artair had charge of," said Erik. "Some

more than others. As with other skills, it had mostly to do with our individual talents. But we were all dragged in by the ear a fair bit of our day."

"I had more dragging than you." Toinette smiled wearily. She, Erik, and Artair's younger children had all preferred other activities to magical study. Cathal would always rather have been fighting; Moiread had enjoyed stories but had been uninterested in the complicated logic of the Upper Worlds. Erik had simply not had the will to command forces most of the time, and Toinette had found the whole matter vaguely troubling, another mark against her humanity.

"And he didn't teach us this spell exactly," Erik said, drawing her back from the past. "When you know what planets govern what, and what angels rule which realms, and the symbols that go wi' all of them, it often becomes a matter of putting logs together to form the house you want."

John gave him a sideways glance. "So, you don't *know* that these swords will harm any of the cursed beasts."

"No," said Erik, too tired to be defensive, as John was too tired to be very accusatory. "We'll not know until we try."

"Hmm," said John, but didn't protest further. "Same with the protective spell?"

"Less so. Wards against surprise attacks are familiar to me, and I know one that will even turn weapons—for a very short time, mind. What they'll do against creatures warped by magic, I couldn't say. But we've not had any threats on the beach, and up in the glen, the house itself should be shield enough."

Watered wine tasted lovely. Toinette closed her eyes and concentrated on that, letting the voices around her fall like raindrops past her ears. The spell hadn't been as draining as the scrying; she thought she was regaining strength with practice, but she also knew there'd been no resistance. That argued for the curse being only a curse, without the will to interfere.

The problem was, she badly wanted to think so. It would be so very good if they only had to find their way to the center, break a skull or throw a ring into the ocean, and be free. Toinette would rejoice to have that be the case—and knowing what she wanted, she knew too that she couldn't entirely trust herself when evidence seemed to lead to that conclusion.

She rubbed at her temples. "Who gets the swords? I'd argue against the two of you, as you've other skills now."

"And not us," said Erik, "for the same reason."

Darkness floated before her eyes. Toinette pushed it to the sides, sorting through her mind for names and impressions, memories of battle. "Sence," she said and felt certain of it, though she knew he was untried. When none of the others objected, she went on with less assurance. "Franz, *if* we can count on him not to be nervy about the magic. I'll have to have a word with him about it. And then…I don't know. Does guile outweigh age?"

"Are you asking, Captain?" Samuel's voice was respectful, but not hesitant.

"I am, if you've any thoughts on the matter."

"Then I'd say to give it to Raoul, and not Marcus. The man who takes one of those weapons will be on the front lines."

"Marcus has been in the midst of a battle or two, if you'll recall," Toinette replied.

"And done well," said John, putting his thoughts in and surprising Toinette as he went on, "but he does better away from them. We don't know yet what the swords will do, or how they'll work. Marcus is most useful in command— assuming you're not around, of course."

"Of course," said Toinette.

Even more than earlier, they didn't speak of plans very far in the future. That day they'd enchanted the swords; the next day, they'd cast the rites of protection; to know what would come after that, they'd need to talk. Nobody mentioned the talk, nor what would come of it, but they would in time.

"I'm willing to go. So are most of us, I'd think," Marcus said, and his glance around the fire didn't leave very much room for protest. "The thing is, Captain, I'm not sure we wouldn't be more of a hindrance than a help."

Naturally it was Marcus raising the issue, Erik thought. He'd have expected no less from the man. He saw too that Marcus's face was drawn tight and his hands knotted together. The *Hawk*'s first mate had no love for what he was saying.

"Even with the swords?" Raoul asked. The enchanted blades lay by the side of the fire, not too close and carefully wrapped. Men's eyes kept darting to them and away as they talked; Raoul's lingered longer than usual.

"The swords might let you kill," Erik said, "but you can still *be* killed much easier than I can, or Toinette. There's little we can do about that here."

Cathal's wife, Sophia, had invented a compound that *would* give considerable protection to mortals, but it was as yet far too costly to produce in quantities and took months for a bottle. Not having anticipated needing it, Erik hadn't bothered to ask; none of them had the skill to make it, nor did the island have the needed elements.

"Also," said Marcus, "there's fire. That tends to spread. If you have to use it, and you have once already, best that you not have to worry about one of us getting in the way."

That sobered even Raoul. There were few among the men, likely, who hadn't seen fire kill, whether from burning arrows in battle or untended hearths in winter. It was a bad death among bad deaths.

Erik stretched his own hands out toward the campfire, felt the warmth distantly, and studied his fingers in the dancing light. He'd a few marks: an English arrow, barbed and ensorcelled both, had pierced the meat of his palm just beneath his thumb; lesser wounds from fighting the elk, though mostly healed, were still red and raised. "As a matter of tactics," he added, "*if* the force behind this all can think, it might not do badly to split its attention. It may send its lesser troops after you. With fire and magic—with plain steel, for creatures more akin to the plants than the elk—you might hold them off well enough. And I'd be saving my strength for the greater foes."

"You?" asked John, looking from Erik to Toinette with narrowed eyes. "I'd have thought you wanted the captain along."

"I did this to you," Erik said with a shrug. He looked straight across the fire at them all, not letting emotion enter his voice. "All of you. I couldn't in good conscience ask *anyone* else to come with me. We don't know what's out there—how strong it is, or what it can do."

"But we've seen some of it," Toinette said, "and what we *do* know is we're the ones best equipped to fight it. Think like a tactician, man, not a monk."

He heard in her voice the echo of her less-diplomatic younger self: *Don't be a fool if you can help it. Hearts don't do anyone any good.*

Erik cleared his throat. "Tactically, then, there are three

points to weigh as I see it. Will both of us stand more of a chance than one? Likely. But should one of us stay behind to defend? And what if we're transformed?"

"Bugger," said John, which seemed to sum things up nicely.

"The Templars' bones were human," said Samuel. "There was nothing twisted about them."

"They *were* human," said Sence. "At the start."

"True," said Toinette, her face blank, "but that could go either way too. Our blood might make us more capable of resisting. At the least, we know a bit of how bodies change."

Erik, who'd thought he would have to make that point, was silent. They all were. Fish cooked untouched on the skewers until it started to blacken and Franz lifted it away from the frames. Nobody made any move to claim it.

Finally Marcus stood up, not to make any great pronouncement but to pace over to the cave entrance and back again. "It's a gambler's question, isn't it? And I say we stake it all, for what good will we gain by holding back? If you fail, we die, and if we die more slowly than otherwise, how much of a blessing will that truly be?"

"And if we succeed," Erik said, "but don't come back? Breaking this spell might take blood. I've heard of such things. Or we and the being behind this might end as Arthur and Mordred did, killing and being killed at the same time. What, then, for you?"

"You can teach us the spell before you go," said Samuel.

"And we can crew the ship," Marcus added, though his face was white and he didn't look at Toinette. "Our numbers won't be good, but we can manage. Men have, before."

"Honestly," Toinette said, though she had to clear her throat before she spoke, and even then her voice was at first the groan of a rusty hinge, "I'm the least necessary of you lot. You've all got strong backs and good heads. Marcus can give as sound an order as I can and can read the sky and the sea just as well." She smiled. The fire didn't quite make it a rictus. "I had been thinking, before this, that it'd soon be time for me to leave him in command. If…well, if things go as Erik says, I'll not even have to fake my death. Saves me a bit of effort, no?"

"Captain," said Marcus, his eyes shining a little in the firelight, "do shut the hell up."

TWENTY-NINE

THE CIRCLE OF PROTECTION AROUND THE CABIN WAS, AS ERIK had said, quite a bit like the warding spells he'd cast around his camp when he'd had few men in strange territory. He strengthened it by mixing in a charm against opposing sorcery and a spell to defend against wild beasts. To his senses, magical and physical alike, the process seemed to go smoothly: power came from the four magicians and settled into a swirling black and gold wall at the circle's outer perimeter, and though the wall turned invisible when the spell ended, Erik could still feel it there.

As with the swords, there was no true way to test the spell. They had done what they could. The rest came down to faith and hope. Those were becoming common enough props of late. Sence or Franz—or Brother Michael, who'd instructed Erik in his youth—might have approved, save that Erik's faith was mostly in his skill and Toinette's, and his hope was for fortune rather than any specific divine favor. If God wanted to intervene, He generally used men as His tools. If they were too flawed to succeed, then that was often the end of the matter.

Yet Erik prayed lengthily and reverently at night, particularly on watch, and even more so before he and Toinette left camp. There was no priest to grant him absolution, but he confessed what he could and took what penance he remembered being assigned in the past. In advance of a battle, you made sure your sword had a decent edge, you checked your armor, and you got as far into heaven's graces as you could manage. With Erik, as with most of the dragon-blooded, the extent of that last had always been debatable—but then, he'd often found both sword and armor less than needful. Accounts likely balanced.

He prayed for the men as well. He'd often done that in war, but never quite so fervently. The men who'd followed him against the English had known precisely what they went to do, and risked no more than a mortal's usual death in wartime, as likely to have been in another leader's levy if he'd never been there. The *Hawk*'s crew was different. *Lord*, Erik asked, *if I should fall, let it be in setting them free*.

And he prayed for Toinette, that he be able to do the same for her, if need be—even more so for suspecting that she was just as likely thinking along the same lines, with herself as the necessary sacrifice. It fretted at his nerves, that knowledge, and yet the forest looked less dark for her companionship.

It was unlikely that any had overheard him, but all knew what was possible, and the knowledge hung over the camp as Erik and Toinette prepared to depart. Success or failure were not the only outcomes.

"There's food here for a fortnight each," said Marcus, handing them packs, "and water as well. It's mostly bread and roots, but there's some dried meat. Eat carefully. Likely as not, this place will turn out to be as large as all of France, and all the rest of the game will be cursed."

"You forgot the sea serpents," Toinette replied, smiling wryly and blinking a few times.

"I wouldn't eat those either, were I you," said Marcus, his voice rough-edged, "but you'll know what's best."

Erik turned away from their goodbyes, feeling an intruder almost on family matters, and made a pretense of adjusting his pack until Franz tapped him on the shoulder. "You should take this, I think," said the other man, holding out his rosary beads. "I had it blessed at Aachen once, at the shrine, and where you go, you will have more need of a blessing than me."

"Thank you," Erik said. At a loss for other words, he clasped Franz's arm firmly for a moment before Toinette cleared her throat and all turned to look at her.

"Wait a fortnight for us, at most," she said. She faced her men at the edge of the path from the beach, straight and tall in the ruins of her red gown, with her hair tied back and a sword belted around her waist. Her face brooked no denial, nor any argument; she gave instruction as she'd done before the storm. "If matters get bad and you can leave before then, do it. Trust no strange sights or sounds. If anyone shows up claiming to be us, question them very thoroughly—*before* you let them through the wards."

"I fostered in England," Erik added, "before the wars. I don't know if an imposter has ways of knowing that, but a man who doesn't isn't me, no matter how he looks."

Toinette hesitated, then said, "And my mother's name is Galitia. Keep yourselves safe. Be on guard."

The men each said their farewell, advising caution or invoking God, all blending into a pool of uncertainty and sentiment. None of them turned away, so it was Toinette who moved first, squaring her shoulders and marching up the path, her eyes resolutely forward.

A few steps into the forest, Erik stopped under a pine and muttered thanks in Latin before breaking off two sprays of needles. "Here," he said, handing one to Toinette.

It was the first either of them had spoken since leaving

the men. Theirs hadn't been an unfriendly silence; rather, for the first part of the journey, speech had felt treacherous to Toinette, equally capable of provoking her to tears or cheapening the memory of her crew's farewell. She didn't know what had made Erik keep quiet—whether sentiment of his own, her own mood being more evident than she'd hoped, or merely concentration on the journey.

She twirled the pine needles beneath her nose, and the smell brought a measure of calm to her mind. "Thank you," she said, and tucked the spray into her bound hair.

"At my lady's service," said Erik with a quick bow but a smile that felt more sincere than joking.

Toinette allowed the answering warmth to linger beneath her breastbone for a few steps. If they lived, she would address that, and what it might mean; if they didn't, it wouldn't matter. Their mission had simplified life a good bit. She had to see that silver lining.

"Almost feels like home now," she said as they walked on, with a gesture to the path around them. Eight people had trodden it for weeks, breaking and crushing the undergrowth. The blood-drinking plants were dead, and while slurred voices still drifted through the brush, Toinette had nearly gotten used to that. "By contrast, I suppose."

"Aye," said Erik, "and by use. We've put our marks here, and they've stayed. There's a safety to that, in the mind if nowhere else."

Toinette nodded. The cabin they were passing had once been wild trees, the ground host to plants no man would have imagined. She'd changed that—she and the rest— with their own hands. They'd made a dwelling that would never have formed in nature. "Like dogs pissing on fence posts, in a way," she said with a quick laugh, "but I won't deny it works."

"We're most of us dogs at heart," Erik said and then winked. "Did no one ever tell you that about men?"

"Wolves, for certain," Toinette shot back.

She knew as well as he did, and knew he knew, that they'd have neither the time for sport nor the safety to indulge in such a distraction. Still it was good to let herself respond to his heated glances. Like the pine, the warmth would be something to carry with her as a talisman against the darkness to come.

"What will you do?" Toinette asked him. "If this all goes as well as possible, that is?"

They'd stopped at noon to eat and drink. Still on the path they knew, they sat with their backs to broad trees and kept wary eyes on the forest. It wasn't very far to the trail of the elk-things and the unexplored territory.

Erik swallowed a mouthful of bread. "How well is 'as well as possible,' do you think?"

Copper eyebrows slanted upward, and the dark eyes beneath rolled. "You know damn well. We break the curse, we find Excalibur or a magic cauldron, we have a calm sea and a following wind, and we're back in France in a month. You take the treasure to Artair, I'm guessing. What then? Back to war?"

It was a question he'd tried not to answer ever since Artair had sent him off investigating rumors. War had an ease to it that matched the simplicity of life in dragon form: the straightforwardness of killing and being killed, the narrowing of vision to the next battle or the next blow, even the visceral satisfaction of victory and survival. A man could get lost there. A dragon-blooded man was in special danger. There were those, Artair had said, who'd become trapped in dragon's shape and seen men merely as prey, and that without the additional intoxication of battle or the fury wounds could cause.

Knowing all this, Artair rarely asked or permitted his kin to spend many years at the front of any war; that was one reason he'd sent Erik abroad. Yet, if the English came again in force...

"I don't know," he said slowly. "He might think he and Dougal will serve well enough by themselves, now that Dougal has sons to carry on after him. There's Cathal too, and Moiread, should matters grow desperate. I've younger brothers, so it's never been a matter of risking the line with me, but...you know the other risks with us."

Toinette's mouth twitched, and she shook her head slowly. "Always the perfect knight," she said, though without the bitterness or the annoyance of their former arguments on the subject. "Oaths are heavy things, I understand. What if Artair leaves the choice up to you? He's not a tyrant, in truth."

"I...don't know," Erik said again, only realizing it himself. Following orders had been simple in its way. "When we signed the last treaty, I thought I'd had my fill of war for a long time. But if my country's at stake, and my people—it truly isn't just Artair's pride. Not for me. Conquerors don't often deal well with their subjects."

"No," said Toinette and sighed. "And I, when I said that..." She laughed shortly. "It's very easy to see a river between yourself and the man in your way, even if there's only a stream. Or less." She drew a line in the dirt with one finger. "Though I'm not sure how pleased he'd be with the comparison."

"Pleased enough," said Erik. "He always spoke well of you in my hearing. If we leave here, he'll be glad to know you've done well for yourself."

"And I hope he does too…and well for the rest of you." Toinette broke a piece of bread in half and stared at the edge. "At times, it strikes me as very odd that men should still seek conquest, after the years we've had. As if inheritance, or rulership, or any of it mattered when they could die spitting blood the next day."

"I don't suppose the English knew the plague was coming when they invaded," Erik said, with what fairness he could manage. "And death's always been on every mortal's doorstep, though the form of it might be less showy. Life's a matter of learning to ignore that, perhaps."

"Mmm," said Toinette, in reluctant agreement. "That's the other half of what I think. Life goes on—and it may be that trying to kill another man for what he's got is as much a part of that as eating or sleeping. Sence, or the priests, would say it's original sin, I suppose."

"So I've always heard," said Erik. "Though my father's priest when I was young was often too deep in the wine bottle to give much instruction on that or any other subject."

As he'd intended, he got a smile from Toinette. "That explains a great deal," she said. Getting to her feet, she brushed away crumbs and shouldered her pack. "And now, maybe we'll see what a pair of near-heathens can do against a greater evil."

"Just hope it's not *too* much greater," said Erik, following behind.

THIRTY

THREE DAYS SINCE THE BATTLE AGAINST THE ELK CREATURES, the site where it had happened naturally bore the marks. Flame had scorched the nearby trees and burned away grass and moss; footprints and the heavier weight of fallen bodies had crushed smaller plants; and dried blood still colored parts of the undergrowth that remained.

In a short time, both Erik and Toinette would look back and find those signs reassuring.

Few would have called blood or burns pleasant, but they meant a world that operated on the natural order. Burnt trees stayed burnt. Crushed plants stayed crushed. Blood seeped into leaves and stayed.

None of that changed immediately as they started to follow the trail of the elk creatures. At first, their route was like the forest they'd come through. The elk had done a decent job of clearing the way for them, making unnecessary the sweaty work with blades and feet that had been so much a part of forging paths before.

When the voices in the trees sounded louder than they'd been, Toinette at first thought it the work of her mind. She knew the forest to be unfamiliar, knew that danger lay ahead, so of course she was paying more attention to any hint of strangeness. She rebuked herself, ignored the sounds, and continued.

After a full minute of high-pitched giggling, as though a demented choir were hiding in the bushes, she looked to Erik. Yes, his face said, he was hearing it too. Yes, it truly was happening. It made little difference—they would continue—but Toinette's skin prickled, and she went on with a hand on her sword hilt.

She saw the first of the blood-drinking vines a short ways after that. They curled around the trees further to the side of the road, pink and white flowers standing out against the darker shades of brown and green.

"Only to be expected," she said, drawing her sword. "I couldn't have gotten all of the damned things."

"They don't look near enough to be a danger," said Erik, eyeing the distance between the trail and the trees. "The elk might've known enough to avoid them."

"Or their blood had no allure. Would you want to drink one of those?"

"I wouldn't want to drink blood at all," Erik said. He drew his own sword and, despite his confident speech, walked warily and to the far side of the trail as they passed the vines. Toinette thought she saw them stir: a lazy wriggle, like earthworms stranded after rain. Even without danger, the motion turned her stomach.

It was midafternoon, the sky bright overhead, and not even a breeze stirred the branches around them. The sunlight was sharp. Toinette shivered and wished that she'd been ruthless enough to extort hose from one of her men. The cut-away skirt left her legs too cold—and too exposed. She could imagine any number of vermin crawling up her boot and onto her knee.

"All right?" Erik asked.

"I truly loathe the wilderness," said Toinette. "I'll be well enough."

"This isn't proper wilderness," Erik said. He didn't say what it *was*, nor did he need to.

Other than that exchange, they didn't talk. It wasn't the

companionable, respectful quiet of their earlier journey. Although they were in it together, and that was a little comfort, their silence was wary.

They'd left the lands they'd come to know, if only slightly. *Terra incognita* was the phrase on maps, Toinette thought, and then, with a laugh that reached her mouth only in a twist of her lips: *Hic sunt dracones*. Except *incognita* wasn't entirely right. They had an idea or two about what lay further up the trail.

Terra pericolosa would have been the real term had Toinette been making a map. If she'd been talking to her crew, she'd have used blunter language still: *enemy waters*.

Motion flickered in the trees as they walked. Glancing toward it, Toinette spotted the black silhouettes of crows, the furry tail of a fleeing squirrel—and then a small white shape that vanished with no sign of actual movement as soon as she looked in its direction. She blinked, and the forest was unchanged.

She didn't walk with naked sword in hand, lest she fall over a rock and stab herself, but she kept several fingers of steel out of the scabbard, and her hand closed around the hilt. Toinette knew herself to be decent with a sword at best—better with knives and fists, not to mention feet, nails, and teeth—but the further away a weapon kept any part of the forest, the better. The feel of it in her hand was a reassurance too, as with the cabin: an object born of men's skill, not the whims of nature or worse.

The light grew gray and faded. Toinette thought of storms, but felt neither wind nor the hot stickiness that went before summer squalls. When she tilted her head up, the sky was still cloudless. It only looked fainter and further away.

"How late in the day is it, do you think?" she asked Erik.

He frowned, peered at the sky, and frowned more

deeply. "I would have said no more than midday. But—"
An upward motion of his hand showed that he'd noticed
the same change in the light Toinette had. "It is darker in
forests. The trees block the light."

"That's not this, I don't think," said Toinette. She
remembered the forest at Loch Arach. The light had been
fainter, but bright and golden in the spots where the leaves
had let it through. Memory was tricky. She hoped Erik
would contradict her.

He shook his head. "No. There aren't more trees here
than there were either."

That was true, and left nothing else to be said. As they
went on, the trees did get closer together, but they shrank
rather than grew, clinging to each other with warped
branches and twisting trunks. The eye found no straight
lines, only snarls that brought to mind staring eyes, or open
mouths, or in a few cases, tangles of innards.

Darkness deepened quickly. After what felt like no
more than an hour of walking from the time Toinette had
noticed the change, night hung around them, without light
of moon or stars. Had she been human, she wouldn't have
been able to see without a torch.

That might not be so bad, she thought, passing a dead
tree whose branches clawed the sky like a malformed hand.

The voices spoke, without any wind to excuse them.
Youuu, they said, and laughed.

Meat.

A white form appeared in the trees again. This time it
had a man's figure, even the suggestion of a beard and a
sword strapped to its back. Toinette stopped and stared at
it, remembered Franz and the plants, and then touched Erik
on the shoulder as he was hesitating too. "I don't think we
should follow that."

"No," he said and then gave an incoherent shout of horror. Toinette didn't blame him. She'd clutched his shoulder at the same time, with enough strength to break a mortal man's bones.

The figure had turned toward them. In an instant, its jaw had dropped to its chest, showing fanged teeth. A long, pointed tongue curled out at them, as if in a child's gesture of mockery, and its eyes had lit with the same eerie green-violet radiance that had flashed in the sky above the island.

Then it was gone.

"Christ have mercy," said Erik and reached for the rosary Franz had given him.

"*Someone* had better." Toinette forced herself to relax her fingers and lift her hand away. "I'm sorry. Did I hurt you?"

"A few bruises at most. Never worry over it, lass." His smile was a pale replica of what it normally was. Toinette felt that they might both be faint copies: echoes of past writing that a scribe had imperfectly scraped away. "I'd have likely had claws in your flesh, had it been the other way round. You've a great deal of discipline."

"I've practiced," said Toinette.

"Petty bastard, is it no'?" Erik asked, gesturing to where the apparition had been. "I wonder what death it would ha' lured us to, if we'd followed? More of the plants, or worse?"

"It couldn't hurt us directly. That's a blessing."

"For now," said Erik.

"You're a cheerful fellow. It's almost like having Marcus with me again."

They kept going. There was really no choice in the matter. They went on through darkness, through cold that got more and more bitter, and past plants that had grown pale and sickly until the leaves looked akin to drowned flesh. Toinette pulled the spray of pine needles out of her hair and held it under her nose for a time. It kept her from wanting desperately to scream.

She began to see different animals too. The squirrels were as pale as the plants. Many were hairless, and their eyes were large and clouded. A birdcall in the trees was thin and choked-sounding.

You, said the voices.

Meat.

She was glad to hear the sound of running water ahead of them, though she'd be damned if she drank any water in this place—likely literally so. The noise was a change, though, and it sounded almost normal. When she saw the stream, narrow as it was, it didn't look to share much of the uncanny nature of its surroundings. It was only a rivulet running through the forest, though the tree roots hanging on to it did resemble fingers.

"Magic doesna' cling well to water," Erik said thoughtfully, sounding more Scottish than usual again. He knelt and examined the earth for a time, brushing aside fallen needles and leaves, frowning. "But the trail ends here. There are others, but I've no notion which to choose."

"You might not need one," said Toinette, looking through the trees in the direction from which the stream flowed. She thought she had seen stone—she ducked around one of the pines for a better view—

—and she cursed, quiet and disbelieving.

There was a temple in the middle of the forest.

It was still at least a day's journey away, which made it all the more astounding. To be visible at such a distance, it had to be huge. Toinette couldn't see details, and the trees did block much of the outline, but she could make out pillars, straight and smooth as ever came from the hand of a stonemason.

Erik, joining her, closed his eyes and shook his head. When he let himself return to vision a moment later, his head was still shaking, instinct denying what he was forcing his mind to accept. "But it would take a hundred men or more to build that," he said, talking in theory to Toinette but truly to any sense of order in the world.

"It would," she said. "And where would they have gotten the stone? Do you know any magic to make that appear?"

"No. Yes." Erik drew the back of a hand across his mouth. "On that scale? I've only heard stories. They don't say a very great deal about *how* to do it, just who does it. That's Solomon, in most of them."

Even *she* knew that name: the king in the Bible, yes, but more importantly the greatest wizard among mortals. Merlin himself, Artair had said, had not been half so powerful, nor had half the command of demons.

"Ah," said Toinette. Once she composed her thoughts, she could speculate on whether Solomon himself had built the structure or an equally powerful unknown or a demon, on what might be the most effective approach for each, and on the next steps. Just then, she could only ask one question, in the terms of her youth: "We're buggered good and proper, aren't we?"

THIRTY-ONE

BECAUSE OF THE DARKNESS, THEY DIDN'T LOOK TO THE SUN TO tell them when to rest. They wouldn't have needed to in any case—full dark simply made colors look less vivid to the dragon-blooded—but Erik had become used to war and making camp before his men's sight became unreliable, and to the hours of the human world as a matter of course. Toinette, he suspected, was even more attuned to those than him.

None of that mattered in the depths of the forest. With only the two of them in the midst of deformed trees and wildlife, it was as though they'd left all the mortal world behind them. The structure ahead didn't count. Whoever had built it had power enough not to be mortal in spirit, whatever his origins might be.

With nothing outside to tell time, Erik could only attend to his body, marking the growth of weariness and hunger—and so, he reflected, mortality came into play again. Or not, perchance. Even God had rested.

He could still hear the stream behind them when they came to a wide spot on the trail. It was nothing so spacious as a clearing, but there was enough room for the two of them to sit and for one to stretch out at a time. None of the blood-drinking vines grew within sight, and the trees were no more warped than ordinary.

"That place," he added to Toinette when she stopped to see why he'd done so, "doesn't look very far away now. Half the morning's walk, or so. We could try to get closer, but…"

"No," she said, anticipating the end of his sentence. "I don't want to sleep too near it either."

The ground rose and dipped, making distance difficult to judge and unpredictable to view, but they could see the overhang of a roof above the pillars and the beginnings of steps below. They made Erik think of Rome and the ruins of the ancient world.

Time moved on and took all with it. The past was darkness and savagery, and yet it stared them in the face a morning's walk away.

Erik averted his gaze, which inevitably led him to Toinette. She blinked. "Yes?"

"You're all I wish to look at," he said, and made a face at the way it sounded.

Understanding, she laughed. "I'd be more flattered… oh, anywhere else in the world." As if to illustrate, Toinette looked around too, and grimaced. "I'd as soon not build a fire. I know it's cold."

"We'll not die of it," Erik agreed. The cold was enough to be uncomfortable, even for them, but they'd take no lasting harm. The attention a fire might draw would likely be worse; even the idea of burning wood from such trees, of looking into the flames or breathing the smoke, held no appeal.

It wasn't as though they had any need to cook either. Their food was dried bread and meat. If using the wood for a fire was an unsettling notion, hunting anything they'd seen was a repulsive one.

They ate sitting on the ground. The meat was greasy, and the bread stale. It would serve. It might have been best. Erik couldn't imagine taking any joy from food in such surroundings. The cold, slimy smell was in his nostrils all the time. Even a king's feast would have tasted of ooze and mud; better to have food not worth ruining.

Toinette ate with her knees drawn up against her chest. When she was finished, she wrapped her arms around her legs, heedless of modesty—though she did pull her skirt down as far as she could. Erik doubted that had much to do with the view. "Come here," he said and held out an arm. "We'll be warmer if we're close."

She needed no more encouragement to curl against his chest, wrapping her own arms around him. The dragon-blooded usually gave off more heat than mortals to the touch, but Erik could feel the chill of Toinette's hands through his shirt, and he suspected the same was true of his. "I thought I'd done with cold places," she said into his neck. "England was bad and Scotland worse."

"What about Muscovy?"

"I only went in the summer. It was hot enough then."

"Ah," he said. "My home's colder than Loch Arach, so I never minded much."

"Ugh. As cold as this?"

"Not really." In truth, it was colder in winter, and so were Scotland and England. But there he'd had fires and thick walls, and the cold itself had been different. Winter was winter. The forest was…emptiness.

Toinette was warmer against him, though, and Erik felt warmer as well. He buried his face in her hair. The scent of her, mingled with the pine needles she'd put back behind one ear, drowned out the smell around them for the first time since they'd entered the darkness. Against his side, her breasts were full and firm, and the long muscles of her waist taut beneath his hand. His cock stirred, proving that joy, or at least desire, was yet possible in one or two areas of man's life.

"Mmm," she said as Erik idly stroked the length of her back. The sound vibrated against his neck, and when she spoke, it was with small puffs of hot air. "This your idea from the start?"

He laughed. "Would that I were that brilliant," he said, and then, reluctantly, for the sound of her pleasure and the slight rocking of her hips were rousing him further, "or that we had another to keep watch. Though that itself might not help matters."

"Bah," said Toinette, "we'd just have him keep his back turned and hum. You don't have much solitude on a ship, and I *was* wed."

She didn't argue the main point, though. Theoretical guards might or might not have let them take matters further, but their lack was a very definite obstacle.

For a time, they settled into a balance between desire and alertness. Neither moved away; neither moved faster or toward more intensity. Erik caressed Toinette's back and sides in a slow, steady rhythm, never truly approaching breasts or arse. For her part, she kissed his neck, stretched against him, and ran her hands over his chest, but kept it all light, not surrendering to urgency—nor even to the idea of a struggle.

It was what it was. Erik's cock pulsed, aching, but there was pleasure in the ache, and the moment would have been most certainly worth any pain.

They lasted like that until the light began.

It was the same unnatural light that Erik had seen from the beach and grown used to there. In the forest, it was far brighter, spreading out in rings of green witch fire from, of course, the temple. No pain accompanied it, but with every flash he felt a vague pressure on… He didn't know what, precisely, but supposed it was the part of him that was kin to beasts, that bled and breathed and ate just as a dog or a horse did.

The light grasped that and pulled. In replacement, it offered…other things. Itself, or the shadow it cast.

No, Erik said inwardly. For him that was all it took. For a man without dragon's blood, he thought rejection might be harder; for an animal, the offer would be no offer at all.

Against his chest, Toinette swore in what sounded like Muscovite. He still welcomed the touch of her breath, still wanted his arms tight around her, but the feeling of pleasant, lazy lust was gone. Neither of them moved.

"Should have expected this, I suppose," said Toinette. "Would have, if I'd thought about it. Where else would the light come from?"

"It explains why part of the island is normal. This power doesn't stay this strong very far out." Erik peered off into the forest as the flares of green radiance washed over him. The oddness of the forest went beyond the darkness, and the power in the temple clearly *could* reach further, or they would have long since been at sea, but the worst of the changes seemed to be where the light fell. "And what happened to the elk. The female and her young went too close. Poor souls. They'd never have understood what went wrong with them."

"That might be better than the other way," said Toinette. "To know what you lost."

"Mmm," he said, neither agreeing nor disputing.

They watched the light. After Erik had refused it once, it had no further pull on him, he found. It was only a change in the sky. "I think," he said, "that it's safe enough to sleep. In watches, of course. And minding each other as well as the woods."

"I'll go first. Let you know if you start looking demonic." Toinette clearly made an effort to speak lightly. When she went on, after a time of silence, Erik first thought she was trying to change the subject, distracting them both from the possibility of transformation—and what the one who remained unaltered would have to do. "How long do women live, if they breed with us?"

"Pure mortals? Two hundred years or thereabouts. So I've heard. I've not seen it firsthand, though Cathal's wife doesn't look past thirty, and she can't be younger than fifty."

"Oh," Toinette said. "My mother may yet live. I'd wondered."

"Likely," Erik replied, choosing his words with care. This was unsteady ground. "When did you last see her?"

Toinette laughed shortly. "When I was almost thirteen. I believe I was one of the last few. She took the veil shortly after I left, became an anchorite. Walled up in Somerset. I made inquiries fifty years back, and she lived then, though the abbot was loath to speak of her. There are those who think she's a saint, for having lived so long, or a prophet." She wound her words out like thread on a spindle, one long unstoppable strand that then came to an abrupt halt: "She's quite lost her wits."

As with the light, Erik had known what was coming, or should have, and yet it left him frozen and staring. "I'm sorry," he managed.

The shoulder beneath his arm moved in a quick shrug. "I didn't know if that happened always."

"No," he said. "No, my cousin took a mortal wife."

"And she's not mad? Well. It was..." She sighed. "I didn't think so, really."

"Did your father cause it?"

"Not to know. She went to his bed willing enough, from what little I did hear, she came out whole, and in the first few years I remember she was..." Toinette searched for a word, shrugged again, and let her hand fall back to her thigh. "Fine. Sad, of course, and ashamed, as an unwed girl with a babe might well be, and even then I think she was jumpy, but we got along."

Erik kept his hands steady on her back, not presuming to hold her closely but not wanting to let her go either. After a little while, she spoke again.

"People see too much. And eight years isn't such a long time—a woman of twenty-five who looks like a maid of eighteen might pass as merely well preserved. We both know that. When that woman never gets a fever or a cough, never has a bad tooth or a cut that festers…people notice. *She* notices. When she's no better than she should be, to start…"

"There were rumors," Erik said.

"There were rumors. She listened. And then there was me. Too strong, too healthy, strange eyes. By the time I was ten, Mam…she went to mass a great deal, and when she wasn't there, even when she was home, she was often… gone. Sitting, staring at the wall, not moving. For hours. The priests would come and feed her, when one of them was feeling kind. I did it otherwise." She stopped and swallowed. The green light washed over them again, making sharp lines out of every shadow. "When I transformed the first time, she stabbed me."

"God have mercy." Erik pulled her closer, and Toinette leaned her head against his chest.

"I can't blame her now," she said. "Her child vanished. There was a monster in its place. She probably thought I'd kidnapped her daughter. It was brave, considering. And she was sorry for it when I turned back. But that's when I thought I'd better leave. I left word with the priests to look in on her."

"And you came to Loch Arach."

.

"I did. After a while."

He could imagine, and couldn't imagine, what *a while* would have held for a girl of twelve, one without the knowledge to control her own transformations, without a known ally in all the world. Erik lifted one hand and stroked Toinette's hair, half expecting the touch of it to burn him, as though he'd lain his fingers on a holy relic. "I'm glad you found us," he said, because he thought she might hit him if he said again that he was sorry or called attention to the wetness on her face.

"Me too." Toinette cleared her throat. "I never thought I'd tell that. I never met the person who needed to hear it. But I wanted to say it before we went in there." A jerk of her head indicated the temple. "I wanted to tell you. I hope the knowledge isn't too great a burden."

"An honor, rather," he said.

For once, she didn't make an irreverent reply or try to shrug off the moment. Her embrace tightened, and then she leaned up to kiss him lightly. "Go to sleep," she said. "I won't let this place have you."

THIRTY-TWO

OF COURSE THERE WERE DREAMS, AND OF COURSE THE DREAMS
were far worse than they had been. Even in the midst of the
nightmare, Toinette wasn't surprised.

The dead wrapped their cold arms around her. They
clawed at her flesh, and the wounds opened onto black
nothing. Pustules swelled on her body and burst. She saw
bone beneath. It shifted in the same liquidly *wrong* way
that the elk creatures' bodies had, lengthened into spurs
and claws, then dissolved again, and the dead slurred in
her ears all the time.

Stinking flesh.

Damned.

This is all.

A dead man's mouth yawned impossibly wide, as the
specter's the day before had done. Inside was darkness that
pulled at her.

"Piss off," she said and struck out at it with one hand,
forming claws almost as an afterthought. The skull broke
under her blow and fell into the hole, which eagerly con-
sumed its own matter. Toinette pulled herself back, shook
free of the dead, and woke to more darkness.

"Well," she told Erik, listening with gratitude to the beat
of his heart beneath her ear, "I'm awake."

They ate quickly and got moving. It was just as cold
in the morning, if morning it was, as it had been, and the
forest looked no different, though the green light had
stopped flashing. Walking was warmer. Besides, the faster

they went, the quicker they could do what they needed and be gone, or die and be done.

Before she'd been walking long, Toinette was sure either would be better than lingering.

Onward, in silence, they passed through the stream and into a trackless forest, keeping the temple ahead of them as a goal. For one stretch, the undergrowth would be clear, and they'd make their way around snarls of wood with comparative ease. Then the plants would close in again, and it would be work for swords: brutal, clumsy slashing that left Toinette coated with clammy sweat.

The sap hardly smelled at all, but she heard faint screams as she hacked at the plants. Occasionally, and worse, she heard laughter.

"We could change," said Erik after the first such encounter, "and burn them."

Toinette shook her head. "I'd as soon not breathe the smoke."

Erik grimaced and made no argument. Changing wouldn't have let them fly either. The branches above them spiked and twined in a painful mating, almost obscuring the sky. Any attempt to fly out would have brought only mangled wings—and one of Erik's hadn't fully healed yet.

So they went on as humans, tired and cold, walking on ground that at times seemed to fade beneath Toinette's boots. When it was there, it felt fragile: an eggshell over a monstrously vacant yolk. If she'd thought it would help, she would have screamed. She might have regardless, except she wasn't sure she would be able to stop.

When they came to another free patch, she put a hand on Erik's arm instead.

He paused, turning his head. "All well?"

"So to speak," she said. "Just wanted to make certain I wasn't imagining you."

It sounded ridiculous, but he nodded in recognition. His face was very white: darkness or strain, Toinette wondered, and did hers look the same? Likely. One of the deformed squirrels stared at them from an overhead branch, then chittered in a singsong rhythm, turned a hairless and raw-looking tail, and was gone.

"If I wasn't real, my feet wouldn't hurt." Erik tried to joke, but neither of them felt like laughing.

Silently, he turned and they began to walk again.

The brush closed in before them, and this time it included the blood-drinking vines. With forewarning, they weren't the menace they'd been before, but they whipped toward Erik and Toinette with a speed as much annoying as disconcerting. No damned *plant* had a right to be that fast. Toinette took to cursing them under her breath, the words falling into a rhythm with her sword.

So occupied, neither of them saw the man step out of the forest.

It was a breaking stick beneath the newcomer's feet that brought him to Erik's attention; else he might have thought the man another phantom.

The figure he turned to face, as the last of the vines fell beneath his blade, was short and starvation-thin, dressed in the remains of a leather tunic and breeches. His hair was long and white, his eyes large and dark, and what skin remained to him was ruddy bronze, wrinkled from weather. That was what Erik could have said about the human part of him.

All else was a sight to inspire profound horror—and deep pity.

The man was changed as badly as the elk had been. His right leg moved with an unnatural fluidity when he walked, and when the ripped leather parted, Erik glimpsed black void beneath it. Spots of blackness dotted his hands and his face, like plague pustules, but these had no tinge of purple, nor any sense of swollen flesh. It was more as though the man's skin had opened, and nothing was within.

In one hand he held a stone knife, but he made no move to use it, nor, at first, to approach. He stared at Erik and Toinette and spoke words in a tongue Erik had never heard before. The tone was universal: desperate, broken hope.

"Sirrah," Toinette began, frowning. "I—"

She stopped as the man took another few steps toward them. The knife dangled from his hand. Erik saw blood on it, but it was gray-red and too viscous. The man spoke another few words, then hesitated; his eyes turned briefly white, but he snarled, what was left of his lips flexing around patches of missing flesh, and shook his head.

The man looked at their swords, took one step forward, then dropped the knife with no reluctance. On that strange earth he knelt, the mismatched meat and shadow of his body moving in a way that hurt the eyes to see, said another word, and bent his head.

"It's all right," said Erik, though he wasn't sure it was. "We mean you no harm. You may rise."

The man stayed where he was and shook his head. He gestured to Erik's sword, disintegrating hand shaking, and then drew that hand across the length of his neck.

"Ah," said Erik, realizing. He would have felt embarrassed for taking so long to work it out, save that he was feeling too many other emotions, none of them remotely comfortable.

Toinette was at his side then, her free hand on his

shoulder but her own sword drawn. "I'll do it if you can't," she said, "but we must be quick."

Erik knew she didn't speak out of concern for their journey, and he knew his heart was hers at that moment, if it hadn't been long before. "No," he said and stepped forward.

He'd long been a soldier, almost never an executioner, but the stroke was a simple one and the flesh horribly yielding. The body crumpled and the head fell; there was, despite a moment of fear on Erik's part, no attempt to reattach. Blood didn't spurt, but flowed sluggishly in a gray-red stream. When he cautiously turned over the head, the eyes were blank, with the look he'd seen on a thousand dead men.

"*Dominus vobiscum*," he said and sighed, cleaning his sword well. "But I don't think we should stop to bury him. I'd consider it no grace to be laid to rest in these woods myself."

"Not much rest either, likely."

Erik remembered his dreams and crossed himself. "No."

Nonetheless, they laid the man out with his arms folded across his chest, closed his eyes, and placed his head between his feet. The gesture was important, as grotesquely *not there* as his skin felt and as sickeningly as his limbs bent. Both Erik and Toinette rubbed their hands against their clothing as they started walking again, hoping to clean off any corruption that lingered.

"I'm glad we didn't bring any of the men," Toinette said.

Erik nodded. "I wonder," he said quietly, "where he came from. He was no Templar. Another shipwreck?"

"Likely. Though from no place I've been, nor met men from—not from the way he spoke. The world is wide." She pressed her lips together. "Or he might have been here long enough to forget all language but his own. Madmen do that at times, I hear, and there's no telling how long he's been on the island."

"Nor how long he was changed," Erik said, though he wished that the thought hadn't occurred to him.

The man had kept enough of his mind to ask for death, and not to attack them. Had his eyes stayed white, Erik suspected, matters would have been different. How many years had he spent fighting off bloodlust? How many feeling the corruption take hold of him, looking at flesh that warped into nothing?

Toinette hacked at a vine, of the immobile sort, and added almost conversationally, "Christian, whoever he was, and more devout than me. I'd have killed myself were I him. Either God would understand, or hell could be no worse."

"I'm not sure he *could*," Erik said, remembering how the elk had kept coming while stuck full of arrows, and how its not-flesh had mended almost as soon as it was cut. A severing blow, with his whole strength behind it, had been the exception—or had the stranger used the very last of his will to keep away the unnatural healing? Erik thought of the stone knife and the dried blood upon it, the same color as the blood that had come from the man's neck. "I think he tried."

Their footsteps were loud against the trail, punctuated by the swish of blades and the snap of plants. "Poor devil," said Toinette shortly but with great feeling.

"No," said Erik. "Poor—but not yet a devil. He saw to that."

He blessed the unknown man for it, but wanted to curse him too, for the thoughts now running the course of his mind. *They'd* delivered the stranger as much as he had done himself. That was well enough, and Erik didn't want credit—but the forest, where they could remain themselves with little effort, was only the start of their troubles.

If the same fate overtook them, was there any salvation, even of the most fatal sort, on the island?

He doubted it.

THIRTY-THREE

THE TEMPLE CAME FULLY INTO VIEW, AND ALL ELSE AROUND IT faded.

It wasn't just by comparison. The trees around the temple were gray and leafless. From their looks, they'd long ago abandoned even such twisted life as the others had possessed. There was no wind, but their branches moved sluggishly against the sky, in patterns Toinette could watch for only a few seconds before the back of her eyes began to ache.

"It's just as well we didn't try flying earlier," she said, looking back down. "Landing through that—" The thought of even a scratch from one of the branches made her shudder. She and Erik both kept very close and used their swords with thorough care.

Cutting their way through didn't take as much effort, despite that. The plants, from wayward moving branches to patchy grass, were all brittle, crumbling at not much more than a touch. The grass was gray too, and the leaves of the plants. That color was more noticeable there, without bark to obscure the shade.

"I think they're all dead," said Erik. "Most likely everything here is. Look."

He gestured to the foot of a nearby tree. Toinette turned her head and saw one of the hairless squirrels lying there, though at first she almost didn't recognize it. Normally that would have been down to scavengers, but as far as she could tell, nothing had touched the rodent—or no animal. It had the same grayish undertone as the grass around it.

Pits of blackness spotted its skin, though, and a larger one, craterous and uneven, sprouted from its side. Toinette had seen a growth like that on a beggar's jaw once, but that had been flesh. The…growth…on the squirrel was nothing, void formed into irregular shapes and fastened onto living flesh. The creature's mouth was open, as if in a scream, and Toinette could see more pitted darkness inside.

She swore and looked down at her own hands, then to Erik's face. She couldn't *see* any dark patches forming, but clothing covered a great deal, and stripping there and then would be foolish.

Nothing moved in the dead forest to either side of them. No birds called. The moving branches creaked slightly, and the stream flowed in the distance, but that was all. Toinette could hear each of her breaths and most of Erik's. "Do you know any spell to protect us?" she asked.

"I don't even know what I'd be protecting us against," he replied. "That is, this"—a quick wave of his hand took in forest and dead squirrel alike—"but I don't know what sent it. Our best defense is most likely speed."

It wasn't the answer Toinette had hoped for, but it was one she'd more or less expected. "The plague didn't touch our kind," she said. "I'll hope that's a sign."

Trees thinned and died, their trunks collapsing into sharp angles in the forest. Toinette's and Erik's footsteps crunched on dry dirt. It sounded like ash, and floated the same way when disturbed, but the smell was cold, wet, and bitter.

Erik spotted more small corpses by the side of the road.

Most were desiccated; a few were only bones, stripped by weather if nothing else. There *was* air in the darkness. It was frigid and stale, but it served its purpose.

A few yards before the temple, the last of the trees vanished. They approached the great steps through a gray wasteland, a wide ring where nothing grew and not even the dead remained. Erik would have felt exposed, with such sparse cover, but he couldn't imagine any would-be attacker coming from his surroundings. He and Toinette felt as unlikely and as much out of place as fish in the desert.

The temple was as gray as the dirt. Each step was surely a full foot in height, and there were at least fifty of them. Above, pillars four times the height of a man stretched up to end in shapes Erik was glad he couldn't make out clearly, then supported a vast conical roof. It seemed to cast a shadow in the darkness, and the shapes from the pillars danced within that deeper blackness.

Toinette's breath hissed through her teeth. "This..." she said, craning her head up and then shaking it in disbelief. "This doesn't *work*. We should have seen it when we were flying over the island the first time. The trees aren't that tall."

Erik wanted badly to argue. The trees might have been on a hill, he would have liked to say, and the temple in a valley, or they might have been distracted and missed the temple, or the sun had been in their eyes. It hadn't been. They'd been looking carefully. And their wanderings over the island had left him in no doubt that the temple was more or less on a level with the forest around it. "No," he said and clenched his throat against a wave of nausea.

"No," said Toinette. She took the pine needles from her hair and smelled them again, prompting Erik to imitate her. It helped, but only slightly.

He reached for her free hand. Briefly she was still, surprised, but then she twined her fingers through his. Toinette's hand was cold, but still warmer than the air around them, her fingers callused and strong. "Best we don't get separated, anyway," she said. A smile like a guttering candle crossed her face. "And if it comes to a fight, I can always use you as a shield, no?"

Erik managed a laugh: brittle, but it counted. They met each other's eyes once, and then began to climb.

Each step was a heartbeat. Their feet lifted and came down in unison on the next block of stone, sending echoes down the steps and through the starved land. Before they'd gone more than a quarter of the way up, Toinette's mind was blank of words. There was only the count: *twenty-five*, and then the strain of leg and thigh as she stepped upward, *twenty-six*.

For the most part, she kept her eyes fixed ahead of her. She glanced from side to side on occasion, alert for possible attackers though she doubted there'd be any, and she listened for any sounds other than footsteps, but she didn't look down. She'd never been afraid of heights. She *couldn't* be afraid of heights: she flew, for Christ's sweet sake.

But she didn't want to look down.

The top of the staircase came as a surprise, not because she'd reached it quicker than she expected—Toinette doubted she could tell quick from slow any longer—but simply because she *had* reached it, and the stairs hadn't gone on forever. Catching her breath, she also made her vision expand out of the tunnel it had fallen into as she climbed.

She and Erik stood in the entrance to a courtyard like the ones she'd seen in Roman ruins. People had walked through those, set up market stalls along the edges, fought and courted and lived in the sunlight. There was no sunlight here, and no people save her and Erik: only ancient gray emptiness.

Erik squeezed her hand, and Toinette wasn't sure he knew he was doing it. They stood together in the shadow of the pillars like Adam and Eve just outside the gates of Eden. What lay behind them had been no Paradise, but ahead would be far worse.

"Won't get better for waiting, I fear," Toinette finally said. Speaking took more effort than she'd been expecting. Her throat felt rusty.

"Ah," said Erik, "and here I'd been hoping."

The courtyard was darker than the forest, which hurt to think about. Toinette couldn't see more than a foot or two in any direction. Judging from what vision she did have, that was no great loss. She saw only the flat, featureless rock to either side, gray and blank. If they'd gotten turned around, she wouldn't have known what direction they were heading.

A shorter walk than climbing the stairs brought them to a pair of tall doors. Despite the lack of light, they had a metallic gleam, but in a green-purple shade that belonged to no metal Toinette had ever seen. A black handle on each jutted out and back in again, forming angles sharp enough to injure any who encountered them with force.

"Should we change, do you think?" she asked, then added, "After we open the doors." Her talons would be too large and clumsy for gripping the handles. Teeth might have worked, but the notion of putting her mouth on that sharp, dark substance made Toinette clamp her jaws together.

"N-oo," Erik said slowly. He was looking at the doors

carefully. "It'd likely be too small inside for us to move well, and we dinna' know what we might have to avoid, and quickly."

"Right you are."

One last time, Toinette clasped Erik's hand tightly, then reluctantly let go. Comfort, as always, took second place to necessity.

The handle was so cold that her fingers stuck to it at first. Toinette swore, let go before the pain could become more than a brief sting, and shrugged one hand up into her sleeve. She wished she'd brought cloth with her, or that she had more of her skirt left to sacrifice. Keeping her arm bent bled off some of her strength, and the door was heavy enough as it was. She had to put her other hand to the handle, keeping it over the first, and set her hips to get leverage before it would budge.

Metal scraped across stone with a scream damnably close to human. As the door only moved slowly, the scream kept going, while the cold of the door handle crept through the cloth and up Toinette's arms. That probably did her muscles good. If Toinette lived to see another sunrise, it would be an immensely painful one, but for the moment cold and fright kept soreness at bay.

Erik's door shrieked in earsplitting harmony with hers. Their breathing, quick and ragged, made up the percussion. Toinette stared at the green-purple sheen in front of her and tried to ignore all of it, until at last they'd opened a passage wide enough to fit through, though they'd have to go in single file.

Beyond was more light than Toinette had expected: a cloudy, half-green storm light that would have had her furling the sails and tying down the cargo had she seen it on the *Hawk*—but at least it was light, and she could see. She was thankful. Her near future, she suspected, would involve often being thankful for extremely small blessings—

—and that would be her future if she was *fortunate*.

THIRTY-FOUR

STONE SURROUNDED THEM. ERIK THOUGHT IT WAS STONE, AT any rate. It was solid gray, thick, and had no metallic shine to it. He could see no joinings or chisel marks, though, nor even any distinct blocks. By his feet, flat wall merged seamlessly into smooth floor. He imagined the same was true at the ceiling, though that was just too high for him to see well.

"No human hand made this," he said.

Toinette shrugged. "Well. Demons, you said."

"Aye, but I'd pictured them laying stones and all. Doing as humans do, but on a grander scale, and getting the rock from elsewhere if it came to that. Not that I had much reason to think I knew one way or another," he admitted, not too unsettled to be embarrassed when he said it. Erik gestured around them. "This, where it's all of a piece, it's as though it *grew*."

"Like a tree?"

"Or a creature."

By her grimace, Erik knew Toinette was thinking along the lines he'd started to, of bowels and throats, and that she liked it no more than he did. "Thank you for that," she said dryly. "How did Jonah end up faring, do you remember? It's been a while since I heard *that* story at mass."

"Repented and was delivered," Erik said.

They continued walking while they spoke; inside the temple, ambush seemed less likely. Their footsteps echoed enough to make Erik sure they'd hear any oncoming attackers, and the light, gloomy as it was, let them see a good distance ahead. The walls to either side were sturdy too, whatever they were—or they looked that way. Erik kicked one of them gingerly, not wanting to touch the stone with his bare hands.

It felt like real stone against his toe. The wall didn't scream either, which was some reassurance, until he reflected on the possibility that they were wandering inside a living creature that didn't feel pain when a large man with dragon blood kicked the inside of its organs.

He was very glad when Toinette spoke again. "Odds are I've committed a few hundred sins in my day, and I can't say that I've been absolved for all of them. You know." Erik did. Most priests wouldn't believe in the dragon-blooded without riot-causing proof, and a fair number of those who were convinced would likely think them irrevocably damned to begin with. Outside of Loch Arach and a few other places, sins committed in dragon form went unconfessed by necessity. "But," she continued, "I somehow doubt repenting is going to get us out of this."

"Aye, well," said Erik, "we're not prophets."

"That's one reason, I'm sure."

The hallway went on, stretched out like melted tallow. Erik thought it shrank as they walked, but if so, it was never enough to make him certain, only to keep him looking at the ceiling and the walls, trying to measure the distance with no marks to serve as guidance.

A sound crept in around their footsteps. Not quite a slurp, nor yet entirely breathing, it was a wet inhalation that at first put Erik in mind of a man sucking on a bad tooth: *shluuuuh, shluuuuh*. Every little while they heard it, drifting through the hallway from no direction that either of them could tell.

"On the *Hawk*," said Toinette, the third or fourth time, "that sort of thing would mean a leak, and a damned bad one. Not quite the same noise, but—close."

"I've heard men breathe nearly that way when stuck through the lungs. Not quite, as you say, but very like."

"Not quite, but very like. That's the whole problem with this place," Toinette said.

"I'd not say the *whole* problem," Erik said, trying to joke. "Surely dark magic and deadliness count a wee bit too."

He knew what she meant, though. Had the sound been exactly one either of them remembered, it might have meant trouble, but it wouldn't have nibbled away at the edges of the mind, drawing attention to what might make it and what was wrong with that comparison. Hearing it was like looking at the temple and comparing its size to the landscape of the island from the air, or watching the elk-creatures move.

The power in the temple blurred edges, even where edges shouldn't *be*. That was as close as Erik could come to describing it.

Eventually, they did come to the end of the hallway: a blank gray wall, and a door to each side wide enough for a single man to pass through at a time. Both doors looked exactly alike, miniature versions of the ones that had led into the temple. Toinette looked from one to the other, then back to Erik, and shrugged. "Have you any preference?"

"No." He frowned and slowly added, "We could try to see magically, but we've not the supplies for a complicated and guarded ritual. And as the less formal sort hasn't worked elsewhere on the island…"

Toinette shook her head quickly. "If it does work here,

what you see is as likely to drive you mad as to be useful."
She didn't know that for certain. Still, the place was quite
bad enough to merely mortal eyes. "Rather not take the risk
to save us a little walking."

"Aye. Right-hand door first, then. And be ready."

With Erik in front of her, and the doorway small, a
sword wouldn't be much use. Toinette shifted her weight
and drew her knife, prepared to throw it if need be, and
staying alert for sounds from either the left-hand door
or the passage behind them. None of that made her feel
truly ready. She suspected that even a troop of armed and
mounted knights wouldn't have done that.

The inner door opened as readily as any in the normal
world. Erik, anticipating otherwise, yanked it hard enough
that it slammed backward into the hall with a thunderous
boom. Toinette winced, gripped her knife harder, and flung a
glance over her shoulder to see what might have responded.

Nothing stirred. Save for the dying echoes, the hall was
quiet. Gradually Toinette let out her breath and followed
Erik across the threshold, where they stopped and stared.

They were in a church.

Arcades stretched to either side of them, arches opening
onto more blank stone. A path led down the middle to an
altar as finely made as any Toinette had seen in her travels,
made of dark wood and inlaid with the green-purple metal
of the doors. Windows flanked it to either side, with stained
glass cut in intricate patterns—but the light through them
was that which had flashed through the forest.

Above the altar hung no cross, but rather a spiky, twisting shape that seemed to change as Toinette looked at it.

She remembered some of the stories about the Templars,
and her throat went dry.

"I don't smell blood," Erik said, clearly thinking along

the same lines she was, "not even old blood. But I'd not touch that."

He gestured to the font near them, where a slick substance glimmered in a stone basin. As Toinette looked down, she saw her face reflected there. It was pallid white, which she could easily believe after her time in the forest, but the features were stretched far too long for it to be human.

She put a hand up and quickly felt her jaw and nose, making sure they were where they should be. "Damned shoddy mirror, whatever it is," she said, trying to sound only irritated.

Erik clasped her shoulder. "Shoddy indeed. You're only a wee bit dirty—still you."

She quickly smiled her thanks, then returned to practical matters. "I don't see a door out, but we might not from here."

Real churches often had doors in the arcades, or behind the altar so that the priest could get to and from his chambers more easily. If the room they were standing in was a real church, Toinette doubted it was to any god she wanted to know about; still, they had to go further in.

Each took one side, stepping under the arches and traveling up the long stone floor. Walking so far apart, they still fell into rhythm with each other. Toinette thought her part of that might have been because she was listening to Erik's footsteps, trying *not* to hear the steady, wet noise that continued around them. Hearing that was like having a slug crawl up her back.

There were no doors on Toinette's side, nor did Erik stop and shout a discovery. Even the places where tapestries would have hung in a normal church were bare—but they flickered as Toinette looked at them, gray stone giving way to black void and then returning again in the blink of an eye.

"Saints defend us," she muttered, equal parts prayer and curse. She'd never thought either would truly be heard before, or at least not answered, no matter what the priests said. Now, after the words had left her mouth, she feared what might listen to them.

They met again before the altar.

"Nothing," said Erik, and watched Toinette shake her head in answer. They stood facing each other, a pose that called to mind the mass after a wedding—though any such joining in this church would certainly be cursed from the start, and the progeny likely monsters from the worst of the old tales.

The similarity only reminded him of the difference and made him long for the true version with a strength that took him utterly off guard. He might have spoken then, had Toinette not already been making for the lectern and the immense book open on it, which likely had nothing to do with any scripture he'd ever heard.

"Too much to hope that they kept records, I—*faugh!*"

She leaned back abruptly from the book, upper lip curling and one hand instinctively raised in defense. As Erik rounded the corner, he could see why.

One page of the book was covered with writing in a small crawling hand. On another yawned a face, one with gaping black holes for eyes above an otherwise featureless dark maw. As Erik watched, the eyes drooped and the mouth opened wider, laughing or screaming, or both.

"Close it," he said, but Toinette shook her head.

"If it's trying to scare us, there's something it doesn't want us to see." She bent her head to the paper, squinted, and slowly began reading aloud. "*The Year of Our Lord*

1308, if God grant my memory serves. Roul ran into the forest, and Amis after him. We found them not, and I fear the worst.

"*It corrupts. I think we have contained the worst for now, but without the Order's greater protections, we may be able to save no more than our souls, if those. Would that this cursed place would meet the fate of Atlantis, and—* What's that?" She looked up and to the side.

"What?" Erik asked. From what he could tell, the rest of the room looked as it always had.

"There was a sort of red flicker. I thought." Frowning, Toinette shifted her weight to get a better view.

As she moved, Erik did see more, but not the red flash Toinette had mentioned. Instead, he noticed the floor below the altar, and how the edges were wavering just around the lectern. A crack shivered silently into being. Another followed.

He threw himself backward with a shout of alarm. Toinette spun around at the noise. She had a knife in one hand, but that wouldn't save her. The floor was crumbling rapidly by then, pieces falling away into a lightless void. Her face went white with fear, and she scrambled backward—too slowly.

The last of the floor around the altar disintegrated beneath Toinette's feet just as Erik wrapped his arms around her. Briefly they both teetered on the edge, balance shifting between solid ground and nothing. Then Erik pulled with all his strength, and Toinette shifted her weight, and they fell, but backward, landing hard on stone whose solidity proved itself along every inch of Erik's spine.

He didn't care.

"Damned well *didn't* want us reading that book, then," Toinette said, getting to her feet and straightening her clothing. "I don't guess it can do that to the rest of the room, or it would have. But I'd as soon not linger."

Erik rose as well. The place where the altar had stood was now a neat-edged hole, bottomless to all appearances. He looked away swiftly. "Back, then, and try the other door. What did you see?"

"A shape made of red light," said Toinette. "I didn't get a very good look at it. It vanished almost as soon as I saw it."

"Perhaps a sign of the room changing," Erik said, as they made their way up the aisle, past the polluted font. "I'd not have expected red, though. Nor the light from that direction."

Toinette nodded. "Nor I. We'd best look if we see it again, though. Whatever it was, it may well have saved us."

THIRTY-FIVE

"Porca Madonna!"

Toinette breathed the blasphemy into the great vaulted hall that lay behind the left-hand door. It was far larger than the church, easily the size of a similar hall in any great castle. She wasn't at all certain how it, the church, and the hallway fit together inside the temple building, but she'd stopped trying to make her ideas of size and place work. That wasn't what had drawn the curse from her throat.

As in any hall, this one had long tables running down the center, with a dais at the head. Figures sat on the benches, and a fire danced in the hearth—but the flames were sickly green, and the figures were all of men long dead. Skeletal hands clasped stone cups. Wispy gray raiment flowed over shriveled shoulders. Their faces, however, were not like any man's, living or dead: smooth black ovals obscured all their features.

Nobody sat on the dais. On its benches, a pile of gray hands filled each place where a person might have been.

"It doesn't smell like the dead," Erik said. He spoke quietly, as if addressing a scholarly point or a detail of tactics. Toinette saw the pallor around his lips and knew his tone for armor. She also realized that he was right, though she'd been trying to avoid noticing any smells. "Only cold and slimy, like the rest of this place."

"Small mercies, yes?"

"Aye."

They both drew their swords before proceeding. The

room was large enough, and though they'd not yet had anything physical attack them, Toinette watched the dead for any sign of movement as she and Erik walked slowly past their ranks.

None of them were missing hands.

The piles on the dais held all sorts. As Toinette passed it, she saw rings, gold and gems shining oddly in the uncanny light, and broken fingernails with dirt crusted underneath. A man's hairy knuckles lay next to the smooth white hand of a lady or a youth. She briefly glimpsed a much smaller hand and was glad it was buried too deep for her to see it clearly.

She saw no blood on any of them, nor smelled it in the room. Even old, that smell tended to linger. "What *is* this place?" she whispered.

Expecting no answer, she started at Erik's voice. "I'm no' certain it *is* a place, truly. Not with a history of its own. Even a dead place would have more life to it. This feels like a picture brought to life, or a child's castle of snow."

"Some child," said Toinette, looking back over her shoulder at the row upon row of blanks where faces should have been, and the wisps of hair falling around them.

"Aye. But look you, did you see a door to the kitchen where we came in? Or tapers on the wall? Or a rood screen in the church?" He gestured downward. "No rushes underfoot either. What's making this only imitates the surface of things, or only wants enough to twist."

"Then those"—she looked back again, taking in hands and men both—"never were people?"

"I couldna' say for certain. I'd not go up and grab one to find out. But I doubt there've ever been so many bodies on the island."

"I'm not sure if these are good tidings or bad."

"No more am I."

There *was* a door behind the dais. Unlike the others they'd passed through, it looked like rough, heavy wood, as would have been fitting for any castle. The handle was still black and spiked, though, and the door opened too easily. The wood it appeared to be should have been heavier.

Toinette took a last glance behind her to be sure none of the dead were pursuing, then stepped through.

They emerged onto a ship.

Erik groaned and shut his eyes. "Are we—"

"At sea," Toinette said, sounding as disoriented as he felt. "And it's raining."

Both were making themselves obvious. Erik closed his mouth against the rain, for what good that would do: he doubted it was water, and having it hit his skin could be bad enough. The swaying beneath him was considerably more pronounced than it had been on the *Hawk*, save for the storm.

They were alone again. At any rate, when Erik opened his eyes, he could see no other figures. The darkness around them could have hidden a great deal.

Toinette was standing with her hands on her hips, sword lowered at her side as she looked up at the white sail rippling in the wind. "Imitation, yes? Nothing real?"

"So I'm thinking," said Erik, although the rain felt cold and wet enough. "Or not made to use."

"What can—" Toinette stopped and shook her wet head. "Sorry. If you knew, you'd have said." She gave the ship a careful look, then said, "This is an old vessel. Small castles fore"—she indicated the wooden plank beneath them, then pointed across the ship—"and aft. And no sealed deck. Meaning no door that makes sense."

Indeed, looking downward Erik saw only flat wood, with no trace of a door. "Then what shall we do?"

"Go where it's least sensible," Toinette said and pointed upward.

Near the top of the mast, almost completely hidden by the rain and the flapping sail, eerie light made a faint square outline.

Erik winced. "I could try to fly in this," he said, thinking of his injured wing, but Toinette shook her head.

"And fall into that water? If it is water? No. We climb."

As she'd told Marcus, Toinette had never learned to climb masts, any more than she'd learned to climb trees or anything else taller than a garden wall. She'd the advantage of having *seen* a number of men climbing in the rigging, though, and hearing a fair bit about it. *Grip the shrouds, put your feet on the ratlines, and hope your arms don't give out* was the sum of the advice, and she went quickly to work, conscious both of their precarious position and of Erik watching her.

The desire to show off, or to not look a damned fool, hadn't passed either after bedding the man or admitting her past. Even in the middle of an evil temple, probably due to die soon, she felt his eyes on her as she gripped the vertically running shrouds, got her feet up on the first of the ratlines running between them, and began to climb.

Most sailors learned to climb in port or just out of it, ideally on a calm day. Toinette had rain blowing horizontally into her face, the ship pitching back and forth beneath her, and the ropes slippery beneath the soles of her boots. Wet hemp had taken most of the skin off her palms by the time she made it midway up, and she'd almost exhausted her supply of profanity.

She kept glancing behind her as she climbed, making sure Erik was still there and whole. For a man who hadn't spent much time at sea, he kept up well—and kept his spirits. Every so often he'd meet her eyes through the rain-swept darkness and nod reassurance: *Don't worry about me*.

Once, when Toinette looked back at her handholds, she saw a faint red light shimmering around them. It lasted through two blinks that time, but not long enough for her to get breath and call out a warning—and then nothing happened. The ship's swaying grew no more violent, nor did the rain get any worse.

No point wasting breath, then, when the storm and the exertion made conversation impossible. She didn't speak of the glow until they reached the top of the mast, where the light glimmered like a trapdoor in the sky.

Then they caught their breaths and hesitated, pure instinct not to tamper with the obviously nonsensical briefly overcoming the knowledge that there was nowhere else to go.

"I wonder," Erik panted, "that there's any way at all to climb. Or a door."

"I saw red around the ropes," Toinette said then. She glanced down and didn't see it again. "Any ideas? As to why, I mean?"

"Aye. But not here. We're only putting off the moment."

Toinette had to admit that. Having admitted it, she had to pry her own fingers off the rope and stick one arm through the phantom trapdoor, which didn't burn it off but rather let her put her palm on a flat stone surface. It was only slightly reassuring, but that was as reassuring as the temple would get.

She closed her eyes when she hauled herself through the portal, fearing the passage and the light more than she did emerging blind on the other side.

"What ideas?"

Briefly Erik was at a loss to know what Toinette spoke of, having been recently preoccupied with sitting down, catching his breath, and wringing a wet substance that he hoped would be harmless out of his hair and tunic. The portal had cast them into another featureless hallway, which he welcomed.

"Oh," he replied, when his thoughts had caught up to the conversation. "I can think of four possibilities. It may be that this place, uncanny as it is, must follow certain rules. Rooms must connect to other rooms as much as they do in a real building, and a room must have most of the qualities of what it imitates. And so on. Or the...being...behind it hasn't the wit to change very much."

"Are those two notions, or one in two parts?"

"Only the one, if you're keeping a list."

"Just trying to follow your speech." Toinette got slowly to her feet. "Argh. And we should start walking again, before my muscles all lock up. Go on."

While Erik couldn't argue her logic, his legs disliked greatly that she'd made the argument. "Second," he added on a groan, "though we don't know what's at work here, if we assume that either this place has its own will or it responds to another's, we may be influencing it with our own minds. Third, there may be another party, one besides our foe and us."

"Or it may all be a trap," Toinette said. Their wet boots squished as they walked. "Could be meat tastes better for the struggle."

"That was the fourth possibility, aye."

Toinette looked at the blank walls around them. "We

don't know that this place thinks," she said slowly, "or that its creator is yet around to do the thinking. But we keep talking as though that's the case."

"That we do," said Erik. "It has that quality."

"Or we do." Toinette shrugged, and grimaced as her soaked gown shifted on her back. "Every sailor speaks of his ship as a woman. I've never come across one that was more than wood and canvas, mortal-built. We make people out of things."

Soldiers in France named cannons, Erik had heard, and his father praised his manor, during storms, as a man speaking of a faithful dog. He nodded. "You think this—"

"I don't know," said Toinette. "But it *might* just be a place men used, and the remnants of that use. Ungodly use, and ungodly men, likely, and made accordingly." She glanced back at the glowing portal they'd come through. "More than likely. Doesn't mean we're walking through more than a ruin. So that's your fifth path."

"That it is," said Erik. "And I'm glad you thought of it. I'd best be careful of assumptions here."

"Best we be careful of *everything* here," Toinette said dryly.

THIRTY-SIX

Less time passed than in the previous hallway, or so Toinette thought. She hadn't yet gotten into the habit of counting footsteps or breaths. After enough time she felt she might pick it up, as little purpose as it would serve. They were there for as long as it took, the labyrinth was as large as it was, and trying to learn too much about the place might well lead to madness or, at best, headaches. Counting would be a way to occupy her mind, as prisoners were said to make marks on the walls of their dungeons. She wasn't that desperate yet.

So she wasn't sure how long they'd been walking when a second hall crossed theirs, and she didn't much care. She breathed out through her teeth and stood with Erik, staring down the options: three more paths instead of two this time, and no doors.

"Thread or breadcrumbs?" she asked, remembering tales she'd heard abroad.

"Cloth." Whether Erik knew the stories or not, he followed the trail of her speech well. He held up one arm. "Cut at the elbow, if you will. I'd rather not take the time to get undressed. And don't have the hand off with it."

"I'll try to resist the temptation," said Toinette. "I'm only glad you volunteered. I've little enough left to sacrifice."

"I noticed." He cast a glance down her figure—lingering at her breasts and then her half-bare legs—that warmed her despite their grim surroundings.

She flashed a smile back. "Don't distract me while I've got a knife."

Cutting off the sleeve without piercing skin was indeed a small challenge, but the cloth did fall without any bloodstains added to the general grime of their travel. Toinette picked it up and began cutting it into strips: small, but with luck still visible on the floor in front of a passage.

"Rightmost?" she asked. "It's not likely to be worse than the others."

"Aye," Erik began, then stopped short and stared. "Look there."

He pointed with his bare arm. The skin above his wrist was paler than the rest by several shades. As he gestured to a blurry spot of red above the center door, he looked momentarily like a saint in a window, indicating a mystery revealed.

In very broad strokes, Toinette supposed there was a similarity. She had no intention of telling Erik as much.

The shape lasted longer. It became a square before it started to fade at the corners, then blinked out of sight, leaving Toinette and Erik frowning at a patch of empty wall above a passage.

"Might be a trap," she said again.

"Or it might not," said Erik. "It's *not* us making it happen, I know that much, for how would we have an idea of what path to take? And if this place must obey certain rules, or was constructed for a particular use, why such indication?"

"Unless it's a warning not to go that way. Or points to the only safe path." Toinette thought of the red glow on the mast and frowned as she spoke. Surely a mere sign, of any sort, would have been on the door or at the base of the mast, not the handholds. It wasn't material. "Six of one, half a dozen of the other. We might as well."

They kept to the middle, though the path didn't remain straight for very long. It twisted around corners, rose and fell over hills, and, as it led Erik and Toinette onward, began to change again. Glimmers began to appear in the walls, like those in the rocks Toinette had seen elsewhere. The stone took on variegated shades.

Erik nearly stumbled over the first roughness in the floor. He caught himself on one wall, pulled his hand back quickly—neither of them wanted to leave their skin long in contact with any part of the temple—and blinked down at the uneven surface. "I'll be damned," he said.

"Likely we both will," said Toinette, but she felt it less inescapably true than she had in the rooms before.

"It's not so foul-smelling here either," Erik remarked after sniffing the air. "Not pleasant, but not as bad as it was."

"I'll take your word for it," Toinette said, but she realized she *could*: the cold stench didn't invade her nose any longer. She'd gotten so accustomed to it that being able to smell her own sweat instead was startlingly pleasant. "If it is a trap, they know how to lure us."

"Thank you for that."

"At your service, my lord," she said with a mocking bow.

The smell kept dwindling as they went on, and the light gradually became dimmer as well. In the forest, that had been another sign of dread to come; this time, Erik welcomed it. Were they underground, which seemed likely, darkness was natural. In a similar spirit he rejoiced as the walls became rougher, though his toes were less philosophical about matters after the third time he stumbled.

Taking Toinette's warning to heart, he didn't let his guard down. For a time they both walked with drawn swords, but the tunnel narrowed as it became more mundane. Letting him take the lead, Toinette switched to her knife. "If I do trip," she said, "this is less likely to end up in your kidneys."

"Odd. I would have thought you'd be glad of the excuse."

She slapped him lightly on the shoulder. "You've not been *that* insufferable. And if I stab you on purpose, it won't be in the back."

With such jokes did they guide each other through the darkness, half reverting to the youths they'd once been—but now, with months of shared work and fear joined to the intimacy of their shared bodies, the jesting words were comfort rather than combat. Any too-strong sentiment would weigh them down and might be a tool for the spirits of the temple. With humor, they kept each other aloft, or at any rate walking.

It was after one such exchange that Erik noticed how the wet breathing was quieter. Their footsteps were no longer steady, broken up by the terrain, but the sound was more of the daylight world. He breathed easier himself, having lost a heaviness on his chest that he hadn't been aware of before.

Then, once again, there were two doors: identical, wooden, and small enough that both he and Toinette would have to duck when passing through either. On one of them, the red light shone more boldly and steadily than Erik had seen it before. This time, he could easily make out the shape: a four-armed red cross, the limbs of equal length and all wider at the ends than the center.

The emblem of the Templars.

Beyond the door was a cave. The entrance was narrow at first, as well as short, but quickly opened up until Toinette could stand at her full height without dashing her skull against the ceiling and walk abreast with Erik. Beyond that, the cave didn't get much larger, and it only stretched back a short way into the darkness.

It *was* dark. The eerie light had vanished. Toinette had no urge to complain. Had she been completely mortal, she would have been blind, but to her, the darkness only came as a relief. She'd stopped feeling the pull of the temple's light after she'd refused it the first time, but its presence had still lingered.

Knife in hand, she looked around and quickly saw the distinguishing features of the cave.

At the end farthest from the door, a row of stalagmites half hid four shapes. Each was covered in cloth, but their size and outline gave their nature away immediately. Toinette went forward not out of any uncertainty but to see what other details she could make out.

From the darkness beyond the shrouded bodies, the skeleton grinned at her.

To any logic, one corpse more was no great matter, even if that one was undraped. That Toinette gasped and her heart began racing when she saw it was therefore damned embarrassing, and she hoped Erik hadn't noticed. As a disguise, she stated the obvious. "So. Five of them. Plus the ones we buried. If there were more, likely they drowned on the way—or died elsewhere on the island."

"So I'd think, aye," said Erik. He drew closer to her, which gave him a better angle on all the bodies. Toinette doubted that was the only reason, just as she knew it was no accident of space that pressed her against his side. They were still solid, still living. It counted for a great deal at the moment.

The skeleton still wore the rusted remains of chain mail

and helmet. He sat with a Templar's shield across his lap and his head thrown back against the wall, and from a distance Toinette could see no clear means of his death. Then she took a few steps closer and spotted the jeweled handle of a dagger protruding from his ribs. One hand still gripped it.

"He killed himself," she said, shaking her head. Toinette had heard of that a few times, mostly in silly stories about young people thinking their lovers were dead and acting foolishly, but she'd never thought to see it done, or even the aftermath. To one bent on self-murder, there were considerably better options—unless, she thought as she looked at the body, there weren't.

"One of them could have stabbed him," Erik said. "A quarrel—"

"What, and then he buried the others with a dagger in his breast?" Each of the shrouded forms had a crude cross over the breast, made of bits of rock carefully laid out. No blood stained the cloth.

"Well—no. A wound like that would've killed him almost instantly, unless it's shallower than it looks." Erik peered at the body and then shook his head. "The spot's just right. And the angle. He'd have been a soldier, of course, but even so, the will it must have taken!"

Toinette thought of the man they'd killed outside the temple. "That's two death-seekers," she said.

"Aye. And this one had sworn himself to the Church."

"Men discard those oaths when it suits them," said Toinette, but still the gravity of it shook her.

They stood silent in the cave. It didn't feel so *wrong* as the rest of the temple, but solemnity was in the very air they breathed. Men had died here, and likely killed as well—and not, Toinette thought, with the heat of a battle.

One had survived to bury the others and then flee himself in the only way he could.

Had they quarreled? Had he killed them in their sleep? Had any of them begun to change already? She remembered the mention of corruption in the book.

A more urgent question: "What do we do here? Why were we sent?" Toinette frowned. "I'd as soon not disturb the bodies, but..."

She trailed off. In that uneasy silence came a scraping sound, and Toinette saw motion out of the corner of her eye. She snapped her head around and then couldn't get breath to swear.

The sound had been bone against rock. The skeleton was moving.

THIRTY-SEVEN

BONES LONG DEAD STIRRED SLOWLY BUT UNMISTAKABLY. THE helmeted head lifted, the shield rose, and the corpse's other hand uncurled from around the dagger's hilt, falling to the side. A reddish glow suffused the bones as they rose, and two points of brighter red shone from inside the helmet.

Draugr, thought Erik at first: the shepherd-eater, the blood-drinker, the monster that had stalked through half the old tales of his childhood. When he drew his sword, he was trying to remember how the walking dead killed, and what killed them.

Memory of the old tales was what stopped him at first. *Draugr* in the stories had always been swollen and fleshy, gray-black from death. There'd never been skeletons. Thus pausing, he further thought that the red light had helped them before, at least once.

Erik stepped back, guarding himself with his sword, until the opposite wall of the cave hit him in the spine. Toinette was there already, eyes and lips narrowed as she focused on the skeleton, knuckles white around her knife.

For all of that, she was the first to speak, in quick, nervous French like a stream in flood: "In Christ's name, whoever you are, we have no quarrel with you. Leave us in peace, and we'll do likewise."

"Ahh," came a man's voice. It was impossible: a man without lungs—and likely without a tongue, though Erik had no desire to lift the helmet and check—could never speak, and yet he did, if only in a sad whisper. "I'll not fight you, child, but there's only one way to find peace in this fell place." Rusty metal squealed and dead sinews creaked as the helmet turned toward the graves.

"Is that how they died?" Erik asked, through a throat so dry and closed he almost sounded like the revenant.

"*Oui*. I was the *turcopolier*, the commander of those who were left, and so, in the end—" The apparition shrugged. "The duty was mine. When the corruption became apparent, we talked it over. They knelt, and I gave them mercy, and then myself, as best I could, and we hoped that would make an end. We knew not that Its power would grow, nor that It would reach out for new prey. Would that any of the chaplains had escaped with us. Would that much had been different."

"It?" Erik asked, noticing the weight of the word.

"Our 'treasure.'" A chuckle emerged from the helmet, likely hollow for reasons beyond the obvious physical limitations. "Whether Philip knew or... But here, I am getting ahead of myself. Sit. Take refreshment as I talk. At the end I'll make you an offer, but I doubt you'll take it without hearing the story in full. I wouldn't have done so, in life."

"Ah," Toinette eyed the skeleton warily.

"I swear by Christ and all the saints," said the dead man, "I'll not raise a hand unless you ask it of me."

And so Toinette sat on the floor, ate dried meat and boiled nettles, and listened to the tale of a dead Templar. She'd never made many plans for her life—a future that might stretch several hundred years was hard to arrange in advance—but what ideas she'd come up with had all been very far from where she found herself.

She took comfort in the minor things: the taste of bread,

Erik's fingers brushing against hers as he passed the wine, the green-blue shine of his eyes even in the darkness. Many such bits of reassurance involved Erik. Toinette couldn't *not* notice. It was far from the time and place to think about what her reaction might mean, and she wasn't sure whether or not she regretted that.

"To begin," said the ghost, "you must understand that I don't know all, or even most. The first part of my story takes place a hundred years before I was born, and I know what the chaplains told me, but they did not have the time or I the rank for them to explain everything. Had they... But there I wish again to change the past, and it cannot be."

Toinette knew the sadness in the phantom voice, even if it was for greater cause than hers had ever been. Had he been living, she would have offered wine. "What was your name?" she asked.

"Adnet, in life," he replied, after a moment's startled pause. "My titles mean nothing here, and I'd as soon not speak my family name in my state. Why?"

"I like to know who I'm talking to." She caught a glance from Erik, and a quick smile, and cleared her throat. "Pray continue."

"The simple fact is this: when my order was but nine men in Jerusalem, a man came to them bearing a great burden. A fisherman had pulled It up in his net, or so the story went, and the history thankfully makes no mention of his fate, nor of those who handled It before It reached us. Perhaps, if they realized the danger and passed It on quickly, they escaped harm—but I fear most men are neither so learned nor so fortunate."

"No," said Toinette.

"What was It?" Erik asked.

"In outward appearance, a wooden chest, with black iron fastenings and many odd symbols. We recognized a few. Over time, scholars told us the meaning of more. None were wholesome. You yet remember the Scriptures, I hope, and the story of the Ark of the Covenant."

"Aye," Erik said slowly, frowning already. It took Toinette longer to call the reference to mind, and Adnet was already speaking by the time she caught her breath.

"This is similar, yet not so. Men built a chest, with much effort and many symbols, and a presence did dwell within it, but the two are as night and day. If the Lord has any kinship to the spirit within that box, all we've heard of Him is a lie. And I do not believe that it is."

Toinette remembered the voice in her dreams, mocking and hateful, and the images of the dead. "What does It want?"

"*Want*," said Adnet, "is a troublesome word. In all our time with the thing, we have never yet known if It has enough mind to want, or in any way greater than a fish wants a worm. It twists, should It get close enough, and devours. It seeks to feed, but so does any squirming maggot on a corpse."

"But It speaks," Erik objected, "and It shows images."

"It spits out what you give it, reflected darkly. Whether that's will or reflex or simply force, I couldn't say." Adnet sighed. "And we truly only realized as much of Its power as we did once we'd had to bring It here. In the Temple, we had spells, material, a hundred years of scholarship containing It, and enough men of God trained to pit their will against It and succeed."

"And how many of you came here?" Toinette asked.

"A dozen. Four had died on the voyage over—we fled with no time to prepare, and no knowledge of where we went, only that we must not let the un-ark fall into the hands of a mortal king."

Erik swallowed his dried meat and asked, "Was he trying for It? Would It be of any use to a king?"

"If one lived who could master It, likely he could turn Its power against his enemies. It would be a terrible thing to face."

To that, Erik said nothing. Toinette studied his face, but found nothing save long thoughts, and couldn't think of the words she wanted herself.

Adnet continued. "All our treasure was only a disguise for what we truly guarded, and it may have been our undoing in the end. Whether Philip knew of the un-ark or not, we fell because men enough knew of our gold, and cared for nothing else. When that became clear, the Grand Master taught me a few of the most basic spells and then sent me away with the others, men low-ranked enough that we could be overlooked. I suspect I know the fate of those who stayed behind."

"The order's no more. I'm sorry," said Toinette. "And the men—"

"Yes. But they would likely be dead by now in any case. I have *some* sense of time, erratic though it often is, and I mark well this body's state."

"Yes," said Toinette. *Dead* was enough. There was no need to tell the ghost about the torture, or the burnings. He'd likely thought of that already: punishments for treason were no secret.

"And you came here," said Erik, "and then the...un-ark...was harder to contain."

"Likely It was slipping past Its bindings once we took It from the Temple. I don't know that the wind that sent us here was chance, and what will It *does* have is likely set against returning to the sea, where It would have even less prey. It prefers thinking beings, you see. It doesn't eat *flesh*."

"Souls?"

"I hope not. Suffering, certainly, and perhaps sanity. Perhaps life as God made it. It undoubtedly blights all such things and twists them to evil. That became clear soon after we landed, and all our protections didn't suffice. In the end"—Adnet gestured to the bodies—"I'd hoped It would starve after us. It's learned to hunt instead. Or to trap. I'm sorry."

He spoke as a man announcing a death.

"You're saying there's no way off the island," Toinette said dully. She'd known that was possible, but having traveled so far, through so much of hell, only to find out now—everything within her wanted to protest. She held it back with what felt like the last of her strength.

"It will not let you leave without It," said Adnet.

That was an excuse, if Erik needed one. Toinette could even halfway agree with the thought. If they had to take the un-ark to save themselves and her men, then it would be hard to blame him for suggesting it. Back on land, skilled magicians—and Artair was one, undeniably—might be able to contain It, or even to use It without harming their own forces overmuch. The English would be most unlikely to win any wars then, or even start any once they'd seen the un-ark's power.

She felt Erik's gaze upon her, and said nothing. There was nothing *to* say; they all knew the same facts. She knew his oath and his loyalty. Toinette looked at the remains of her food and waited.

His breath echoed in the cave. "Well, then," he said, "how might we destroy It? And what would happen if we did?"

Erik had tried to put his feelings about Toinette, and what he knew she thought, to one side when he decided, and thought he'd largely succeeded. The facts of the matter were weighty enough. Even Artair, when he heard them, might well agree that the risk was too great. If not, which was quite possible, Erik would bear the displeasure of his clan's patriarch and survive. The man was no tyrant. His final decision was rational, or so he hoped.

Still he glanced at her after he spoke, and rejoiced in her smile.

Adnet's next words banished pleasure quite effectively. "We tried," he said. "Over the years. Destroying the box will likely banish the spirit within, though none know if It can die as mortal flesh does, but no weapon could leave a mark on it. My predecessors dropped a block of stone on it once. The block shattered. The chest remained."

"Fire?" Erik asked.

"The records say that came closer than most other methods. The wood smoldered, but the flame died, and the burnt places healed in a matter of months." Adnet shrugged, armor and bone moving together with a discordant screech. "We tried holy water and the relics of saints, and if they wounded either the box or the being inside, none could see it. We tried exorcism. Seven men went mad."

"Magic?" Toinette was chewing on her lower lip, looking less sunk in despair than Erik was beginning to feel.

"Such spells as we could discover. Most of ours went to protection and to defense—it's why I can keep a small part of this place less uncanny than the rest. And it kept that thing from feeding on us, in the end." He touched the dagger's hilt. "We tried, in truth. But it did no good. Human flesh and blood can barely stand against the un-ark enough to keep It imprisoned. To make an end of It..." He shook his head.

"Well," said Toinette, lifting hers, "neither of ours is entirely human."

THIRTY-EIGHT

"The Watchers?" breathed Adnet. If he'd had eyes, they'd likely have been wide as cart wheels.

"That's one of the stories I've heard," Erik said. The book of Enoch talked about angels mating with mortal women and producing children: giants in the Bible, but who knew what might have gotten lost with the ages. "Among others."

"We're dragons," Toinette said quickly. *Here are the facts. Let's have them out.* "When we wish to be. We heal quickly. We live long. We see in the dark, and I'm surprised you didn't wonder about that."

"I hadn't realized it was so dark," Adnet said. "Although it must be. The mind does not rot as the body does, but certain perceptions—and the expectations with them—do fall away."

That raised questions, the same that Erik had been contemplating ever since the ghost had made his appearance, but they would have to wait. Practical matters were at hand, which Toinette confirmed by speaking again. "We also can breathe fire," she said. "It's stronger than most flame and killed a few of the creatures this thing touched."

"And," Erik put in, thinking of the light in the forest, "we've a bit more resistance to Its power than most men, from what I can tell. Our kin are old too, and well-versed in magic. I don't know as many spells as I might, but I could likely manage an attack on that front, or enchant a weapon to strike at this power."

Adnet hesitated, or so Erik thought. What made for hesitation in a moving skeleton was far from clear. He was silent for a while. Erik and Toinette ate the last of their food without speaking, until another thought crossed Erik's mind. "If you don't believe we can destroy It," he asked, "why did you guide us here? Only to tell us of our fate?"

"To offer you the chance to change it," said the spirit, "if only for yourselves." With a grating noise, he plucked the dagger from his ribs and held it up. "In this, one of our enchantments yet holds. If it gives a man his fatal wound, that man's death won't feed the un-ark, nor will It be able to make any use of his body. I came back to offer that mercy to any who made it this far, and to fight the un-ark back with what power I yet have. Now that you speak…" He sighed. "If the hope you offer is true, then I rejoice in it, but I *had* thought my duty clear."

"I am," said Erik, "a bit familiar with that sentiment."

Toinette reached across the gulf of crumbs and stone to squeeze his knee.

"You are, in truth, the first to travel so far." Adnet turned the dagger over in his fleshless hand. "And you're unchanged, which speaks to your claims. It's still a great risk."

"Aye," said Erik.

"It's one I'd take," said Toinette. "And I know it's not only me, but in time it won't be only us. Men are traveling more, to Araby and the Indies and to trade with the Mongols. It won't be very long before they try to cross the ocean this way as well, and the spirit reaches forth to take prey. We can chance striking at It now, before It gains in strength life by life. I'd roll those dice."

Adnet stepped forward, his dragging footsteps across the stone unsteady and quiet. In front of Erik, he stopped and held out the dagger, hilt first. "Then I bid you take this. Should you fail, you may yet have a moment to grant mercy to yourselves and to the world."

The dagger's gold hilt felt sun-warmed when Erik took it, far as the cavern was from any sunlight. Holding it, he could neither smell nor hear the signs of the un-ark, and he bowed his head before Adnet, knowing the value of the gift. "You're most generous, sir. I vow, one way or another, that presence will have neither of us."

If it came to that most desperate of circumstances, he vowed silently to see Toinette's soul safe before his, and to do it when she didn't know, that she might have the better chance of heaven. Even the idea made him want to snarl and smash the cave walls, but he forced himself to practicality.

"Outside this door and through the one opposite," said Adnet, "there will be another passage. Take the rightmost turns, and you'll come to the center. The place of the chest. I cannot tell you what It'll put in your way, nor may my power approach the nexus of Its strength, but I'll give you what aid I can."

"Thank you," said Toinette, getting to her feet. "We owe you our lives already, and we may owe you our souls in the end. I wish there was a chance of paying you back, but it doesn't seem likely."

"Might there be *any* service we can do you," Erik asked, "before we go from here?"

"The ground here is too hard for burial, and you've no cloth for a shroud," Adnet replied. "Yet if you would lay the sign of our Lord over me, as it is on my brothers, I would count it a kindness."

"Gladly," said Erik, and then had to ask the question every man would have wondered about. "What *is* it, on the other side?"

Despite his permanent, lipless grin, Adnet managed to

convey a smile. "I haven't gone the whole way, nor will I unless you win your battle, but I've seen what I cannot speak of, nor you hear save at great cost to your mind and perhaps your body. I will say only this: it is not what the un-ark would have you believe."

Remembering his dreams, Erik found the relief of that answer quite satisfactory. "Then I'll go with more hope," he said, "even if the worst happens."

"Hope is always a strength, applied well," said Adnet. He lay down by the side of his shrouded companions, straightened his legs, and folded his arms across his chest. "Farewell," he said, "in the truest sense of the term."

Slowly, the red light faded from around his bones. By the time it vanished, Toinette was already picking up chips of stone from the cave floor.

"Hold," said Erik. "We'll need *some* cloth to put them on. Use my other sleeve."

If they did walk out victorious, he thought, there was a decent chance that they'd both be naked as Adam at the rate they were going. Toinette's nudity always made for a pleasant sight, but that particular situation sounded uncomfortable. All the same, he held still as she cut off the other sleeve of his tunic and helped to spread it carefully across Adnet's chest.

The cross they made on top of it was less even than the others, owing to the proximity of ribs beneath the cloth, but it was clear.

When it was done, and both of them stood over the bodies, Toinette took Erik's free hand. "You know," she said, "if I must be here at all, there's nobody I'd rather have with me."

Out of the cave, behind the opposite door, they walked through the passage Adnet had mentioned. It was no worse than the rest of the temple at first. The smell and the sound picked up, but Toinette had thought they would and braced herself. In truth, when Erik walked beside her holding the dagger, it wasn't so bad.

They turned right when the tunnel forked, walking through a small maze of twists and turns that all seemed much alike. Time drew out in a thin unending thread. Toinette tried to get her mind around the presence they were going to face, the thing for which she now had a description and a name: *un-ark*.

To name a thing, Artair had told her in her youth, gave you power over it. But a true name counted more than others. She doubted that *un-ark* would count for much. "It didn't sound," she said to Erik, both of them knowing to what she referred, "like anything you've heard of, did It?"

"Not particularly. The greater demons, or the specifics of them, are vanishingly rare. I'd not thought to ever meet with any. There's a great deal in the worlds that even those with magic never hear about."

Toinette could understand that. Even dragons didn't casually cross the Alps, and the elemental messengers Artair and his kin used took a great deal of effort and the right sort of ground, or so she recalled Agnes saying. Even most of the MacAlasdairs hadn't crossed the Channel. A magician in France or Muscovy was likely to be a surprise to them, and him to them.

"You could all stand to journey more," she said.

"Aye, look how well this turned out," Erik responded, half joking. Then he drew closer, and while Toinette was glad, she knew it wasn't out of either lust or comfort. "When we reach It," he said under his breath, "we'll use the Greater Exorcism, then the Conjuration of Fire, then change and breathe flame. Do you object? Do you know the spells?"

Closing her eyes, Toinette cast her mind backward, seeing cramped writing on old parchment, hearing her own voice reciting the procedures back to Artair. "Yes," she said slowly. "Enough to follow your lead."

"That will be a change," Erik said with a grin as they went around a corner.

All at once, they were standing on a city street.

It was no city Toinette knew, and it was every city. The buildings shifted as she looked at them, blooming and shrinking like wax in water. She recognized London and Paris, and thought she saw a hint of Rome's basilica.

Figures walked the streets. Most of them were faceless, as those in the great hall had been, but when Toinette stared at one, features lay themselves over the black void: a man's face, purple-black with plague, eyes dazed with agony and the knowledge of his approaching death. He fell to his knees by a church and began to shriek wordless pleas to the sky.

Bodies lay all around them. Flies buzzed, landed, feasted.

It was mirage, and it was memory.

"Blessed Virgin have mercy," she said, her voice hoarse. "It's taking things out of my head now."

"Or mine," said Erik, looking at her with eyes grown dark and hollow.

And the hell of it was, Toinette couldn't tell which. There was no part of the city she could point to and say *I knew that man* or *This didn't happen when I was there*. The dead filled the streets, the living wept and pleaded and waited to die, and it was all a memory either of them could have claimed, from almost anywhere.

She wiped her dry mouth with the back of her hand. "There must be a thousand doors here, and they're all changing. And behind the wrong ones—"

"I know."

Sword in hand, Toinette started toward the first of the buildings. Erik's hand fell on her shoulder. "No," he said, as she turned to blink at him. He was holding the dagger, white-knuckled. "I think I can find our way."

"Come back," Toinette said.

She opened her mouth as though she wanted to speak on, but swallowed and shook her head, and Erik could think of no response. There in the abattoir of a dozen remembered streets, the mingled sounds of feasting insects and human misery around them, jokes offered no protection.

He took her in his arms and kissed her, not out of lust—it would have taken a twisted man to feel desire in such a place—but to hold her, to know the feeling of her beneath his hands and lips. That, as much as the dagger, would be his shield.

Erik stepped back, calmed his breathing, and spoke: "*Visio dei.*"

The dagger's power answered his call in lieu of the normal spirits of vision, as he'd hoped it would. It shielded his mind too. A golden radiance cut through the clinging green-purple fog around him and kept at bay the shadowy forms twisting there, waiting for an unwitting traveler to open the wrong door. Erik averted his eyes all the same. Men weren't meant to see all the forces of the world, and if they won the day, he wanted no clear memory of those beings, whatever they were.

Finding their route was bad enough. A distance down

the corpse-strewn street pulsed a hollowness, a shifting rip in the world that led to a malign and hateful *no place*.

"There," Erik pointed.

Toinette's hand closed around his elbow and gripped tight. "I think I see it," she said. "A couple steps closer. Then you can let go."

The steps in question took an eternity. He moved his feet through sucking fog, stepping over phantom bodies that felt and smelled like reality. Only the dagger's light and Toinette's presence at his side seemed solid; the rest was a pit where he could spend his days scrabbling and flailing, lost forever.

"Here?" Toinette echoed him.

"Aye." The door was unremarkable, but he felt the presence behind it.

"Then don't linger, for God's sake."

Glad to oblige, Erik dismissed the spell. The city became marginally less horrible. He steadied himself with his hand on one wall, taking deep breaths and being sure to do so only through his mouth.

"Tell me when you're ready," said Toinette. She held her knife in one hand, and her eyes sparked with gold.

The color reminded Erik of the dagger he carried, and how its light had pushed back the fog of the un-ark. It was still warmer in his hand and heavier than it should have been. Notions of power crossed his mind, uncurling like bright ribbons and leading his thoughts onward.

"In there," he said, drawing close to Toinette and lowering his voice again. Given that the un-ark could evidently pick memories out of their minds, he wasn't sure whispering served any purpose, but old habits died hard, and he had no wish to take chances. "After the exorcism, give me a moment before the invocation. I've an idea."

"That makes one of us," said Toinette.

"I *can* explain, if you'd like."

She shook her head, pushed back wayward hair, and smiled grimly. "The less we speak, the better we might be," she said, echoing his earlier thoughts. "Besides, I trust you. Magic's your ship. If you think you can get us through the storm, I'm glad to help you do it."

"I'll only hope to do as well as you've done all these years," said Erik. He wanted to say more, but the circumstances would have made any confession seem cheap: words he didn't think he'd have to live by.

Instead he fixed her image in his mind. In a moment he memorized the small, weary, defiant grin, the fire of her hair, the way she held herself although she was as tired and afraid as him. "Well, then," he said. "Let's have this done, aye?"

Beyond the door was cold like Toinette had never imagined, not even in the depths of winter at Loch Arach. It stopped her breath at first, and her whole body tensed, as though her skin and muscles were trying to burrow inside her for warmth.

It was not winter.

It wasn't the ocean.

It was *nothing*.

A thin stone path ran from the door to a square platform, and nothing supported it. Nothing was around it. Platform and path hung in the middle of a void lit by occasional twists of purple-green radiance, which came from nowhere and disappeared almost immediately.

In the middle of the platform sat a chest about half the size of a man. Black metal bound strange pallid wood, winding around it in three thick strips. Purple-green fire flickered along the edges of that metal, and those edges blurred as Toinette looked at them.

The sound of wet inhalation was everywhere, and loud.

"*Oh*," Toinette exhaled, a sickly gut-punched moan. She felt dimly ashamed of it in front of Erik, but she could no more help herself than the dying men in France could have stifled their groans. At extremes, the body took over, and the body knew that the room was *wrong*, a fever-dream place that belonged in front of no remotely human eyes.

She glanced back over her shoulder, though she knew flight would do no good. The door was gone. Everything was gone. There was only the path.

And so she forced one foot to rise, one leg to swing forward, and then the other. She did look down. The void was awful, but it was better than the chest.

The stone echoed beneath her feet. From the darkness beneath it, faces swam up to meet her. A few were those she recognized. All were dead. All were rotting.

The way of all flesh, came a wet voice from around them. *You are this. Only wait.*

It was an observation, not a threat. Toinette sought for a witty reply, or at least a profanely defiant one, of the sort she'd made in her dreams. Nothing came to her. There was only walking, and the path.

She stepped onto the platform and felt the call of the light again, as she had in the forest. This time it was more forceful. It sought the center of her mind, the weariness and the pain of her walking, the bleeding blisters on her feet and the bruises on her arms from when Erik had grabbed her. It *pulled* at those spots, working not on her mind but on her body.

The way of all flesh.

Toinette yanked back. "My form is *mine*," she snarled. Artair had given her that when she'd been fourteen, and whatever she'd said to Erik, she doubled the amount of her debt to the patriarch in that moment. The light, startled, relinquished its grasp.

Defiance cleared her head. The room was still horrible, the chest more so, but she could make her way to the far side of the platform and straighten her back. She could remember words, including the ones she needed.

She didn't look at the chest, nor at the faces coming out of the void around her. She met Erik's eyes instead. "On your mark," she said.

They began.

THIRTY-NINE

"STRONG AND MIGHTY SPIRIT OF HELL," ERIK BEGAN, SENDING his voice out from the bottom of his chest as he'd been taught to do in such rites.

As soon as he began, the words started to slip his mind. It took an effort of will to call them back, and more effort yet to shape each one. His tongue hung heavy in his mouth. Around him, the air was both cold and thick.

The thing in the box was fighting back.

He pushed onward. Toinette's voice rose with his, low alto mixing with his baritone. "Go back into thine own place. Return to the Pit that spawned thee, O abomination, and trouble this world no more."

The faces around him rotted, crumbled, formed back on themselves but hideously altered. His father stared at him through eyes embedded in his cheekbones. Gervase's crushed flesh parted in a grin, and he held out a mangled red blotch of a hand, reaching and inviting at the same time.

Come to me, said the clotted voice of the room. *Love dies. Faith dies. Truth dies. In the end is screaming meat. Do you think yourself different?*

Erik couldn't answer. He couldn't break the ritual, and if he could have, what would he have said? *No, I think you're wrong*. But the words sounded small in his mind—sounded human.

"In the name of Azazel, I send you back. Power of judgment have I over you. In the name of Kokabiel, I banish you. Power of the stars have I over you."

Indeed, power answered to Erik and Toinette's call. It pierced through the dark, slimy air of the room, flowed through their words, and struck at the creature in the box.

Connection was an inescapable part of combat. Steel met steel, or even bone, and the blow numbed the arm of he who dealt it at first. This time, in this combat, Erik caught a glimpse of the thing in the box, and of the shrieking knot of hunger and malice that served it for a mind.

It needed no food. It ate for the joy of it, or such joy as It knew—reveling in torment and consumption, in the painful return of existence to the nothingness It loved and hated at the same time. Given twenty years, It had made the island Its own. Given another century, It would grow, until It ate through the world and out the other side, returning in triumph to the place of tumorous angles It called home.

Erik's soul screamed within him at the knowledge. His mind shuddered and wished to turn away, to seek comfort in madness or death.

The dagger was in his hand. Power held him up. Toinette's voice yet sounded in his ears.

It is not what the un-ark would have you believe, Adnet had said, and if that was so, then there was a force beyond the one that pressed on his lungs and his mind. Erik could cling to that.

"In the name of Shamsiel, I bar this world to your presence. Power of the sun have I over you," he continued, breathless at first and then no longer so. Force was speaking through him, and it had no need to breathe. "In the name of Sariel, I bar this world to your mind. Power of the moon have I over you."

The chest shuddered now with every word, blows that came from inside, as the spirit hurled Itself against Its vessel in pain. Erik went onward, invoking Tamiel and Uriel,

Arakiel with the power of the land and Penemue with the power of wisdom. He knew they were hurting the un-ark, and he knew it wasn't enough. He and Toinette were landing blows that bruised, but none that pierced the armor.

The first pass, he thought. *Both strike, but stay in the saddle.*

He drew breath and power, then let it out in the final verse of the exorcism. "And above all I compel you to leave this world by the God of those virtues and potencies, who dwelt in the Heavens, who rideth upon the Kerubim, who moveth upon the wings of the wind, he whose power is in Heaven and in Earth, who spake and it was done, who commanded and the whole Universe was created; and by the holy names and in the holy names, *Iah, Iah, Iah, Adonai Tzabaoth*."

As the last syllable rang in the chamber, dispelling the slurping sounds and the voice alike, Erik ran forward to the un-ark. It aided him, though he suspected unwillingly; close at hand, It had a pull like the tide. He saw twisted letters on the black metal bands, forming an incantation he never wished to read, and noticed that the white wood was the same color as a drowned corpse's face.

The dagger was hot enough against his palm to have crippled a normal man. Erik raised it over his head and then stabbed downward with all his might, sinking the blade hilt deep into the center of the box.

Winter-dawn quiet filled the room. It lasted just long enough for Toinette, staring at Erik and the dagger, to notice the stillness.

Then the screaming began. It came from no human lungs, and so had no pauses or hitches, no moments of respite. The voice that had insinuated earlier abandoned words and howled in the rushing shriek of a waterspout.

Don't like that, do we? Toinette thought, and her lips stretched in a killer's grin. She remembered her men, and the Templars with their brave pathetic crosses of rubble, and she laughed out loud. *Keep wailing, you wretched beast—you've lots more pain due, and I'll pay you all the interest I can.*

The words to the Conjuration of Fire were Latin. She'd learned them long before and had had no occasion to use them since her girlhood—but when she started speaking, they came back to her vividly, with the feeling that *she* wasn't exactly the one remembering them. For some spells, anger was a great asset.

Now the shapes on the walls were *them*. Images of Toinette and Erik rotted, or sickened with plague, or underwent all the tortures of the damned. Her guts spilled and vanished. Erik's mouth became a bloody hole.

Toinette didn't look away, but watched and was glad. She knew what the un-ark was saying, and *I'll kill you, you son of a bitch* was always the first threat of any man who'd gotten a fist to the nose or a knee to the bollocks. The angrier they sounded, the more they were hurting.

She raised her voice, pitching it to cut through the screaming just as she'd done to make herself heard over gales and pounding waves. The names of angels twisted on her tongue.

They called on fire beyond fire. Beyond the world, Mars governed the true essence of flame, the fire that danced on the wings of the seraphim. So Artair had explained it when he'd taught Toinette the ritual, with a quick smile for the notion of flaming serpents as angels. Toinette hadn't given it much thought at the time, but as she and Erik chanted, she felt that fire within her veins.

Even the lair of the un-ark wasn't beyond the reach of all aid.

Still, when the shapes faded from the walls and the screaming quieted, Toinette didn't believe they'd won. All but the stupidest of creatures knew how to gather strength.

She braced herself as she kept chanting. When light began to fountain out of the box, she was glad she'd done so—and knew it might not be enough.

The light pressed on her mind. Senses and sense buckled under its formless weight, caving in slowly to a force they were never built to withstand. Toinette clung to the words of the conjuration. Every syllable took conscious effort, deliberate motion of her lips and tongue, and deliberate awareness of the word's meaning. All other meaning was slipping away: Jehan's face, oranges in Iberia, the words to prayers, the feeling of flight at dawn, Erik's lips against hers. She would have wept. She might have been weeping. She could barely feel her own face.

Purity and wisdom, light and inspiration, protection and destruction both.

The chant rose in pitch. Power rose with it. Toinette knew that she was almost done. One more line, then one more task, and—then?

The thing before her had to perish.

All else was fog and phantoms.

Spirit of flame, hear us and aid!

She screamed the last phrase. Clarity, a light unlike the green-purple radiance around them, burst into her brain, driving the other force back for a few precious breaths. Toinette felt her body again: wet cheeks and cracked lips, blistered feet and bruised arms.

The un-ark's power was entering there. She could feel the flesh falling away, and the icy void that replaced it.

You want change? she thought at it. *Fine.*

As Erik had plummeted from the *Hawk*'s deck in the storm, Toinette turned and dove off the platform, arrowing her body into the void. As she fell, she opened herself, embracing the power of the flame and the power of her blood together, and letting them fill her from the inside out.

She fell.

Then she flew, and her wings had no need of wind.

FORTY

RISING, TOINETTE SHONE IN THE DARKNESS. THE GOLDEN SPARKS in her eyes glimmered throughout her body, shining among her ebony scales. Her wings beat slowly, but she hovered midair with no visible struggle, her neck curving long and graceful to let her look down at the un-ark.

Erik would have held still just to watch her if he could have.

He himself had started changing while on the platform. Luckily, he'd been halfway through when Toinette had hurled herself into the abyss; he'd had no chance to panic, only to gaze awestruck as she ascended.

The light yet flashed around them, trying to compel, but it found no purchase. If it had ever been used on other than mortal flesh and blood, that time was aeons past. It was already fading as Erik left the platform, flying through a void at once more stable and less resistant than air. He caught a glimpse of his body as he bent his neck forward and saw that he was glowing too, but far more faintly than Toinette.

Between one blink of an eye and the next, giant hands made of shadow and lined with purple-green light lashed up from the depths.

The too-long fingers clutched at Erik. He recoiled, just out of reach of nails like sharpened tree trunks; from across the room, he heard Toinette's roar and whipped his head around to see her. She'd escaped the worst of the attack, but the second hand had caught her across a hind leg. It dissipated back into the wall, but the damage was done. Blood dripped, hissing and smoking on the platform and glowing molten red.

The spirit of fire was with them. If it was to do any good, there wasn't much time left.

Erik turned his gaze away from the hands and breathed deeply, summoning forth the flame. He saw Toinette stretch out wings and neck, her chest swelling, the glow steady in her eyes even as the hands began to re-form behind her.

Fire poured out from each of their mouths, striking the un-ark dead center on two of its sides.

A hand of shadow wrapped itself around Erik. Its fingers bound his wings to his sides, and wherever it touched him, he felt not just cold but blighted, as though the mere contact took away a bit of his vitality. He tried to escape, tried to rake at the hand with his claws, but to no avail. It clung. It began to squeeze.

Bands of shadow clasped Toinette too. Her body thrashed frantically, vainly trying to escape—but her flaming breath was steady and strong.

Good it is, Erik remembered his mother's father saying, *to end a stout life with a stout death.*

Wing-bound, he would fall. But he would fall in fire. Erik ceased his struggle and thought only of the foe before him, the blot that must be purged so that men could live more safely in the world. He bent all of his strength toward that destruction.

Lungs aching, vision blurring, he saw the bleached wood kindle and flare.

The hand's grip slackened.

Erik took the reprieve and hauled more air into his lungs, keeping the fire blazing forth from his open jaws.

The flames around the un-ark took on a greenish hue.

No, Erik thought, with no energy left to shout it even in his mind. There was only flat denial left, and pointing the power he channeled at the discolored flame. The force riding his body doubled, racking his bones and muscles with pain. Flesh, dragon or mortal, was an imperfect vessel.

Yet the fire flared a deep red-gold, banishing the taint of green, and that sight was worth every heartbeat of pain.

Wood, though transformed by the fell spirit within it, was still wood, and fire was fire. Once the fuel had caught, the flame spread rapidly. From each side of the un-ark, it roared up and around, meeting in the middle and forming a half-sphere that wavered less than most wood fires and glowed more. Within it, wood crumbled away, and even the metal bands began to melt.

The hands broke up as well, fading back into unformed darkness. The spirit that had animated them was withdrawing Its power, discarding all forms and shapes in favor of one last bitter fight for endurance.

Erik could almost see It as the box crumbled. The flames clouded his vision, and he was grateful for that, but within the broken shell of the wood he could faintly make out a presence like darkness given matter: a void that squirmed and huddled against the walls that had given It a home for so long. He had the sense that It was bigger than his eyes allowed him to see, and less solid as well; he knew, though he couldn't say how he knew, that It was wounded.

Although he could tell that the thing was gathering strength, he couldn't have said what for, and the sudden cessation of flame from Toinette's side filled him with a jolt of alarm. He looked up, found her gone, and knew fear all through his body until he spotted her again, smaller and human, thrusting her hands into the flame to grab the un-ark.

"You go down with your ship," she snarled, her voice nearly equaling her roar in dragon's form. "No slipping away." Shoulders straining with the effort, she wrenched the un-ark up from the table and held it in midair. Adnet's dagger yet remained in the lid, and Franz's rosary hung now from the hilt, silver cross glowing in the midst of dragonfire. It and the blade had both begun to melt, but from within, like no metal Erik had ever seen. As he and Toinette were, they were vessels for power; as they were, cross and dagger were likewise imperfect.

Toinette turned with a speed that belied her burden, spinning so that the largest hole in the box faced Erik, and he saw clearly the spirit within. "*Now*," she roared.

And faced with the void's eyeless, consuming regard, hoping but uncertain for Toinette's life, Erik spent the last of the power he could channel in one piercing gout of flame, narrow and blue-white with heat.

The flame spread out as it touched the spirit: not as fire might catch and spread, but as a thrown net unfurled around its prey. It covered the writhing blackness in a mesh of fine light that knit itself together, pushing the creature behind it back at the same time: back, but Erik could not say to where, and wouldn't have wanted to try. He knew only that the thing faded from his vision, that the sense of cold hungry malice went with It, and that the world where it had been seemed mended: a scar, but no longer an open wound.

When he sunk to the platform, out of breath, he noticed that the smell was gone, and the sucking noise as well. The only sounds were the crackling of flames as they devoured the rest of the box, and the harsh, gasping breaths he and Toinette took: one set louder than the other, but both labored, both in harmony—and both signs of people very much alive.

Thunk went the un-ark back onto the platform, only a flaming shell now and without a passenger to worry about escaping into the stone.

Thwap, more softly, went Toinette's arse onto the floor, and *thunk* again, less controlled and more bruising than she'd have liked, went her back onto the side of the altar. Her arms shrieked at her about muscles and blisters. Dragonfire wasn't as fatal to other dragons as it generally was to humans, but it hurt like hell nevertheless.

A part of her, the girl from London, wondered whether the flames had burnt especially, and *her* especially, because they were holy. She doubted that small voice would ever truly die, any more than had the spirit in the un-ark, but she could tell it to sod off with far greater ease than she'd have managed a month before.

She'd called on the angels. They hadn't turned away. For a little while, she'd been part of something much greater—and she'd been in it with Erik.

As though her thoughts had summoned him, he knelt at her side, as human in shape as her, and stroked the side of her face. "Thank God."

"I'm looking no worse than usual, then," she joked, but she turned her head and laid a kiss in his palm. "You?"

"Well. Better than I'd thought either of us would end this. The dagger's vanished, though, and the rosary with it."

"Huh." Toinette got to her feet, groaning, and stared down at the box. Indeed, it was only a pile of charred wood now, and that rapidly becoming ash. No trace of metal was left. Before long, there would be no sign of the un-ark at all.

For the first time, she noticed that the platform no

longer stood in a void either. Toinette couldn't see a floor below, but rough stone walls, the sort that might appear in any cave in the world, surrounded them. The air was chilled, but no more so than she'd have expected from being underground.

"It went to good use," she said, watching as the wood burned. "I'm sure Franz will agree. If we can go home now, I'll go to the shrine myself and get another blessed for him—oh?"

Distracted as she was, she didn't notice Erik stepping up behind her until his hands settled on her shoulders and he turned her around. He did so gently, careful of her injuries, but there was nothing diffident about his face. Feeling filled his shining eyes and splashed a smile across his face, astonished and joyous at once.

"You," he said. "If my journeys took me ten times as far as yours, I'd never find another with your spirit. Not man or woman, dragon or mortal."

Sentiment hadn't figured largely in Toinette's life— Jehan had been a swift interlude in the march of years— and to hear so much, from Erik of all people, struck her dumb and dizzy. She hoped her answering smile spoke for her, as for a breath or two she stood staring into his eyes.

"You—you were damned impressive yourself," she finally managed, and wished, for the first time since her girlhood, for more poetic gifts, or a heart that spoke more easily. In the absence of either, she could only lift a reddened hand and stroke his hair back from his forehead. "I feared that you'd not know what I meant, at the end, but I should've known better."

"I knew well, my love," he said, and Toinette's breath caught, "but I'll be glad if I never have to do such a thing again." Erik took her hand carefully in both of his, looked down at it, and shook his head. "I'd not have harmed you for anything less than the world."

"I know," she said, "and I—"

But a *crack* cut through her words, one too inhuman, too loud, and too instantly recognizable for either of them to ignore.

Erik, facing the back of the cave, was the one to see what had happened. One arm still around Toinette, he pointed, and Toinette turned again.

A stalactite had fallen. The one that Erik had noticed had been small, but in the instant when they stood staring, a chunk of the ceiling shivered and fell. It landed in a heap on the opposite side of the altar, just where Erik had been standing during the ritual.

"God's blood," said Erik quietly.

Above them, the ceiling rumbled again, and the platform shook below them. The path to the door was still there, but the pit below it, even if only material and mortal, was very deep.

"Let's run now," said Toinette.

FORTY-ONE

FLIGHT FOLLOWED, BUT VERY MUCH NOT IN THE DRACONIC sense: flight on foot instead, through a series of winding caverns too low even to run through properly. Flight with the sound of falling rock behind them and the earth trembling under their feet, all too aware of the weight of stone that likely lay overhead.

Why?

Erik couldn't know. Had they, by taking dragon form earlier in a cave naturally too small for any such creature, broken through some vital support? Without the un-ark's spirit to sustain it, was the temple's natural structure enough of an affront to the world that it couldn't survive? Or was the collapse one last trick of the spirit, a trap for any who might truly manage to destroy It?

Any might be true, or parts of each. There might be another explanation entirely. Erik could wonder all he liked, as his boots struck stone and he forced overworked muscles into yet more service, but the darkness gave him no answers.

The phantom town they'd come through before was desolate on their return. A few buildings yet stood as Erik and Toinette ran past, but they looked flat and simple: sketches from an untalented hand. Stairs climbed into a rock wall. Windows opened onto stone, or blank space. One of the roofs caved in behind Erik. The sound was softer than falling rock should have been.

Mostly, he didn't look back. There were all kinds of

stories about what happened to people who did, and he hadn't even Orpheus's reason. Toinette ran at his side when the path was wide enough, easily keeping pace with him. When they had to go single file, she was just behind, her ragged breath and running footsteps signs of her presence.

There was no longer a door at the end of the town. A cave entrance just opened onto the junction, and two more faced it. Erik could glimpse shrouded bodies through one of them, and through the stalagmites he thought he saw Adnet's bones lying at rest. *Goodbye*, he thought, with no time to stop or breath to speak. *God grant you peace at last*.

Onward down the long passages they ran, and the world fell apart behind them.

"The ship," Toinette panted. "How do we get back through it?"

The thought struck Erik mid-chest like a blow. He couldn't stop to talk—even as they ran, he heard smashing behind them, the world's longest and largest avalanche on their heels—and could barely manage to think. His blood pounded in his ears. "Find the portal ourselves. Force it. We'll not have much time."

He rasped in a breath and grabbed for what scraps of his power were left, but Toinette interrupted him.

"*Visio dei*," she said. Her voice wavered considerably and was far higher than usual, but there was power in it.

Aware of how disorienting the visions were, Erik reached back and grabbed her arm, pulling her along the corridors with him. He hadn't the leisure for gentleness, nor even to regret the violence of his grip, but he did hope he wasn't injuring her.

She would heal, if he did.

Would either of them survive a rockfall? He didn't know, and the thought of it was more horrifying than death itself. How far below the surface were they? *Where* were they?

"Here," Toinette said abruptly, and gestured. "Down. The floor's...not false, but..." She bent forward, chest heaving. "You have to think where you want to be."

"Aye," said Erik quickly, for it hurt his heart to hear her try to speak. "I take your meaning. Go."

She slipped through the portal as if it were the surface of a pond. Erik jumped after her, thinking *out of here*, and then they were on rock, running away from the rotted hulk of a ship and toward a door in the middle of a beach made of stone.

Ah, said a part of his mind that sounded like Artair, *shapes have power even in their death. Fascinating*.

Erik wasn't particularly fascinated. He looked away from the door only to glance at Toinette, seeing that she was still keeping up. Her leg dripped blood as she ran, but slowly, and she *did* run. That would have to be good enough. The ship was groaning as it died, wood buckling and twisting under no force that Erik could see; chunks of timber fell and flew, making him and Toinette duck.

The door crumbled at his touch, falling to fragments and becoming a cavern entrance. He'd just ducked through when he saw the lintel buckle. Again he grabbed for Toinette, but she was already leaping through, her foot clearing the doorway as the whole structure came down in a crash and a cloud of dust.

Destruction was moving faster.

In the great hall, the high table lay tipped onto its side. The figures were gone, and the hands with them. The other two tables were dissolving into the stone. They melted as

Toinette saw them, like fog in sunlight. No great loss—but she looked away swiftly, dizzy from the sight.

All was failing beneath the earth. Or all was returning to the way it was meant to be. The world reclaimed the wreckage of twisted magic with a speed that might have been heartening had Toinette and Erik not been caught in its midst.

On and on they ran, dashing across the great hall and into the passage on the other side, past a cavern mouth with the ruins of a church beyond it. The symbol had fallen off the wall, and all the windows had shattered, revealing more stone beyond.

Toinette's cut leg hurt less. At first she thought that fear had pushed her beyond pain—she knew the wound couldn't have healed so quickly, not when she'd gotten it from the un-ark itself—but the rest of her body still protested every motion. Only her legs and feet had it easier than they had before.

The impact of feet against stone jarred less, she realized. There was less stone *to* jar. Even as the ceiling fell in behind them, the floor was growing softer.

Beyond shame, Toinette would have sobbed with terror, save that she had no breath to manage it. They were going to die. They'd come far, they'd won against all odds, and now, even in victory, they'd be buried alive, never to know air or light again.

Her mind gibbered. Her body, wiser or at least less complicated, bolted down passageways through rock that became gravel and then dirt. She had enough mind left to know that Erik was with her, and to keep making sure of it, glancing to her side every so often. Otherwise, she put her head down and ran like a spooked horse.

The great doors lay fallen from their frame, the metal

twisted and molten. Some shapes lingered. Others didn't. Toinette didn't know why and didn't care. She hurdled the wreckage and landed on the other side, almost stumbling in the loose dirt. It was falling down into the earth, filling the cavern from whence it had come. Like the tide, it tried to carry all before it.

Toinette's vision went red halfway across the courtyard. Her face was wet; she wouldn't have known sweat from tears then, or either from blood, and didn't bother wiping the moisture away. She didn't need to see. The edge of the steps was a few feet away, a few feet that felt as though she were treading water against the waves.

Dimly she thought of wings, but she had no strength to transform, and none to take off if she had. More weight would only have sealed their doom.

They made it to the edge of the steps and threw themselves over, running headlong downward. Halfway to the bottom, the dirt was soft and sucking as quicksand, and Toinette's legs worked no longer.

She turned and grabbed Erik's shoulders. "Jump," she managed.

They clung to each other and leapt, not down but outward as far as their collected strength could manage.

Toinette felt her feet leave the sand. Through a red mist she saw the distance between them and the steps grow, and the steps themselves collapse in on themselves, buckling and bending in a way that no stone had ever done. She felt Erik's arms tight about her, and buried her face against his neck, shielding the back of his head with her own arms.

She closed her eyes.

They landed hard, with a solid *crunch* and a stab of pain through Toinette's wounded leg, not to mention a blunt impact that jarred her whole body. Her teeth clicked together with enough force to chip one; her shoulder hit a good-sized rock, which tore through the cloth of her gown and half the skin of her upper arm.

But they *did* land, on firm, solid ground that moved not at all. They landed, and lay for a while as the temple's final collapse roared behind them.

FORTY-TWO

Having come to a stop, Erik couldn't rise again. He told himself that he should, that they'd do well to keep walking, but the earth was too nice and flat, his bones too heavy, and Toinette's head too welcome against his chest. All he could do was roll onto his back, pulling Toinette with him, and stare up at the sky.

For a change, there *was* a sky, one the mundane gray of low clouds and lit by the faint sun of midafternoon. *What* midafternoon was a mystery. Based on when they'd eaten, they'd spent only half a day in the temple, but Erik had heard many tales. Time worked differently in such places. They could have emerged weeks or years later than they'd gone in—there was no way to know.

He hadn't the strength to worry.

Small things occupied his mind instead. Air, for instance: real, clean air, smelling vaguely of the sea beyond the island and vaguely of pine. There were no trees around them—the ring around the temple was a wasteland yet, if not so sinister as it had been when Erik and Toinette had entered—but after so long with nothing but the un-ark's smell, Erik thought he could have caught the scent of a plant in England.

Toinette breathed as deeply as he did, the motion steady against him. It reassured him where her closed eyes might have otherwise given alarm, as did the slowing beat of her heart. Her hair fell across his face, and tickled, but he made no move to brush it away.

In time, though Erik couldn't have said in how *much* time save that the sun hadn't set, Toinette groaned and sat up. "Praise the saints," she said and licked cracked lips. "And we're…mostly…each in one piece."

The whites of her eyes were as red as Erik suspected his own were, and her voice as hoarse as his throat felt. The cut on her leg was a raw-looking line of red, but it had mostly stopped bleeding from what he could tell. "Aye," he said, "and glad to hear it from you. Though I fear we left the wine behind us when we changed, and the food as well."

"Bah," said Toinette, but good-humoredly. "And we're quite lacking in mead and fowl as well. Inhospitable, I call it."

Erik laughed, though it hurt his throat and his ribs alike. They'd both gone without for longer. Survival was food and wine enough.

"We should walk," he said, though. "Get to the stream, clean your wounds."

"Clean everything we can, after that run," Toinette replied, getting to her feet with another groan. "Just poke me in the ribs if I fall over on the way. You'll never carry me in your condition."

He might have protested, but knew it for the truth, and was in no shape to speak very much. Instead, when he stood, he wrapped an arm around Toinette's shoulders and, careful of her burns, leaned his weight a little on the one she offered.

Thus supporting each other, staggering sore-footed like a pair of drunks in the small hours of the morning, they retraced the paths they'd taken.

Dead trees stayed dead, and nothing moved among them. Time and nature might reclaim the woods around the temple, or the blight might remain. Not all scars healed. It was enough for Erik to know that the dead forest *was* a scar, to look through the trees and see the red light of the setting sun, and to breathe in nothing sinister as he walked.

Likewise, though the trees and wildlife in the livelier part of the forest were yet deformed, no phantom shapes appeared among them. The wind was chilly, more so as the evening approached, but the bone-deep cold was gone. A malignity had made its home nearby, and the land yet bore the marks, but It dwelt there no longer. The forest Toinette and Erik walked through was empty, and then twisted, but it was *free*.

They walked wearily enough that night fell when they were hours from the stream. Erik glanced down at Toinette as the sky darkened, and she shrugged beneath his arm. "I'd rather keep going. You?"

He nodded. Given the thing that had inflicted it, he didn't want to sleep without cleaning Toinette's wound, and his thirst was almost as great as his tiredness. More than that, the stream had become a symbol as they walked, a border. Once they made it there, they'd be back in the world they'd grown to know.

That was all sound reasoning, but by the time they finally dragged themselves to the water, Erik had questioned it to himself on several occasions. Even getting his head down to take a drink was an effort.

Yet the water did help. He was far beyond the reach of a second wind, but after minutes of drinking, when his stomach felt swollen from water, he knew himself to be alive again and possessed of human limbs, not rusty mechanisms. Erik dipped his face into the stream, washing away blood, sweat, and dirt alike, then turned to Toinette.

She sat barefoot and wet-haired on the bank, cupping

water in her hands and pouring it over the slash on her leg. Blood ran anew as the scab broke open, and Toinette hissed in pain, but she kept going.

"Let me," Erik said, kneeling at her side.

Without a word, Toinette leaned back on her hands, staring up at the sky as Erik took over her task. The wound was deep, and running had done it no good, but *only* blood ran from it. Erik saw no odd colors, smelled nothing unusual, and was cautiously relieved. "How does it feel?" he asked.

"Not bad," she managed, and though her voice was unsteady with pain, Erik knew what she meant. "It hurts worse than a knife would've, but there's nothing odd about it. Nothing cold, or…well, you know."

"Aye, I do."

The scraps of his sleeve they'd have used to mark doors, unused thanks to Adnet's aid, made decent bandages. While Erik saw to her leg, Toinette lay on her side, soaking her burned hands in the water. "My pride," she said, glancing down the length of her body at him, "may never recover."

"Just as well. Pride's a sin, they tell me."

"Are you taking credit for saving my soul?"

Erik tied the final knot, sat up, and looked at her: bruised, cut, wearing only the dubious remains of her gown, in need of a far more thorough wash than her brief dip in the stream could provide, and utterly beautiful. "I'll save you any way I can," he said, "if there's need."

At that, Toinette turned and rose to face him, silent for a long minute before she spoke. "I love you too," she said, "if you hadn't worked that out. Now let's get back onto land before we fall asleep and drown."

They slept on the ground that night. It was hard, and colder than even the sand of the cave, but they could hear the stream running nearby, and Toinette curled into Erik's arms, warm and loose-limbed. He couldn't have voiced any complaints.

However she'd tried to hope, Toinette had truly thought she'd never see morning light again. Waking to it made up for the taste in her mouth and her hunger, just as having Erik pressed against her back outweighed the lack of mattress or blankets.

It was a good morning. It got better when they stripped and bathed in the stream, as cold as it was. Toinette wrung out her hair and rinsed it twice over, feeling that she rid it of invisible slime as well as the normal sort of filth.

Sleep and her nature had done well. Her hands were still sore, but no worse than they'd been after taking the wheel during a storm. The minor bruises and cuts had vanished. The wound from the un-ark had stopped bleeding, and didn't start again when Erik cleaned it. It'd take days to heal fully. It would doubtless leave a scar. But it was on the mend.

Erik's hands on Toinette's leg were as gentle as the sunlight on her shoulders. She watched him as best she could from her angle, marking the muscles in his bare arms and chest as he worked and the fall of his hair over his face. He was very serious just then.

She smiled and waited, and then, when the bandages were back on her leg, turned and stretched, pointing her toes and parting her thighs. Erik's head lifted. Although her view wasn't what she would have wished while he was kneeling, Toinette thought she saw motion between his thighs as well.

"Ah," he said, his voice low in the morning air, "we haven't celebrated our victory properly, have we?"

"Tragically." Toinette ran a hand down from her neck, tracing her fingers around one pointed nipple, and over her stomach to brush the auburn curls above her sex. "And it's always important to mark these occasions."

Erik agreed, she saw, as he turned toward her. His cock had risen to press against his stomach, and swayed a little when he moved. He stretched himself out by her side, kisses hot down her neck and hand sliding between her thighs. "Only," he said, "you'll lie quiet this time, like a good lass."

"Is that what you like in your women?" she teased, drawing her nails slowly up his spine. "How clerkly you've become."

"I'll show you clerkly later, love," he growled into her shoulder. "Only you're too tall for me to carry back, so I'll have to leave you in shape for walking."

And so they did go slowly, gently, in the steady rhythm of the running water near them. Toinette—looking up into green trees and blue sky as Erik thrust inside her and she felt herself falling into that final dissolution—thought, *This is right*, and knew she was thinking of more than pleasure or even love. The golden morning and the land itself were a part of what she and Erik did. It was life, and renewal, and a final triumph over the forces that would deny such things.

She did lie still, or still enough not to damage her leg further. *Quiet* Toinette didn't manage at all. Before the end, she was crying out with joy in a voice that likely carried to the treetops.

FORTY-THREE

"THEY'VE COME BACK!" RAOUL BOLTED UPWARD FROM HIS former seat on the rock and started forward to meet Toinette and Erik, until John caught him by the arm.

"So it seems." The happiness in the older man's face was tempered by caution.

Both looked hale enough, and no more aged than Erik remembered them, setting his mind at ease about how much time the journey through the temple and the battle with the un-ark had really taken. The swords at the men's waists gleamed with the purple fire of their spell, lighter and more bluish in hue than the un-ark's magic had been, and both, now that John had delivered his warning, waited warily as Toinette and Erik drew within human conversational distance.

"Captain?" Raoul asked.

Toinette nodded. "My mother's name was Galitia. You signed on in a tavern in Bordeaux. John there spends half his pay on beads and ribbons for his wife. Tried to bring a monkey back to his children once, but it died a week out. For Christ's sake, let us come in and eat something."

"And I was fostered in England," Erik added.

John and Raoul began to laugh, and Toinette joined them. Exhausted as he was, and perhaps because he was exhausted, Erik was swept up in the wave of mirth as well. They stood laughing together on the beach as the other men came to see what the commotion was, curiosity becoming surprise and then elation.

Perspective is the damnedest thing. A mostly whole dress, a skin of water, a side of roasted fish, and a good half-pound of boiled nettles made Toinette as content as she could imagine any king being on his throne—maybe more, considering kings and kingdoms. Being able to sit down, take off her boots, and stretch her feet out in front of a fire had her making noises of bliss around each mouthful she took.

"You both look like you've been dragged backward through hell," said Marcus.

He'd taken Toinette's face between his hands when she'd first sat down and peered into her eyes for a long time, until she'd swatted at his arms and said that if she was evil, she'd have killed them all by now. "That's not why I was looking," he'd responded, but had refused to say more.

"Not inaccurate," Erik replied. "Best we tell all the story later. But we did win."

"Of course," said John, who'd been the first to embrace Erik after they'd all stopped laughing.

Samuel passed another slice of fish over to Toinette. "We saw the light go very bright two evenings ago," he said, "and then it turned red, and finally vanished. The woods haven't been as bad since."

"We've not had dreams either," said Raoul, and then looked embarrassed, "saving the normal sort of nightmare, that is."

"Plenty of fuel for those," said Erik.

Toinette remembered the church, and the faces the un-ark had shown her, and grimaced. Memory faded, though. That was one of the good things about being mortal, even as vaguely mortal as she and Erik were.

"Then we've done well," said Sence, in a tone that suggested that was all the question that would ever need settling.

Franz, eating quietly, looked as though he agreed. When Toinette had apologized for the loss of his rosary, he'd smiled. "No bowman gets all his arrows back," he'd said.

"But you're wounded," said John.

Toinette shrugged. "Nothing that won't heal in time. And you should see the other fellow."

After dinner, they bathed in the ocean. Salt water would counter any lingering magic, Erik thought, and was good for wounds, Marcus said. Toinette invoked several different saints during the process, but the tone she used wasn't likely to get help from any of them.

It *did* sting, besides being almost freezing. Clothing and a place by the fire were very welcome afterward.

Then, all precautions taken and with full stomachs to hearten them, Erik and Toinette told the men what had happened in the temple. It was Toinette who did most of the talking, while Erik chimed in with details every so often. They addressed her crew, he thought; she should be the one in charge of it.

She skimmed over details, saying only that the inside of the temple "made no sense" and "changed to be places from memory," but she did speak of the man they'd killed, and of Adnet and his fellow knights. Silence crept in around her tale then: her audience, as she and Erik had done at the time, thought long of the Templars and their fate. Sence and Franz crossed themselves first, with most of the others following suit.

Of the light, neither of them spoke much, nor of their contact with the mind of the un-ark. The memory of that hungry, hateful version of intelligence would likely stay with Erik until his dying day. He wouldn't wish it, even secondhand, on anyone else.

"…and we came away just as the whole lot of it fell in on itself," Toinette finished.

"Then," Samuel said, "are we free?"

"It stands to reason," said Erik, "but there's no way of being certain until we try."

"So hope," said Marcus, "but not too high. And no matter what, be glad we're not sharing the place with that thing any longer. That'll be a good thought to take to sleep."

He spoke with the force of command, and none there gainsaid him. Raoul went out for watch, while the others took their accustomed places by the fire—all except for Toinette.

Rising from her seat, she lifted her chin, then came over to settle herself against Erik's side. At first her limbs were tense, as though she waited for a challenge, but none came and she let out a breath when Erik put his arms around her. He saw her look across the fire, meeting Marcus's eyes, and then saw the other man smile rather triumphantly.

"Hmm?" Erik asked Toinette under his breath.

She made a face. "He was right, the bastard. Bless him."

Battered, patched, ransacked for supplies, the *Hawk* still floated, and Toinette still stood steadier on her deck than anywhere else. With her hand on the wheel, she scanned the cloudy sky above and then looked to the crew at their places.

The wind was right. The tide was right. *Visio dei* had shown that the island's center was oddly empty, but the black-purple web from before had crumbled entirely away.

Unless they waited through the winter, there was likely no better time.

"Very well," she said. "Let's cast off."

She held her breath as the ropes dropped away and the sails snapped out. She would have wagered that every man aboard did the same.

And yet it was *easy*, almost the smoothest launch Toinette had ever made. The *Hawk* caught the tide at once, with never a bump or a sense of dragging the bottom. Wind filled the sails almost immediately. Perhaps, Toinette thought, the spirits of wind and water were themselves glad to be free, eager as long-tied dogs.

Within a few minutes, they were out past the point where the wind had turned before. They'd almost made the open ocean before Toinette recalled herself and grabbed the wheel, laughing. "Bring her about!" she called to a crew who'd stood as astonished as she'd been. "We've a day of provisioning still to go."

She didn't add anything, not wanting to tempt fate, but the rest of the words were in her heart regardless: *And then we make for home*.

"Right now," said Erik, "I can see why you take so much joy in the sea."

In the dawn light, the island receded behind them. The cabin would stand empty. Perhaps one day others would use it for shelter and wonder who'd come before, just as they might survey the graves on the beach. Perhaps the woods would retake the cabin before another set of human eyes looked on the island.

The wind was chilly against Erik's face, but he wouldn't have traded it, or the smell of salt and the feel of their brisk passage through the ocean, for any moment of stillness by a fire.

Toinette turned and smiled at him. With her hair and gown blown back, she could have graced the prow of a ship herself, save that she was far more vividly colored than any figurehead. "Just now, I think you've a place here any time you'd like."

"Certainly so," said Marcus, looking up from coiling rope, "especially as I fear we might be in sore need of hands soon. John, at least, wants to spend a year or so raising crops and children, and Raoul's been speaking more of his girl back home."

"Undeserving wench," said Toinette. She turned the wheel and then went on. "Though I admit the idea of a few seasons on land appeals more these days. Perhaps," she said, not looking at Erik, "it's time I saw what summer looks like a little further from the coast."

"I know of a place or two that might suit," said Erik, putting a hand on her shoulder. He looked at Marcus. *Eros* was not the only sort of love—his education had been classical enough to cover that—and loyalty was a great treasure itself. "And I'd wager that half a score of strong men would be welcome there. Men who've seen the world and proven their worth particularly."

"A man does have to consider his old age," said Marcus. "I'd very much enjoy spending mine in the company of friends, and among those who've seen…some of the stranger corners of the world."

"Then put the word out," said Toinette. She raised a hand to cover Erik's, squeezed it, and added with a grin, "And know that it's likely to be cold."

"I always knew you'd lead me to a bad end, Captain."

Laughing, they made for home.

ABOUT THE AUTHOR

Isabel Cooper lives in Boston in an apartment with a silver sword and a basket of sequined fruit. By day, she works as a theoretically mild-mannered technical editor; by night, she tries to sleep. She's never been to sea properly, but would like to manage it one of these days.

NO PROPER LADY

The Terminator meets *My Fair Lady* in this tale
of black magic and ball gowns

In two hundred years, demons will destroy the world…
unless Joan, an assassin from the future, can take out the
dark magician responsible. But to get close to her target,
she'll need help learning how to fit into society.

Simon has his own reasons for wanting to destroy Alex
Reynell, and Joan may be his perfect revenge. But as each
day passes, Simon is less sure he wants her anywhere near
Reynell. Because no spell in the world will save his future
if she isn't in it.

"A genre-bending, fast-paced whirl."
—RT Book Reviews, 4.5 Stars TOP PICK

For more Isabel Cooper, visit:
sourcebooks.com

LESSONS AFTER DARK

Meet the X-Men of Victorian England in this tale
of black magic and ball gowns

For years, Gareth St. John put his supernatural talent for
healing in service to the British Army. Now he's the
doctor at a new school that helps others learn how to hone
their abilities.

Olivia Brightmore never expected to discover real
magic as the school's newest teacher. She tries to keep the
handsome doctor at arm's length, but she can't resist the
urge to get under his skin. But it doesn't take the Sight to
know something is growing between them...

"Cooper's worldbuilding is solid and believable."
—RT Book Reviews, 4.5 Stars TOP PICK